Praise for *The Last Train*

'I found this book enthralling. I   beautifully told.'
Lorraine Kelly, UK broadcaster

'Lawrence's parallel plotlines advance in lock-step with each other . . . with spooky similarities but also crucial differences, until they're entwined to great effect towards the end.'
Sunday Herald Life

'A gripping tale.'
Daily Record

'. . . a deft mix of vivid storytelling, intriguing mystery and building momentum, skilfully interwoven with the history of the Tay Bridge disaster.'
Scottish Field

'Un-put-downable'
Dundee Courier

'A very enjoyable read . . . and a fascinating insight into the history of Dundee's famous bridge disaster.'
Kirsten McKenzie, author of *The Chapel at the End of the World*

'Sue Lawrence swaps cookbooks for suspense and has come up with a winner.'
Scots Magazine

'A brilliant historical mystery.'
Literary Dundee

Sue Lawrence was born in Dundee but lived and went to school in Edinburgh, before returning to Dundee to study French at university. She then trained as a journalist with DC Thomson.

Having taken time off her career when her three children were small, she took up writing again after winning BBC *Masterchef* in 1991. She was cookery columnist for the *Sunday Times* then *Scotland on Sunday* and also wrote for several magazines and appeared regularly on TV and radio.

She won a Glenfiddich Food and Drink Award in 2003 and two Guild of Food Writers Awards, in 1998 and 2001. She was President of the Guild of Food Writers from 2004–2008.

She is author of 15 cook books, including *Sue Lawrence's Book of Baking*, *Scots Cooking* and *A Cook's Tour of Scotland*.

For Diana,
Hope you enjoy!

The LAST TRAIN

SUE LAWRENCE

Best wishes,
Sue Lawrence

ALLEN&UNWIN
SYDNEY • MELBOURNE • AUCKLAND • LONDON

First published in Australia and New Zealand by Allen & Unwin in 2018
First published in the United Kingdom by Freight Books in 2016

Allen & Unwin
83 Alexander Street
Crows Nest NSW 2065
Australia
Phone: (61 2) 8425 0100
Email: info@allenandunwin.com
Web: www.allenandunwin.com

Cataloguing-in-Publication details are available
from the National Library of Australia
www.trove.nla.gov.au

ISBN 978 1 76063 086 7

Set in Plantin by Freight
Printed and bound in Australia by Griffin Press

10 9 8 7 6 5 4 3

In loving memory of my father, Robert Anderson, ever proud of his home city of Dundee.

Chapter 1

Sunday 28 December 1879
7 p.m.

The storm raged on. In the pitch black, the thunder cracked as a roaring gale whipped through the narrow wynds and filthy closes of Dundee's tenements. The wind ripped trees from their roots as it continued east, howling round the dingy buildings as slates and chimney pots crashed to the ground. Roofs from the bathing huts along the shore flew off as the wind rushed along the River Tay. The deep, tormented waters heaved upwards and crashed into foam-crested waves.

Above the maelstrom on the river, and far from the squalid homes of the poor, a large stone house was feeling the blast. Though neighbouring houses were gothic in style, this was classical, with pediment and pillars. The wind battered against the windows, rattling the casements. A flash of lightning forked through the bleak sky as a figure appeared upstairs at a window. The woman pulled the curtains open and placed the lamp on the table behind her. She beckoned to the children by the fire, their eyes wide with terror.

'Come over here, my dears. There is nothing to fear. The storm sounds dreadful but it is simply the noise of the wind.'

As she spoke there was a crash as a slate smashed onto the cobbled path beneath. She took a deep breath and put her arms round her son and daughter, who had scuttled over to join her.

'Shall we see Pappa's train?' James tipped his chin up in an attempt to see more clearly through the window.

'Will the train blow over in the big wind, Mamma?'

'No, Lizzie, it will not. Pappa shall be here as usual for your bedtime prayers.' Ann lifted up her eight-year-old daughter and stood her on the window seat, adjusting the girl's long nightgown as she did so. She tried to help her son but he clambered up onto the plump cushions himself. 'I am ten years old now, I don't need help,' he muttered.

They gazed out through the whirling wind at the heaving waters beyond. The full moon was obscured by dark, scudding clouds.

'There, see. Lights!' said James, pointing across the river, towards Fife.

Ann turned to check the longcase clock behind the lamp; it was nearly quarter past seven. 'It's a little late, I do hope it won't speed.'

She watched the lights of the train as it rounded the curve at Wormit and straightened up onto the bridge. 'It has passed the signal box now,' Ann whispered.

'Pappa says it must slow down over the bridge.'

As they watched the train continue at full speed, Ann clenched her hands tightly together. The train entered the high girders and she held her breath.

'Look, more lightning, Mamma!' Lizzie cried, cowering into her mother, whose mouth opened wide. For Ann saw not lightning, but a brilliant sheet of flame from the iron girders and a comet-like burst of fiery sparks from the engine. In one long trail, the streak of lights and fire plummeted downwards. And then, nothing. All was dark on the river.

There was a sudden hush in the room while the rain continued to pelt against the window and the wind howled and swirled.

'Stay here,' said Ann, coming to her senses. 'Do not move. I shall fetch Mrs Baxter.'

She fled from the room and ran downstairs to the kitchen, flinging open the door. 'Go and sit with the children, I must go out at once. I fear the train is over the bridge!'

Chapter 2
2015

'Mum, it was really cool on the bus. We got juice and crisps and Jenny Baird was sick so the driver had to stop really fast, like a racing driver.'

Fiona looked round from the sink, drying her hands. 'Sit down and tell me all about it,' she said, flicking on the switch of the kettle. 'Was it a good trip?'

'Yeah, it was okay. It wasn't the Peter Pan museum though, just the house where the man who wrote the book was born.'

'J. M. Barrie. So what did you see there then?'

'Stuff about when he was a child and things. And how they used to live in those days. Well, the teacher said it was a big house for rich people and that the ordinary folk wouldn't even have had a toilet inside the house.'

Fiona made a pot of tea and opened the cake tin. 'Bit of cake, Jamie?'

He nodded and rushed over to the kitchen dresser, peeling off his school sweatshirt as he went. He opened the drawer and pulled out a pad of paper and a box of coloured pencils.

'I'll draw you a picture of the statue they had in Kirriemuir. It's Peter Pan with his pipe or flute, can't remember what Miss Robb called it.' He began sketching then slurped some tea.

'Don't be so noisy, Jamie, where are your manners?'

'That's how Pete drinks his tea.'

'Yes, well, some grown-ups think it's okay to have bad table manners, but it's not.'

Jamie glanced up at the clock. 'When's Pete home?'

'Oh, yes, I meant to say, Pete won't be home till later tonight so I'm cooking. You up for pizza?'

He looked up from his drawing and grinned. 'Cool.'

She planted a kiss on his cheek as she headed for the door. He wiped it away with the back of his hand and leant over his piece of paper, pencil poised.

★ ★ ★

Later that evening, once her son was in bed, Fiona poured herself a glass of red wine and stood looking out the window. It was a beautiful May evening, the sun low in the sky and the top of the hill still bathed in bright light. She took a sip and wished Pete wasn't working so late. She'd love to go and climb the hill, but didn't like leaving Jamie alone. It was a small and friendly village where everyone left their doors unlocked all the time, and the neighbours said he'd be fine – some even suggested that she was being overprotective – but there was no way she would leave him by himself.

Her love of walking was new, developed since she and Jamie moved to Glenisla two years previously. When she arrived she had been a city slicker from Dundee who hadn't donned hiking boots since school; now, though, she was hooked – and was even a member of the local hillwalking club. She'd been unsure when Pete had asked her to move with him to Glenisla, but Jamie soon loved living in the country and made friends easily at the village school.

She looked at her watch. Pete would have finished service by now; he must have become embroiled in the bar chatting to the locals. Fiona switched on her iPad and Googled J. M. Barrie. He had been born in nearby Kirriemuir but she knew very little else about him. Thank God for Wikipedia, she thought.

She put down her empty glass on the coaster, which read The Old Chain Pier, and smiled. This was the pub where she'd met Pete some three years before; she had been taken in not only by his looks but by his easy Antipodean manner. She hadn't had much fun since Iain had died. It had taken her years to get over his death but now at last she felt secure and happy; and Jamie adored Pete, though he didn't call him Dad.

★ ★ ★

Fiona was in bed by the time Pete got in, propped up against a pile of pillows with her iPad on her lap. She pushed her glasses up over her forehead.

'You're late. Busy night?'

Pete threw his jacket on the chair and sat on the bed to take off his trainers. 'Yeah, and loads of bookings over the weekend.' He leant over to give her a kiss. 'What're you looking at?'

'J. M. Barrie. You know, the Peter Pan author? Jamie was on his school trip today to Kirriemuir today. He enjoyed it but the best thing seemed to be some little girl vomiting all over the bus on the way home!'

Pete smiled as he disappeared into the bathroom.

'Oh,' shouted Fiona. 'Before I forget, there was a phone call a couple of hours ago. Someone called Cress – or was it Lettuce – anyway, a woman with a silly name. She was from The Scotsman, must've been that girl who was up a few weeks ago. She told me she couldn't get through on the hotel phone. She said to let you know the restaurant review's going in the paper tomorrow.'

Pete came back into the room, toothbrush in hand. 'Did she say if it was any good?'

Fiona smiled. 'I obviously tried to probe but got nothing. I'm sure it'll be a rave review though.'

Pete returned to the bathroom and continued to brush his teeth.

Fiona leant forward so her voice would carry. 'I was thinking how brilliant it is we're all online now. Instead of having to post the newspaper cutting to your folks in Melbourne, you can just send them the link. I could do it tomorrow if you give me an email address.'

There was silence, followed by the noise of Pete spitting out his toothpaste. He wandered back into the bedroom and pulled off his T-shirt. Fiona noticed the rolls of fat around his midriff; too much tasting his good food.

'I don't know why you don't tell me more about them. I mean, that's three years we've been together and I've never even spoken to your parents on the phone.' Fiona smiled. 'Do they actually exist?'

Pete sat down on his side of the bed and slipped off his jeans. 'What time does Doreen get the papers in on a Saturday?'

'Well, the shop opens at eight, but the papers only come up from Alyth about half nine. If you're desperate to see the review you could check it out online first thing.' She put two pillows back to his side, popped a couple of pills in her mouth and swigged from her water bottle, then switched off her bedside lamp. 'Anyway, come to bed. You'll need a good night's sleep – if it's a five-star review, Michelin may well come calling!'

'To the sleepiest village in Perthshire? Bloody doubt it.' He slipped into bed, gave her a kiss and rolled onto his side. 'Night.'

A couple of minutes later, he turned and whispered, 'Fi, you know I love you, don't you?'

'Of course I do, darling.'

$\star\ \star\ \star$

Next morning, Fiona woke up to the sound of the phone ringing. She looked at the clock: 08:30. How had she slept so long? She ran downstairs and grabbed the phone. It was Mrs Cumberland, the receptionist at Glenisla Hotel.

'Is that you, Fiona?'

'Yes, is everything okay?'

'Well, no, not really. Sorry to bother you on a Saturday, and when he's got a late night tonight too, but can you tell Pete to get over here as soon as he can? That new sous-chef can't get the grill on and a guest's wanting kippers. Pete's always saying not to do them in a pan as they stink everything else out.'

'Sorry, Mrs C, he's not here,' said Fiona, walking through the cottage. 'No idea where he's gone.' She frowned; usually on a Saturday morning he loved long lies. 'I'll call you back.'

Fiona went back upstairs to the bedroom and pulled open the curtains to let the daylight in. As she looked around, she noticed that his drawers were pulled open and half-empty. She rushed to the wardrobe – an overnight bag had been taken. How could she not have heard him open the creaky wardrobe door? Then she remembered that she was taking antihistamines for her hay fever and had slept heavily, as if drugged. She glanced at the packet of Piriton on her bedside table and then noticed the envelope.

She eased herself onto the bed to sit down, put on her glasses and ripped it open.

Fi, like I said, I love you, always will. But I've got to move on. Give Jamie a hug and tell him to keep up the drawing. He'll be an architect one day like his dad. xx

Fiona stared at the note, then pulled open Pete's bedside table drawer. She rifled through letters and bills then let out a long breath. His passport was missing. She ran downstairs and opened the front door. His car was gone. Fiona staggered back inside to the kitchen table and sat down, her hands at her head. He's bloody well done a runner, she thought, as she heard the noise of the toilet flushing next door. How the hell would she tell Jamie?

Chapter 3

Sunday 28 December 1879
7.30 p.m.

Ann Craig yanked her cape from the coat stand and threw it over her lilac gown. With clumsy fingers, she buttoned it up in front of the mirror. Her face looked paler than usual, framed by her dark hair. Usually this was where she preened, tilting her head from right to left, pinching her cheeks to add colour; at this moment though, grooming was far from her mind. She fastened the hook at the collar and strode towards the door.

'Wait, Mrs Craig,' said Mrs Baxter, heaving her bulky frame as fast as she could along the corridor. 'Donald will go with you.'

Donald Baxter emerged behind his wife. Normally smart with his hair neatly combed, tonight he looked windswept. He pulled his cap from his pocket and said, 'I'll come too, Mrs Craig. I'm just in. There's a commotion down by the shore, no one's sure what's happened.'

Ann pulled her hat firmly onto her head and opened the door. As the wind whirled around them, her hat blew off and she ran to fetch it. It was caught in a rose bush so she ripped it from the thorns and rammed it once again onto her head, holding it in place with her hand.

'Will you not let me go down myself, Mrs Craig, and find out what's going on? This isn't a night for a lady to be out.'

'Don't be ridiculous, Baxter. I am perfectly capable. Here, take my arm.'

He reached out his arm and together they battled against the lashing rain and blustery gale. As they headed for the river, they came across others, heads stooped low against the wind. They tumbled along together over Magdalen Green towards the signal box on the shore.

The wind continued to howl furiously as Ann and Baxter slithered down the slope towards the path. She lifted her head and stopped, peering ahead. She could see the huge signal post was bent over like a bowed willow branch. She pulled Baxter's sleeve and shouted in his ear. 'I shall remain by this lamppost. Go and ask at the signal box.'

Baxter cowered low and took careful steps across the Green.

'Hurry!' she shouted, wrapping her arms round the post. Shoulders stooped, she listened to the almighty roar as waves higher than houses crashed against the shore, throwing great sprays of water over the gathering crowd. It was impossible to see the bridge through the dark; Ann tried to put aside visions of the train plummeting into the murky, cold depths of the Tay.

Some ten minutes later, she looked up and saw a hunched figure approach, arms held out at either side for balance.

Baxter came right up to her and shouted, 'A man climbed up to the signal box. Signalman told him he'd got the usual signal from the other side as the train entered the bridge. Since then, nothing. No more telegraphic communication, he said.'

Ann stared at him. 'But what's to be done?'

'No one can do anything right now, Mrs Craig.'

She pulled back the hair that had blown over her face and yanked it behind her ears. 'We shall continue at once to the station. They must know more there.'

Baxter began to protest about the gale, that a lady should not be out on a night like this, it was much too far to walk, but she struck out her elbow for him and said, 'It's barely a mile, Baxter.' One glance at the resolute look on her face and he realised he had no choice. He took her arm and off they staggered through the howling gale towards Tay Bridge Station.

* * *

As they approached, Ann saw crowds of bedraggled people standing outside, huddled round the gates. Even over the moan of the wind she heard wails of anguish. Ann looked up at the large clock over the entrance: it was just before 8 p.m. and the train was well overdue. The crowds parted a little as she headed for the station gates, which were firmly shut and padlocked.

'Come, let us continue,' she hissed to Baxter.

She leant through the bars of the gate and rapped on the wooden door and some of the throng turned to her.

'They've locked us out.'

'Station's closed.'

'Flung us all out.'

Ignoring the pack, she whispered to Baxter, 'Go round the back to the side stairs and then to the stationmaster's office on platform two. Tell Mr Smith I wish to see him.'

'But Mrs Craig, he will not...'

'Go, Baxter. At once!'

Baxter shuffled away and headed round the back. Ann stood up straight and surveyed the crowd. She was used to being taller than most women but now she seemed to dominate everyone before her; the crowd was stooped, heads bowed as they huddled for shelter from the storm.

After what seemed an interminable time, Baxter appeared and whispered to her to follow. She set off behind him, head held high, pulling at her skirt which had become trapped under someone's walking stick. She turned to check the crowds were not following then hurried down the side steps towards platform two and stationmaster Alec Smith's office. At the foot she came to an abrupt stop as she noticed a glint at her feet: broken glass. She looked up and noticed that part of the glass roof had shattered. She lifted her skirt a little and continued, stepping with caution towards the office as Baxter swung the door wide for her to enter. Here was a strange sight. Two railway men, dishevelled and windswept, were staring silently at the inert telegraph machine as if willing it to stutter into life. A third man sat at the desk, his head in his hands, snivelling like a child.

'Mr Smith, what news is there?'

He sprang to his feet, wiping his forearm across his flushed face. 'Mrs Craig, I'm sorry you were barred from entry. I had to take the decision to close the station. I am unsure the rest of the roof will hold.' He took a deep breath. 'I've just been out to the signal box – there's been no signal from the south box since the train left, only a few minutes late. Together with my engine-shed man I tried to get along the tracks, but the wind was too strong.' He turned towards the men by the telegraph machine. 'Jimmy, tell the lady what you saw.'

One of the men swivelled round and whipped off his cap. 'Nothing, nothing but broken ends of the rails pointing down into the river.'

'Mrs Craig,' said Alec, now more composed. 'I must go and speak to the provost. The bridge is down and the train with it.' He turned to grab his coat from a hook on the wall then nodded as he passed her with the two men.

'But, Mr Smith, can nothing be done? Surely a boat can be sent out? Passengers must be rescued?'

The stationmaster ushered Ann out and locked the door. 'On a night like this, there's nothing to be done. I fear they are all at the bottom of the Tay.'

Ann Craig swooned and began to fall. Baxter caught her just before she hit the ground. 'Come away home, Mrs Craig, there's nothing more to be done tonight.'

Chapter 4
2015

'Why am I going to see Mrs C with my pyjamas on?'

'She's going to look after you for the morning, I've some things to do.' As they walked across the street to the hotel, Fiona tapped his number on her phone again. It was still switched off.

'Mum, I want to show Mrs C my picture of Peter Pan.'

'No time to go home, Jamie. She'll give you paper and you can draw her another one.'

'Okay, she's got new colouring pencils in her desk.' He skipped across the road and they headed for the hotel entrance.

'Fiona, any idea what's happened to—'

'Let's discuss it in a minute, Doug,' she snapped at the rotund man standing by the door, pointing down at Jamie.

She marched towards the office. 'Here he is, Mrs C,' she said, forcing a smile.

'Come away in, wee man. Let's get you settled. My, is it a sleepover you're here for?' She laughed and pointed at his pyjamas.

'Mum said there was no time to change.'

'Mrs C, would you mind taking him over the road for his clothes, but no rush, whenever you've time.' She dropped a key onto the desk, leant down to kiss the top of Jamie's head then turned back to face Doug, who was pointing at his watch.

'Where is he, Fiona? He was due in over an hour ago and his car's gone. He's never been late and we're fully booked tonight.'

'Honestly, I have no idea. I need to go off to try a couple of places. Please bear with me, I'll let you know.' Fiona looked out the window as a white van passed and parked across the road outside the village shop. 'Doug, the paper van's here, you know the review's in today?'

Doug smiled. 'I had no idea,' he said, patting his trouser pockets to check he had some change. 'I'll go and get a copy. Will I pop one through your door in case she runs out?'

'Thanks, Doug,' Fiona said. 'Back soon.'

★ ★ ★

She drove south much faster than the speed limit. God, she looked rough, she thought, glancing in the rear-view mirror at her messy, fair hair and sallow skin. She ought to have at least taken a minute to brush on some blusher; she looked like death.

During the hour-long journey she ran through every possible scenario of what might have happened, where he might have gone, but her thoughts kept returning to the same thing. She turned into Dundee airport, parked at the far end of the short term car park and ran into the terminal, rushing over to the City Flyer check-in desk.

'Hello, sorry to bother you but what time did the London flight leave this morning?'

The girl in the navy jacket and red cravat looked up from her crossword and removed her glasses. 'Left on time, eight twenty.'

'Can you tell me please if a Peter Gibson boarded this morning?'

The check-in girl shook her head. 'Sorry, I can't give out that kind of information.'

'But he's my partner, er, husband,' said Fiona, deciding that embellishing her status might help.

'Sorry, not allowed.' She put on her glasses again and returned to her crossword.

Fiona opened her mouth to ask another question but realised there was no point. She trudged back out of the terminal and headed towards her car. Once again she tapped out his number on her mobile phone and listened. 'Hi, Pete here. Leave a message and I'll get right back.'

She stood by her car and shouted at the phone. 'Pete, where the hell are you? Ring me!'

Between two terminal buildings and over the river she could see Fife bathed in the morning sunshine. This was the sort of day she loved Dundee, with its vista over the water to the low rolling hills on the other side. But there was no time to linger; she needed to get back to Jamie.

Fiona was about to get into her car when she noticed two policemen standing by a red vehicle at the other end of the car park. One was peering inside as the other circled the car, taking down details.

God, she thought, that's Pete's car. He must have been on the flight after all. She looked at her watch. If she alerted the policemen to where she thought he was going, could they stop him? Stop him boarding the next Melbourne flight? But why would they do that? Apart from abandoning his car, he had done nothing criminal.

She climbed into the driver's seat and sat back, mulling over whether to talk to the policemen. She would look pretty foolish if there were some plausible explanation for his disappearance. After all, he loved her, didn't he? And she loved him; he had made her life worth living again since Iain's death.

Fiona started the engine and drove slowly towards the policemen, winding down her window as she approached. She smiled and attempted a casual tone. 'Has someone forgotten they're in the short term car park?'

'No, that'd be for the wardens, not the police,' said the older man, bending down at the back of the car and scribbling in his notepad. The younger man sidled over and winked. 'Stolen. Been found at last.' Then he coughed and turned away as the older man stood up.

Fiona put the car into first gear and eased off, her mouth open. She looked at the registration number in her mirror. Yes, it was definitely Pete's car, she could even see the Superman air freshener Jamie had insisted he buy, dangling in the windscreen. How the hell could it be stolen?

She opened a can of Diet Coke, took a slug then tried to arrange it all in chronological order in her head. It was the end of May now. He'd sold his old banger during Jamie's Easter break and had bought that car the following week. He'd said he got it for a bargain after some mate recommended a local garage. So, he had had the car for a month. It couldn't be stolen, it would've been noticed before. Though when she began to think about it, she realised he had been nowhere in the car other than round the village or north towards Glenshee for a day's walking in the hills.

As she headed into Alyth, she remembered that she needed cash. She stopped outside the RBS in the town square and parked the car. She pushed her debit card into the machine and tapped in her pin number.

She hit the button to select fifty pounds and an error message popped up: Insufficient funds. Strange, she thought, and tried again. The same thing happened. Feeling slightly panicked, Fiona clicked through to check her balance.

Nothing.
He had taken all their savings.

Chapter 5

Sunday 28 December 1879

10 p.m.

Donald Baxter helped Ann out of her wet cape and ushered her into the morning room on the ground floor. He stoked up the fire then went to the door. 'Jeannie,' he shouted, 'come and give us a hand.'

The noise of heavy footsteps drew nearer and Mrs Baxter entered the room. 'Mrs Craig, you look like a drowned rat. Warm up by the fire and I'll fetch a hot toddy.'

'Are the children all right, Mrs Baxter?' asked Ann from the depths of the chair.

Mrs Baxter nodded. 'Aye, fine.'

Ann sat up and stretched out her hands towards the flames. 'Baxter, I've been thinking. I need you to go to the harbour, they must surely put out boats to rescue the passengers.'

Mrs Baxter lifted off her husband's coat with two hands. The wool was a dead weight, sodden with rain.

'Fetch your other coat, Donald!' she said, placing another log on the fire.

'Aye, I'll do that, Mrs Craig, but I don't see how even a big ship could make it out there in this wind.' He turned to his wife, who was raking the fire. 'I'll be back as fast as I can.'

'Are the children asleep, Mrs Baxter?'

'Like I said, the bairns are fine,' she said, poking at the logs. 'Took a wee bit o' time to get them over but they're sleeping away now.'

'Good.' Ann sat back from the fire and stretched her neck. 'I think I should like that hot drink now.'

'Right you are,' said Mrs Baxter, bending down to lift the hemline of Ann's gown. 'This grosgrain silk is drenched, it doesn't dry well. You'll get poorly if you don't go and change.'

Ann nodded but remained sitting.

Mrs Baxter struggled upright, her hand on her lower back. 'Mrs Donaldson next door sent her girl Aggie round to see if we needed anything. She heard about it from Billy the gardener when he came back from the evening service.'

Ann didn't reply, her eyes shut tight, lips moving as if in silent prayer.

'Mrs Craig, d'you think there was any chance Mr Craig wasn't on that train?'

Ann sighed deeply and opened her eyes. 'As you well know, he has taken the four fifteen Edinburgh train for the past six weeks after visiting his aunt in Fife. I cannot see why tonight should have been any different. I do not feel any good can come of this, none at all.'

Ann bit her lip as she considered the future. If the situation was as dire as she presumed, how on earth would she survive without her husband? Without his income?

* * *

Baxter emerged from Whale Lane and crossed over towards the harbour. Noisy crowds had assembled, people shouting at each other over the wind. Baxter pushed his way towards the lights and movement surrounding a large boat that was preparing to leave the harbour. Everyone was clamouring for news, and snippets of it began to reach him.

'The harbourmaster's sending out a steamer.'

'The train's in the river.'

'I heard there's some folk clinging to the piers.'

'There she goes!'

The powerful steamer moved off through the choppy river. The wind was still severe, though at least the thunder and lightning had ceased. Baxter looked up to a large clock above the harbour building. It was quarter to eleven, three and a half hours since the train had disappeared. Was there still the slightest chance that anyone had survived in those icy black waters?

During the interminable wait, the gale began to subside. Eventually someone shouted, 'Look! There's the boat coming back in!'

People in the crowd bellowed questions to the men on board the ship as they threw thick ropes and tied knots round the mooring bollards and soon more rumours began to fly.

'The wind was too strong, couldn't get near enough.'

'The current was against them.'

'I heard the ship got out there, saw a whole section of the bridge had collapsed.'

'They tried to look for passengers but there were none.'

'Everyone's drowned.'

'Nobody kens that, my Johnnie'll be fine.'

Baxter nudged his way through the jostling crowds towards the gangway. There was a seaman coming ashore, his head bent against the wind that continued to lash the waves into foam. He looked up at the expectant crowd, holding onto his cap, and shouted, 'Gone, the train's gone, down into the water.'

'Nonsense. How could you see in the dark?' called an anxious woman.

'We were lowered into the lifeboat, got as near as we could, looked all around. There's no sign of life. No one survived.'

'But could they not be hanging onto the piers?'

The seamen shook his head and walked away.

'No survivors,' he repeated, as the captain appeared at the top of the gangway and the provost and harbourmaster rushed forward to meet him.

Baxter cupped his hand round his ear to hear better as words were exchanged and heads shaken.

'No survivors.' The provost shouted it loud, his voice breaking with emotion: he was very sorry for their loss, but there were no survivors.

Wails were heard from the crowds, paroxysms of grief as those awaiting loved ones heard the news they had all expected but somehow hoped could not be true.

Baxter tied his scarf tightly around his neck and headed off home. How could he tell his mistress that her husband was at the bottom of the river?

Chapter 6
2015

'Even though Glenisla is miles from anywhere, it is well worth a visit to taste talented chef Pete Gibson's food. His is a gift that few of his peers possess. His lightness of touch results in sauces that are the very essence of the flavour but without the heavy richness too often used by classically French-trained chefs. Self-taught, he takes quality Scottish ingredients and converts them skilfully into masterpieces that last in your memory long after your meal is over.

Starters, such as crab bonbons with saffron aioli or venison and rabbit terrine with sweetcorn ice cream, have true, defined flavours yet leave you wanting more. And for mains, his seaweed-crusted lamb loin and hand-dived scallops with cauliflower korma will leave you simply gasping for breath, so exquisite is each mouthful.

But you must leave room for dessert. Just one taste of Aussie Pete's rhubarb and elderflower syllabub with ginger macadamia shortbread will…'

Fiona flung the paper across the table. For God's sake, was he sleeping with the woman? She remembered the day the journalist arrived at the hotel, allegedly incognito. The tape recorder sitting on the table gave it away; that and the fact that she dined alone. Fiona had taken one look at her inappropriate attire for a country hotel – high stilettos and décolleté neckline – and knew who she was.

Fiona sat back on her chair at the kitchen table and looked up at the ceiling. He'd been out late that night, what had he been up to? She was beginning to doubt everything about Pete now. Perhaps she should contact the paper and try to speak to the reporter.

Just then the phone rang.

'Yes? Oh, hi, Mrs C, I was about to come back over the road. Good, glad he's been okay. No, I'll give him lunch here, thanks.'

She tried Pete's phone again – nothing – then she stretched for the paper to see the journalist's name. Cressida Scott, that was it. She headed for the door, her gait weary. How dare he do this to her, to Jamie. She could kill him.

* * *

Jamie sat down at the table and grimaced. 'Why're we having soup, Mum? Mrs C said I could have pizza and chips at the hotel.'

'You had pizza last night. Soup's better for you. Eat up.' Fiona snapped.

Jamie glanced up at his mother's face, her features set rigid. He took one spoonful then plonked the spoon back into the bowl, spilling some soup over the edge.

'Watch what you're doing, will you?' Fiona tapped at her phone then flung it onto the table.

'You said phones weren't allowed at the table, Mum. And why wasn't Pete at the hotel? Mrs C said he's run to do an errand. What's that?'

Fiona sighed. 'Jamie, I've no idea where Pete's gone. Not a clue. He hasn't told me, but I've a feeling he might have gone home to Australia.'

'Without us?'

Fiona shrugged and ripped off a hunk of bread.

'But he always said he'd take me and show me Sydney Harbour Bridge and the kangaroos and that cricket place...'

'Well, it looks like he's gone all by himself.'

Jamie finished his soup in silence. Fiona drummed her fingers on the table and glanced at her son. A single tear ran down his face as he gazed into his half-empty soup bowl.

She scraped her chair back and knelt down beside him. She reached over and hugged him tight. 'Jamie, darling, I'm sorry.' She stroked his curls. 'Sometimes people let you down and it looks like Pete's let us down. But I've no idea why.'

'Was it because I tied his two shoelaces together that time and he never laughed like you did?'

Fiona smiled. 'No, it was certainly nothing to do with you. And today in the paper there's this brilliant article raving about his cooking, so it seems a strange time to go, but...'

Jamie sat up straight. 'Mum, why don't we go to Australia too? Go and find him?' His dark eyes were shining. 'Like an adventure.'

Fiona shook her head. 'We've no money, we can't do that. In fact.' She stroked her son's cheek. 'I've been thinking, we'll need to leave here. Doug'll let us live here for a bit but, when they get a new chef, we'll have to leave the cottage.'

Jamie wandered over to the drawer and returned with paper and pencils. 'But where will we go?'

'We might need to go and live with Granny and Pa in Dundee.'

'I don't want to live in Dundee. I want to live here.'

'But their house is big and... Oh, remember how you can see the Tay Bridge from Granny's bedroom window? Well, they're making a room in the attic above there; she might let you have that room as your bedroom.'

Jamie started to draw a picture of an aeroplane with lots of tiny windows. Fiona took the dishes over to the sink then came back to peer at the picture. Jamie had just completed all the windows and began to draw a head in one at the front.

'Is that Pete?'

'No, that's the pilot. I've forgotten what Pete's face looks like.'

Chapter 7
Monday 29 December 1879

Ann Craig sat in her armchair, gazing out of the drawing room window on the first floor. Dressed in dark grey crêpe, her face was ashen, her eyes red-rimmed. It was late morning and for the past hour she had sat there alone, contemplating the tranquil vista, taking deep breaths. She was trying not to panic at the thought of what might lie ahead for her and the children. She looked at the river, calm now, the water scarcely lapping against the esplanade. The storm had eased the night before, around midnight. It was as if the howling wind and lashing rain had been a dream, or rather a nightmare – until she looked over again to the far end of the bridge. Ann took up the field glasses on the table and peered into them, once more focusing on the broken piers.

There was a soft knock on the door. 'Mrs Craig,' said the maid. 'Mrs Donaldson is here to see you.'

'Thank you, Jessie. Bring us in some tea.'

Margaret Donaldson, dressed in a dark grey gown and black redingote, bustled across the room and embraced her friend. They were an incongruous pair, Ann tall and statuesque, Margaret reaching only up to her shoulders.

'My dear, it is too terrible. What's to be done?'

Ann sighed and dabbed her eyes with a handkerchief, indicating that Margaret take the seat opposite. 'Thank you for taking the children this morning. They are distraught but also do not fully understand.'

'They were playing nicely with the twins when I left just now. James already had the paper and colouring pencils out in the nursery. They may stay for luncheon, and indeed the afternoon, if you wish.'

'Thank you.'

Margaret sat down and glanced out the window. 'You are sure that Robert was aboard that train?'

Ann gave her a weary look. 'If he was not, why is he not home, Margaret? Or why have we not heard from him?'

There was a tap at the door and Jessie came in carrying a broad tray, which she set on the table beside them. ''Scuse me, ladies, but Mrs Baxter says she's put out some of her yellow cake for you.' She began clanging with the silver teapot and china cups and saucers as Ann stood up and went over to inspect the tray.

'Have some of Mrs Baxter's cake, Margaret. It's always excellent.' She put her hand to her throat and swallowed. 'I for one cannot eat a thing.' She turned to the maid and gestured to the decanter of Madeira on the cabinet. Jessie scuttled over and poured two glasses.

Margaret lifted her glass to her lips. Over the rim, her beady grey eyes were just visible. She was blinking uneasily. 'Ann, have you heard a diver is going down this afternoon?'

Ann's blue eyes widened. 'I hadn't. Do they still think there might be survivors?'

Margaret shook her head. 'They do not, but the diver might find some clue about the bod… the passengers, Ann.'

'I simply cannot understand how this ghastly accident can have happened,' said Ann, ringing the bell on the table. 'Jessie, have Baxter come here at once.'

'There's talk the structure of the bridge was weakened by the wind,' continued Margaret. 'I don't recall such a storm, ever. Certainly not in my lifetime. Archibald's mother reminded us of the terrible gale in the winter of 1853, when the Tay was almost frozen over for weeks. But she said even that was nothing compared to last night's wind.' Margaret put down her glass. 'It's remarkable how her memory fails her on day-to-day matters but events years ago she never forgets.'

'And yet consider the change today, the river is like a millpond.'

'Ann, might it be worth sending a telegram to Robert's aunt to confirm that he left the house at the usual time for that train? To eliminate all doubt?'

Ann nodded. 'A good idea. Why did I not think of that? She too will be worrying; the news is bound to have travelled far and wide.'

'Yes, I heard that Her Majesty the Queen had even sent a message to Sir Henry, expressing her sorrow at the calamity.'

'Sir Henry could never have imagined his work as provost of this great city would cause him to encounter such sadness.' She looked up. 'Enter!'

Baxter stood at the door, overcoat on, cloth cap in hand. 'Mrs Craig?'

'Baxter, I want you to go and find out what news there might be after the diver has been in the river.' Ann took a sip of her Madeira. 'Also, I need you to send a telegram for me, asking Lady Cruickshank if my husband did indeed leave her at the allotted time to catch the usual train at Ladybank station. Shall I write down the address or can I leave it to you?'

'There's no need, Mrs Craig, I can do that fine, I ken her address from Mr Craig's letters. Kirkmichael House, Ladybank, Fife. I'll do that first then go from the post office to the harbour and find out anything more.'

'Thank you, Baxter.'

★ ★ ★

That afternoon, Ann was still up in the drawing room, striding back and forth, stopping occasionally to straighten an ornament or move the curtain an inch. Margaret had agreed to keep the children till teatime to give Ann time to consider her options. Ann decided that she would go to the station first thing the next morning and speak to Mr Smith herself. She had had enough with hearsay and rumour; she needed to speak to someone in authority. Alec Smith would have information, surely. She had been acquainted with him for some years – he would help her. The way he looked at her, admiring her, he would definitely be of use.

She picked up the field glasses again and turned at the knock on the door.

Baxter walked in, still with his overcoat on. He had his hat in one hand and as he removed his coat, Ann noticed his black armband.

'What news do you bring?'

'Well, Mrs Craig, the Fairweather – the tug that took the diver out there – set sail at two o'clock. The diver went down at the far end there.' He went to the window and pointed to the south end of the bridge, now barely visible in the dying light of the late afternoon. 'Twice he went down. First time he came back up he said he found the first class carriage.' Baxter stopped as Ann Craig gasped and collapsed into her chair. That was where her husband would have been sitting.

'It was lying on its side, about fifty feet east from the fifth broken pier.'

Ann lifted her fan from the table and began to fan herself with wide sweeping movements.

'Shall I continue, Mrs Craig?'

She nodded.

'Then he went down again and this time found the engine. Same eastern side, just further along. They say the train's lying there along the river bed, from the fourth to the fifth pier.' He pointed out the window. 'The diver found nothing more. No bodies.' He bowed his head and stood still, absorbing the silence of the room.

Eventually Ann put down her fan. 'I want you to come with me tomorrow morning to the station. I wish to see Mr Smith in person for a full assessment of the situation. We shall leave after early breakfast, once you have taken the children next door to the Donaldsons.'

'Very well.'

'And Baxter,' Ann said, her fingers upon the jet brooch at her neck. 'Remove the armband, if you please.' She sighed and continued, 'I appreciate the sentiment but until we have confirmation, we shall not attend to the etiquette of full mourning. I do not wish to upset the children until we know more.'

★ ★ ★

Ann sat between her children's beds and closed the book she had been reading. Every time she read to her children she thought back to her own childhood. Her mother had never read to her, nor indeed cuddled her; she could barely remember any physical contact at all. She bent over to kiss her daughter's forehead then put her arms round her and squeezed tight.

'Mamma, I have been thinking,' said Lizzie, releasing herself from her mother's grasp.

'Yes, my darling?'

'You know how Alice has all these adventures? Well, surely she must have been away from her house for a long time?'

'What do you mean?'

'Well, she fell down the rabbit hole then so much happened to her that the people in her house – her mamma and pappa – must have missed her for many days?'

'Yes, probably.'

'So, I wonder if perhaps Pappa is having a big adventure, like Alice, and he will soon be back home with us once the adventure is over?'

James sighed. 'You don't understand, Lizzie, it's just a book. Mr Carroll made it all up.' He slithered down under his covers and pulled the sheets up to his nose.

'Lizzie, dear child, you have such a wonderful imagination. But now you must say your prayers. Sit up please, James, and put both hands together.'

There was a crash as the door was flung open and Mrs Baxter burst in, red-faced and panting.

'Mrs Craig, come down the stairs at once, Donald has news!' She gestured to Ann to draw nearer. 'They've found a body,' Mrs Baxter hissed. 'They've found a body in the river!'

Chapter 8
2015

Fiona slammed the passenger door shut and turned for one last look at the village where they had lived for the past two years. There was a low mist so she could not see the hills, only a shadowy tunnel of trees, leaves dripping with morning dew. She waved again at Mrs C and Doug, standing at the entrance to the hotel. Doug gave her a thumbs up and beamed. Mrs C bent her head down and waved with both hands at Jamie who sat in the front, unsmiling.

'Wave at Mrs C, Jamie!' Fiona whispered, slipping into the car beside him.

He turned and lifted his hand, attempted a half-smile, then returned to face straight ahead. As they drove away, Fiona looked back in the mirror. The winding road from the village up the glen was still steeped in the lingering mist. She saw the two figures disappear into the hotel and the wooden door shut.

'So, here we go, off to stay with Granny and Pa. Excited?'

Fiona glanced at her son's features, rigid with indignation, and put on the radio. It was the same Radio 4 programme she had heard four weeks before when she discovered Pete had gone.

She had given up trying his mobile and had had nothing back from his email. She had spoken to the two guys he knew in Alyth who insisted they knew nothing and, strangely, she believed them. There was one other person she was going to try once they were settled in Dundee, but until then, she had her son to consider.

The previous day had been the last day of school and she had been so proud as Jamie crossed the little stage in the hall to collect the prize for art again. He had smiled when the teacher had given him his prize but that smile had become rare. Ever since Pete had left, Jamie had been quiet, often morose. She hoped that living with her parents would bring him out of himself. When they had stayed at the house in Magdalen Yard Road for a weekend, he had loved playing with Jack next door. Perhaps the long summer holidays would help him move on from their life up the glen. She wished she too could move on, forget about Pete. Had he just taken her for a ride for three years? Told her he loved her even though he didn't? Did she ever really know him? She shivered as she contemplated the fact that he might be a criminal. If you steal a car and remove £3,000 from a joint account, what else could you be hiding? Every waking moment in the past month, she tried to go over everything he had ever said, searching for a clue about why he might have gone. Nothing.

The only good thing about living back in Dundee was that, once Jamie was sorted and at his new school, she could start work again. She had missed going out and doing something for herself. There had been no chance of finding work as an art curator in or near Glenisla, but in Dundee, with the new V&A opening in a couple of years just along the waterfront, she had hopes of a proper job. Besides everything else, she needed the money.

Fiona slowed the car down as they approached the ring road in Dundee. Jamie, whose eyes had been shut, feigning sleep, sat up. 'Did you remember to pack my skateboard, Mum?'

'Of course.' She peered into the mirror. 'In fact, I can see it poking up above the plants in the back.'

'Good, I want to show Jack next door. Will he be at his house today?'

'No idea, but Granny'll know.'

Jamie's face no longer wore the forlorn look of earlier. Hopefully things were going to turn out fine, she thought, as she turned left along Magdalen Yard Road. She parked the car and followed Jamie's gaze towards the Tay, the water shimmering in the mid-morning sun. On her other side was the home where she had spent the first twenty years of her life, the sweeping driveway leading up to a solid Victorian structure. She chuckled as she thought of a stranger's first impression of the pediment and pillars, perhaps of a household of stately grandeur. Inside the cold stone exterior, however, was the homespun shambles she knew and loved.

★ ★ ★

'So, this is where we thought you could sleep, Jamie. Right at the top of the house,' Dorothy said. 'That suit you all right?'

Jamie tore across the polished floor and straight to the window. 'Cool, thanks, Granny. I can see right to the end of the bridge!'

'When we heard you and your mum were coming to stay, Pa said you had to have this room,' said Dorothy, ruffling her grandson's hair. 'He was converting it into another room for all his drawings, but he can carry on using the study.'

'Thanks.' Jamie turned back from the window and beamed. 'It's huge!'

'About the size of our entire Glenisla cottage!' Fiona laughed.

'Oh, and when Pa gets back, he's going to set up his old Scalextric set and lay it out for you over there. Remember he had to keep taking up the track when he had it out on the kitchen floor.'

Jamie rushed round the large attic bedroom, opening and shutting drawers and cupboards. 'They're all empty.'

'Just waiting for you to unpack, sweetheart,' Dorothy said, drawing him into her droopy cardigan. Jamie allowed her a brief hug then extracted himself and started unzipping his bag.

'Lunch in a bit, Jamie. I'm just going to show your mum into her old bedroom.'

Fiona shook her head and laughed. 'I'm going to be a little girl again.'

'Oh, I forgot to say. Pa's left you a present, Jamie.' Dorothy looked around. 'Now, where did he put it? Ah, yes, he said the clue was "snakes".'

Jamie frowned and looked around, then his eyes lit up and he ran over to the bed and fell to the floor. He lifted up the edge of the duvet and pulled out a package.

'Snakes?' Fiona turned back to her mother.

'Remember Jamie used to be frightened of snakes? Dad said he used to do a weird snake dance for Jamie at bedtime to get rid of any hiding under the bed. Your father's more than a little crazy.'

Jamie sat on the floor with his legs apart and ripped off the newspaper wrappings. 'Wow, look at these, Mum!' He pulled out a pair of binoculars and ran to the window.

'I can see the bridge really well. I'll be able to time all the trains coming across.'

'Maybe not all of them, Jamie,' Dorothy laughed. 'Pa said the binoculars aren't new, but they're the ones you always used to play with when you were little. He thought you might like them up here.'

'They're great, Granny. I can't wait to show Jack.'

★ ★ ★

'So what are you going to do about a job, Fi?' Struan walked over to the kitchen window and opened it a fraction before pulling his pipe out of his jacket pocket. He began to pack it with tobacco then tamped it down and lit it, sucking in and blowing out great puffs of smoke.

'I'm going to see Martha on Monday, she's at the Museum in Albert Square now, says she's going to put feelers out. They're planning a new exhibition on the Tay Bridge disaster, so they might need help with that. Then I need to speak to the V&A people about getting an interview set up sometime in the next few months.' Fiona took a sip of her wine. 'Dad, you're not going to smoke inside when Jamie's around, are you?'

'No, Miss Prim, I am not,' he said, puffing as he threw the match into a bin. 'My grandson will see only the clean, fit me, not the old wreck who has taken residence inside me of late.'

Dorothy shook her head. 'Ignore him, Fi, he keeps pestering the GP with his imaginary ailments, but he just needs to give up that pipe.'

Fiona scraped some risotto to one side and put her fork in the middle of the plate. 'That was delicious, Mum, thanks. Good to be home.'

'Good to have you, sweetheart.' Dorothy looked at her plate. 'But why d'you always leave a tiny amount of food on your plate? That's not the way you were brought up.'

'Sorry, I'll revert to the inner child soon.' Fiona grinned. 'Be swapping my jeans for dungarees next.'

'Nothing wrong with dungarees, I still wear mine around the house, so comfy.' Dorothy looked down at her thick black tights and poked her finger through a hole at the knee. 'Hand me the sewing basket, Stru,' she said, pointing to a corner cupboard.

Struan walked over to the cupboard, lifting an empty Coke can from the counter and throwing it in the bin. Dorothy stood up and opened the bin, extracting the can. 'Recycling, Stru, how many times do I have to tell you!' She shook her head and headed for the outhouse.

'Tell you what, Fi,' Struan said, studying his daughter while puffing out little wisps of smoke. 'If you promise to give up that hideous fizzy drink you're addicted to, I'll think about giving up the baccy.'

Fiona laughed. 'Now, let me think, what's worse for the health? A few cans of Diet Coke every day or an entire packet of pipe tobacco inhaled into your lungs?'

'Well, I agree with you about the smoking, sweetheart, but have you seen how bad Coke is for your teeth?'

'That's why I drink from a straw!' Fiona downed the last of her wine.

Dorothy took the sewing basket from her husband and sat down, leaning back into her rickety chair as she opened it.

'You need to superglue these chairs again, Struan, they're falling to bits.' Dorothy shook her chair from side to side then pulled out a needle and black thread.

Struan walked back to the table and gave his chair a shoogle. He sighed then returned to his pipe. 'Okay, how about this, Fi. Let's start tomorrow after breakfast – no more cans of killer Coke for you, no more pipe for me.'

'So, no more rancid fumes all over the house?' Fiona smirked. 'Sounds like a plan.'

'I'll just nip along to the petrol station for a last pack of Condor then that's it. Sunday is the start of a new life. In fact, I thought I'd teach Jamie to fly that big red kite tomorrow. It's been sitting in the garage for ages. We could take it onto the Green,' he said, grabbing his coat from a hook by the door. He put it on and patted his pockets. 'Christ, no bloody money, where'd I put my wallet, Dot?'

'Dad, you've got to stop swearing when Jamie's around.'

'What, like your bloody Aussie fugitive?' Struan said. 'First time I met him, I thought he had Tourette's syndrome.'

'Ignore him, he comes out with some strange things these days,' said Dorothy, as Struan disappeared out the door. 'You know he won't be able to give up his pipe either.'

She leant down to snip off the thread with her teeth then replaced the needle in the basket. 'But it'll be so good for him to have Jamie around, he looked better today than I've seen him in weeks.'

'Good.' Fiona smiled and started to load the dishwasher. 'Mum, I was planning to get the train to Edinburgh on Tuesday, got a few things to do there. You okay to look after Jamie?'

'Of course, sweetheart, any time. That's why I'm so glad I left the school last year.' She shook her head. 'Retirement doesn't seem to suit your father quite as well though.'

Chapter 9
Tuesday 30 December 1879

The doorbell rang and Jessie ran across the tiled floor. Mrs Baxter had told her they still hoped for a message to say Mr Craig was alive, that he had been detained somewhere and missed the train.

'Good Morning, Jessie.' Mrs Donaldson bustled in, handing her gloves to the maid.

'I shall keep my coat, I can't stay. Tell Mrs Craig I have news.'

Jessie showed her into the morning room then ran upstairs, taking the steps two at a time.

Ann rushed downstairs and into the morning room. 'Is there news?' She sat down opposite Margaret and arranged the heavy material of her gown around her.

'There are two pieces of information, one good, one not so good and...'

'I know about the body, Baxter told me last night.'

'Ah, well, that was the bad news. The good news is that we must continue to pray for Robert's safe return. This morning my housemaid went up to Perth Road first thing to collect the newspaper.' She shook her head. 'The Scotsman is full of the disaster. I suggest you do not even attempt to read it, my dear.'

'Yes and...' Ann urged.

'Aggie passed the end of Miller's Wynd and saw such a commotion. A woman was shouting out like those common fishwives down by the harbour to anyone that would listen, that God had answered her prayers. Her neighbours had all gathered around, many still in night attire, as she stood clutching a piece of paper to her bosom. Aggie approached and asked a neighbour what had happened. Apparently, she'd been grieving since Sunday night and, along with many others, had been waiting at the station for news. She had just gone back to her home – you know those horrid tenement blocks between Perth Road and Hawkhill – to find a gentleman waiting, with a telegram.'

'What did it say?'

'She had been awaiting news of her seventeen-year-old daughter's body. But the telegram was from the girl herself, asking her poor mother's forgiveness as she had decided to stay overnight in Edinburgh on Sunday instead of taking the train home to Dundee. She was – she is – alive.'

Ann let out a long breath. 'It's so refreshing to have some good news. How fortunate is that woman. But surely I would have heard by now, Margaret.'

'Not necessarily. Until you have definite proof, my dear, there is always hope.' She raised an eyebrow. 'I cannot imagine the scene between mother and daughter on her return as surely there was a young man involved. Her mother must have been overjoyed at her return yet angry for her disobedience.'

'I would forgive Robert anything if only he walked through the door,' Ann said, turning towards the window. Her icy blue eyes narrowed at the thought of being destitute.

'Of course you would.' She looked up at the clock. 'Now, it is only ten minutes before Baxter is due to bring the children to the house. Shall I wait and accompany them myself?'

'Oh, yes, that is kind. It is now becoming more than simply an inconvenience Miss Graham taking this week off work.'

'Yes, but Ann, my dear, you are so fortunate to have such an excellent governess. Our Miss Bryden is, I fear, rather too lenient with the twins.'

That is because you are so strict with them, Ann thought, standing up. 'Your kind offer means I can set off earlier for the station with Baxter. I intend to apprehend Mr Smith and find out what is going on.'

Margaret frowned. 'You know they are setting up the refreshments room as a...' She swallowed. 'A morgue. Are you sure you want to do this?'

'Yes, I must.' Ann pushed her fingers through her long wavy tresses. She knew Margaret was looking at her, judging. She had overheard one of Margaret's Women's Guild friends whispering to her that Ann Craig was coquettish. Well, so be it, at least I don't look dowdy, she thought, tipping her head back to shake out her loose hair.

'But first I shall go upstairs to finish my toilette. I shall send the children down presently.'

Watching Ann rush to the door, Margaret put her hand to the back of her head, clamping her fingers over her tightly braided chignon.

★ ★ ★

Ann and Baxter approached Tay Bridge station and stopped at the edge of the crowds. A policeman stood by the entrance, barring people from entering.

'Go and ask what is going on, Baxter. Surely they must let relatives go down into the station.'

Donald nudged his way though the crowds, tipping his hat as he pushed past any women. Ann watched him speak to the policeman then wend his way back through the throng.

'All relatives are allowed in. Follow me, Mrs Craig.'

He held an arm out at right angles as he jostled his way through the throng, so that Ann did not have to shove people aside herself. She strode on, head held high, the exotic plumes on her hat making her a foot taller than everyone around her.

'This is the lady I told you about, sir,' Baxter said to the policeman.

The policeman pushed the heavy wooden gate behind him open. As she passed, she heard him whisper, 'Sorry for your loss.'

She nodded acknowledgement and continued on towards the main steps. Inside the station the broken glass was gone. Someone had at least attempted to clear some of the debris from the storm; it would be a long, slow process. There were people waiting on the platform, some sitting and some standing, all eerily silent, as if they had been struck dumb. The door to the third class waiting room was open. Ann peered inside and saw a dozen or so persons, all dressed in black, most staring at the floor. One man lifted his head and as she glanced at him she saw his expression; it was one of long-suffering supplication.

Ann pulled her handkerchief from her pocket and dabbed her nose. She was appalled at the sight of these poor people, waiting and wondering. Could nothing be done? And then she saw a man on his knees, consoling an old woman in the corner. It was Alec Smith.

Ann waved her hankie in the air and he came towards the door.

'Mrs Craig,' he said, wringing his hands together. 'I was just telling the relatives the Fairweather has been out on the river again, with the diver.'

'Yes, I heard.'

'Will you come to my office? I have a few minutes before I must leave.' He gestured the way and beckoned for Baxter to follow.

Inside the little office it was cold and empty, the telegraph machine silent.

'Mrs Craig, have you heard there is a body?'

She nodded. 'Baxter here told me, but I have no details, only that it was a woman.'

'Last night, just before sunset, a mussel dredger was out on the river, about three miles from the bridge, north-east of Newport. One of the men on board noticed something drifting between sandbanks. He rowed over to it and saw it was a body.'

He opened his mouth to continue then looked down at the floor.

'Mr Smith, I am not so feeble that I cannot hear the unpalatable truth.' Ann removed her gloves and flicked them impatiently between her hands.

Alec Smith gazed at her soft, pale hands. 'He saw it was a woman, her poke bonnet was still tied beneath her chin and her black skirts floated around her. He managed to fish her out with a hook.'

Ann pressed her lips together and grimaced.

'The body was brought here. It is yet to be identified.

We have made the refreshments room into a mortuary. Now there is one body, we expect many more.'

Ann nodded. 'Has anything else come ashore?'

'Yes, I was along at the harbour earlier and the master told me there's all sorts come ashore a couple of miles away at Broughty Ferry beach. Items are being washed up on the sand at low tide.'

'What sort of items?'

'Gentleman's vests in a package, a woman's handbag containing a bible. A pair of spectacles, shoes, several full mailbags.' He paused. 'A child's handkerchief.'

Ann began to tremble but forced herself to sit up tall. She took a deep breath. 'What is to be done next?'

'My staff will lay out all the flotsam in the refreshments room so that relatives might lay claim to them and then, eventually, identify their loved ones.'

There was a tap on the door and they turned to see a tall, ginger-whiskered man, wrapped in a thick woollen overcoat. He removed his hat on seeing Ann.

'Excuse me for interrupting, Mr Smith, but as I indicated this morning, I need to return to Aberdeen today and you said you might have information on when trains northbound shall return to regular timetable.'

'Of course, Mr Fletcher, come away in.' He gestured for the man to enter. 'This is Mrs Craig, her husband was on board the train. One of only two passengers in first class, we believe.'

The man stared at Ann, his dark eyes narrowing. His expression was difficult to determine but as he inclined his head and held out his hand to her, she realised it was not the usual admiration, but pity.

'Mrs Craig, this is Edward Fletcher, the diver who

went down yesterday.'

Ann stood up and faced him. 'Can you tell me what you saw? Please.'

'I've done many dives in my long career. The Tay has always been a challenge as it is so fast flowing, and from the bridge it is also tidal. I was taken out in the boat and then I descended.'

'Excuse me asking, Mr Fletcher,' interrupted Baxter, 'but I've aye been curious about divers. How d'you keep out the cold, what d'you wear?'

'Leather suit with brass helmet bolted on and weighted boots.'

'How do you breathe?'

'The air is pumped down by a manual pump on board.'

'I read something in the newspaper recently about diving bells,' Ann asked. 'Do you use those?'

'No, they'd have been no use at those depths, so I just went down myself and communicated with the men onboard by standard procedures. Four tugs on my rope means I need to come back up. I managed to stay down there for six to seven minutes each time. On the second dive, I found the coach.'

'What could you see?' Baxter leant closer to hear the softly spoken man.

'Nothing, it was dark and murky. All I managed to bring up was some of the upholstery, a piece of cloth from the seating in the first class carriage.'

Ann sighed and sat down with a thump. 'Mr Fletcher, do you think bodies will be recovered soon?'

'I cannot say, I am sorry.' He turned to address Alec Smith. 'Mr Smith, is there an Aberdeen train soon?'

'My apologies, sir, of course. Normal timetables are not

yet resumed for northbound trains but we are planning on having one leave on the hour.' He glanced up at the clock. 'You have plenty of time. Platform four.'

'Thank you.' Fletcher nodded at Ann and headed for the door, where he pulled the stationmaster aside. 'I talked with some whalers last night at my lodgings. They say a drowned body wouldn't rise to the surface till after seven days, because of the trapped gases. Usually it would be three to four days but at this time of year, in the cold, it would take longer.'

'But that woman?' Alec Smith tilted his head towards the mortuary along the platform.

'Her body must have drifted into the shallow waters. If the others are lying on the riverbed, it could be a long wait.'

Alec Smith watched the diver stride along the platform then turned back towards Ann.

'I heard that, Mr Smith. So we must truly wait a week for news? What will you do with all the relatives?'

He looked out at them. 'Unless the provost or harbourmaster have any other ideas, I intend to call in the minister. All we can do is pray. There is nothing more to be done.'

Chapter 10
2015

Fiona and Jamie wandered along the sandy beach, hand in hand. The warm water lapped onto their feet and the sea sparkled in the midday sun. They both smiled and looked up towards the dunes to see a red kite flying over the sandy ridges. Fiona stopped and Jamie began to run towards it. Then they saw whose hand held it: it was Pete, in his favourite beach shorts and a tatty old T-shirt. He beamed when he saw them and Fiona felt a surge of happiness flooding over her like a wave of warm water. But as she watched him approach, she also noticed he kept looking over his shoulder. She found herself unable to walk; the sand was impeding her steps. But Jamie was running towards the dunes and Pete kept turning his head over his shoulder. He stopped and looked round one last time and Fiona could just make out some blurred figures behind him. She wanted to shout to him that she loved him, she missed him, but then as Jamie was about to reach him, she woke up.

Fiona opened her eyes wide and felt a tide of sadness sweep over her. The dream had been so vivid; she wanted to get straight back into it. She frowned as she remembered how keen Jamie was to see him, running over the sand, and she realised how much she missed Pete. What surprised her was that she missed him now more than Iain, who had been her husband for ten years.

Theirs had been a happy marriage, until Iain's cancer had arrived unannounced and he was gone within weeks.

She felt sweaty, the sheets and her pyjamas were damp. She looked at the clock: six o'clock. Why was it you had such vivid dreams just before you woke up? It was something to do with REM sleep – her mum would know. She'd ask her, though she wouldn't tell her she'd been dreaming of Pete. Dorothy might think she wasn't coping well. She wondered if she was coping at all. Sometimes it felt like she kept putting on a brave face for Jamie when all she wanted to do was sob.

Fiona slipped into her flip-flops – thongs, Pete used to call them – and as she headed for the stairs she remembered she had been carrying the same flip-flops in the dream. The house was silent but the early morning light illuminated the wooden stairs as she slapped her way down. Even before she opened the kitchen door, she could smell it. She pushed open the door and shook her head. There at the back door stood her father, in his ancient silk dressing gown, pipe in hand. He was looking out towards the Green and the river beyond.

'Dad, what are you doing? You promised.'

Struan spun round and grinned. 'Cup of tea, Fi?'

'You're a big cheat, Dad. I've given up my cans of the fizzy stuff.' Fiona muttered, flicking on the kettle.

'My house, my rules.' He continued to puff out wisps of smoke. 'I thought if I did it now, there's a good two hours till Jamie's up so he won't smell it.'

'Bit extreme, but cunning idea, Dad.'

Struan pulled his matches from his pocket and had just begun to relight his pipe when he turned to look at his daughter.

She was pouring boiling water into two mugs, scowling.

Struan put his pipe on the window ledge outside and strolled into the kitchen. He tousled Fiona's hair and sat down on the rickety chair. 'Your mum's right, these chairs are falling to bits. That's today's job. What are you up to?'

Fiona sipped her tea then sniffed. 'I can still smell the smoke in here, Dad.'

'That's why I had a smoke now and not later when the Little Prince will descend from the high turret of his stately castle and breath only fresh Dundee air.'

Fiona grinned. 'I'm off to Edinburgh today, got some folk to see.'

'Wouldn't be anything to do with Bruce's sudden exit, would it?'

'He used to hate when you called him that.' She leant over the table, both hands round the mug. 'Might be.'

'Can't you just let him go? A disastrous part of your life but one that's over now?'

'Dad, I can't just shrug off three years, the things we did as a family. Jamie adored him.'

'Not what he said to me on Sunday when we were out with the kite.'

Fiona glared at him. 'What do you mean?'

Struan shrugged. 'Just that he said he was sometimes scared of Pete.'

Fiona stared at her father. 'What did he say?'

'Mentioned something about tying shoelaces together and putting salt in his tea?'

Fiona's shoulders dropped. 'Oh, is that all? Of course he was mad, who wouldn't be? Jamie was just being a pain in the neck. Pete was great with him.'

'If you say so, sweetheart.'

'Do you know any different?'

Struan put down his mug and looked out towards the river. 'One weekend when you were down staying here, you were out with Mum. Pete was on his laptop on the table here and Jamie was drawing one of his pictures beside him. I was in the hall, unbeknownst to them. I was trying to figure out where I'd put my wallet or keys or something. Anyway, I suddenly heard Pete bellow at the lad, can't remember what he said but it was loud, so I opened the door. Jamie looked terrified. Pete laughed when he saw me and made light of it, said something like Jamie had nearly ruined something he was doing on his Facebook page.'

Fiona sat back onto her chair. 'Pete wasn't on Facebook. Everyone used to take the piss out of him for living in the last century.'

Struan shrugged. 'Just repeating what he said.' He leant over to pat his daughter's shoulder.

'Why'd you not tell me?'

'You and Mum came back full of the joys of spring, didn't want to ruin the weekend. Then it was only after Bruce buggered off that I remembered.'

Fiona shivered. 'If I got my hands on him, I could actually kill him.'

★ ★ ★

Fiona sat back in her seat and looked out the window as the train drew to a halt: Leuchars station, she'd just read about that. She delved into her bag for the book that Martha had given her, remembering that this was the station where, in 1879, the last passenger had disembarked from the ill-fated train. The exhibition the museum was planning on the Tay Bridge disaster was to tie in with the memorial erected on Riverside Drive. Martha was putting it all together and had recommended Fiona to the museum for an assistant position. She was so grateful to her friend, thought Fiona. What would she do without her?

Fiona flicked through the book to the section about Leuchars. As the train pulled out, she turned to look back down the platform towards the main road to St Andrews, trying to imagine the scene that night in 1879.

The train from Edinburgh had been a couple of minutes late due to the high winds and had to delay even longer as one of the first class passengers had arranged for a coach to meet him at Leuchars to take him to St Andrews. On arrival at the station however, there was no sign of coach or coachman and so the gentleman climbed back into first class, having decided to continue on to Dundee instead. Above the noise of the ferocious storm, the passengers on board heard the knock-knocking of the stationmaster's hammer as he went along the train, tapping the wheels in each of the five carriages. Once he was happy the train was sound, he pulled out his whistle and was about to blow it when he looked east to see the lights of an approaching vehicle, hurtling along the road at speed. It was the gentleman's coach, so the stationmaster rushed to first class and helped him and his luggage off the train and onto the platform.

What a lucky escape, Fiona thought as she continued reading. The next stop on the track north – and the last one before the bridge – was St Fort. It was here that all tickets were collected and although these were later counted, there were some passengers without tickets: off-duty railway staff and children accompanying adults. This was why the final number of deaths was never known. There were fifty-nine names on the memorial but it was reckoned that many more had died. St Fort was only two miles from the bridge and as the train increased its speed to try to make up time that stormy evening, the catastrophe awaiting those poor passengers loomed.

Fiona shut the book and looked out at the rolling Fife landscape. She must bring Jamie on this train, he would love the journey. She pushed the book into her bag and pulled out her iPad to look up Edinburgh buses to Granton.

* * *

As the bus swept round the corner into Granton, she looked out over the Firth of Forth and recalled the passage in the book about the doomed train leaving from Granton pier. Having left Edinburgh Waverley at 4.15 p.m., the train had stopped at Abbeyhill, Leith Walk and Trinity, then at Granton at 4.35 p.m. Here the passengers boarded the paddleboat ferry, the William Muir, to Burntisland where they continued on the train through Fife and eventually to the River Tay and their fate. She gazed out over the river towards Fife, barely visible in the morning haar.

Her bus stopped just after the Old Chain Pier and she got off and looked at the pub in amazement. She'd heard the place had been gutted in a fire, not long after Pete had left the kitchens there for Glenisla, but the transformation was startling. The roof was new and there was a conservatory, all freshly painted. There were even tables and chairs outside on the pavement. What a different place from the ferry booking office it was in the nineteenth century, and from the dark dingy pub it had been before the fire.

She swung open the door and walked in. The room was brighter than she remembered, though the stale beery smell was much the same. She checked her watch. It was eleven o'clock, so there ought to be someone around.

She cleared her throat loudly and headed for the bar. The kitchen was at the back, but she didn't like to just go in. She was about to cough again when a door opened.

A man in his early thirties appeared behind the bar, staring at Fiona. He put his tattooed arm up to his head and scratched under his white chef's hat. 'Christ, is that you, Fi?'

Fiona smiled and nodded. 'Hi, Ross, how've you been?'

He came round the bar and threw his arms round her. 'Where's the hunk? He with you?'

Fiona drew herself away and looked at him straight in the eye. 'That's why I'm here. I tried to call but they kept saying you weren't here so I thought I'd come down myself and try to find you.'

'Been back home for a month, just got back at the weekend.' He swallowed. 'Mum died, I'd to sort stuff, funeral and things.'

'I'm so sorry. Was she ill?'

'Nope, car crash, all very sudden. Dad's not coping too well, but I had to come back, got to get on with things now.'

'That's awful, I'm really sorry.' Fiona looked up at him, at his earring glimmering under the light above her head. 'Where was home for you, was it Sydney?'

Ross shook his head. 'Noosa, up the coast.'

'Of course, Pete said how beautiful it is up there.'

He ushered her to a seat. 'Coffee?'

'You got time?'

'Sure, won't be any lunch customers till twelve. Debs'll be in soon for the bar.' He went over to the coffee machine and started to fill the metal filter basket.

'You've not heard then?'

He slid the filter into position and looked round. 'What?'

'Pete left, did a runner, just disappeared. No idea where, took all our savings and...' Fiona felt tears start to fill her eyes. 'Sorry,' she said, taking a deep breath.

Ross's mouth was open as he stared, incredulous, at Fiona. 'What?'

She nodded, and then continued to tell him about the day, six weeks before, when Pete had upped and left.

Ross stirred a sachet of sugar into his espresso and leant over the table. 'I just don't get it. I mean, why? Why the hell would he leave you? And, Christ, how's that cute boy of yours taking it?'

'Jamie was pretty gutted. We're living at my mum and dad's house now in Dundee. He seems to like it there, great mates with the boy next door.'

Ross shook his head. 'D'you know, I did wonder why I'd not heard a thing, after Mum... But I wasn't in contact with anyone while I was away. So where d'you reckon he's gone?'

Fiona shrugged. 'I presume back to his folks in Australia, but how would I know? Heard nothing and not likely to. The hotel staff were all livid, had to promote Tom the sous chef too soon – and Pete had just had a brilliant review.'

'Of course, I saw that, I remember thinking I must get in touch, then there was the accident and...'

'Did you have his folks' contact details in Melbourne, Ross?'

'Melbourne? He was from Tassie, Fi.'

Fiona looked up at Ross over her coffee cup. 'He told me he was from Melbourne and his parents lived there.'

'He had a Tassie accent, they speak differently down in Hobart. He used to take the piss out of my northern drawl. And he never spoke about his family.' Ross took his phone from his pocket and scrolled down. 'Got his mobile number on my contacts – but you've obviously tried that.'

'Endlessly.'

'Weird, no email for him. Did he not have one? Surely he's on Facebook, at least?'

Fiona shook her head and tucked a loose strand of hair behind her ears.

The door swung open and a girl with spiky turquoise hair came in. She smiled broadly and said hello, revealing a glint of metal on her tongue.

'Hi, Debs,' said Ross. 'Be with you soon.'

There was the hiss of a can opening. Debs stood with her tanned shoulders and broad back to them, tipping her head back as she swigged from the can.

'Debs used to work the bar when Pete started work here, only came back last year,' explained Ross. 'Debs, can you remember anything about Pete? This is his partner, Fi. Seems he's done a runner.'

Debs swivelled round, her face flushed. 'No, what happened?'

'She just woke up one morning and he was gone. A note saying he was off. Passport and everything gone too.'

'Fucking idiot, always thought there was something…' Debs stopped when she saw Fi's expression.

'Sorry, out of order. He was a good guy but he had these crazy moments. Remember that time, Ross, we were all pissed after a late night and he suddenly got kind of weird and forced us to agree the three of us would head down under the next day. I didn't even have a bloody clue where he was from – New Zealand, was it?'

Ross shook his head. 'Australia.'

'So, you can't remember anything else about him,' said Fiona. 'Did he mention his family?'

Debs shook her head and took another swig from her can. 'Better get on. Presume you need onions peeling?'

'Yeah, cheers, Debs.' Ross leant back on his seat. 'She never cries when she peels onions, so I get her to do a whole bag before service. Chops them too. Me, I'm crying like a baby if I go near a raw onion.'

Fiona smiled. 'So you don't know anyone else who might know where he's from?'

'Can't think of anyone. I met him one night when we were drinking at the Granton Arms. He said he'd done some cheffing so I asked him to join me for a shift and that was it. He was only here for a few months.'

'But he must've talked to you about home? Family?'

'Not what blokes do, Fi, sorry.' He stood up and put his hand on her shoulder. 'But if I think of anything, I'll let you know. Fi, I'm really sorry but, to be honest, I know nothing about him. Not a bloody clue.'

Chapter 11
Wednesday 31 December 1879

'That's a beautiful picture of our house, James. The windows and the pillars at the front door are so exact. Thank you. Can you draw me another please? Perhaps the Donaldsons' house next door?'

'I will try, Mamma, although theirs is not as easy. Pappa told me ours has classical lines, theirs does not, it is not symmetrical. But I shall try.'

Ann ruffled her son's hair. 'Good boy.'

James pulled out another sheet of paper from the pile on the table. 'I shall do one of the house with the dog at the window.'

'Why do we not have a dog, Mamma?' Lizzie snuggled into her mother's lap as she lay across the window seat, her stockinged feet stretched out.

'Hush, dear child,' said Ann, stroking her hair. 'You should be sleeping. Remember you promised that if you had extra pudding at luncheon, you would have a quiet time this afternoon?'

Lizzie screwed up her eyes to close them tight, then yawned. 'I know, Mamma, but I am not sleepy.'

Ann wound a finger through her daughter's ringlet. 'Then why are you yawning?' She peered over at James, who had drawn four solid lines for the walls of the house.

Hearing the clip-clop of horses, she turned back to the window and looked down to the street. A carriage drew up outside their gate and the horses whinnied as they were brought to a halt.

'Is that a horse?' Lizzie sat up and knelt on the window seat cushion to look out. 'Oh look, a carriage. Who is it?' Her eyes opened wide. 'Is it Pappa coming back from his adventures?'

James dropped his pencil and ran to the window, where he jumped up to join his sister on the seat.

A man stepped down from beside the driver to open the carriage door. A figure, dressed in black, descended, pausing on each step as if it were slippery. There had been a sharp frost that morning and there was an icy blast coming straight off the North Sea and down the river. Once on the road, the figure straightened up, revealing her face.

Ann gasped. 'It is Lady Cruickshank. She must have received my telegram.' She stood up and brushed down her skirts then ran to the mirror above the mantelpiece, sweeping her fingers through her hair and pinning up some straggly locks. She sighed as she noticed her grey pallor, then pinched her cheeks to try to revive some colour. 'Why has she come? Has she news?' she muttered to herself.

The children ran over to her, excited. 'Why is that lady here, Mamma? Does she have news of Pappa?'

'I don't know, but you two must remain up here while I receive her.' Ann took a deep breath and looked at her hands; they were shaking. She opened the door then turned to her children. 'Play quietly, please. You ought not to be in the drawing room at all. She would expect children to be in the nursery.'

Ann closed the door behind her and rushed to the top of the stairs; she looked down to see Mrs Baxter shambling along the hallway to the door. 'The morning room, Mrs Baxter! Put her in there.'

Mrs Baxter looked up and nodded, stopping to remove her apron and ram it in a drawer in the hall.

'Bring tea!' Ann hissed, before shuffling backwards so that she could not be seen.

The door swung open. Mrs Baxter inclined her head and ushered in her master's aunt. 'Please come this way, my lady. Mrs Craig shall be down presently.'

Ann peeked round the banister to watch Lady Cruickshank peel off her gloves, remove her cloak and thrust them at Mrs Baxter. Ann appeared at the top step, nodded at the housekeeper and began her descent. She wondered what news she brought. If it were good, why was her attire the black of mourning?

Ann entered the morning room and walked to the window where Lady Cruickshank, dressed in a dark tea gown, stood looking out onto the rose garden.

'It always surprises me that one's gardeners must cut the roses back quite as much. And yet, every year in the summer months, they bloom with reliable certainty. Nature is a wondrous thing.' She stretched out a hand and Ann took it, glancing up at the sexagenarian, whose lined face betrayed no emotion. Ann's hands were sweaty and all of a sudden she felt weak.

'Please sit down, Aunt Euphemia.' Ann gestured to the comfortable armchair by the fire. 'Are you feeling better? You look well.'

She frowned. 'I am always well, Ann, I never allow myself the indulgence of illness.' She started to fan herself with her hand. 'Fetch me a fan, will you. It is stifling in here.'

Ann handed her the fan from the table behind her then reached over the table for the bell and rang it. 'Shall you take tea?'

'What's that? Tea, yes. And cake.'

Ann sucked in a deep breath. She wished the woman would not treat her like a servant.

Lady Cruickshank looked around and towards the window again. 'That is an extremely sharp wind out there. But thank the good Lord Sunday's storm abated. I had the impression our walls were to come tumbling down, like Jericho.' Her wrinkled face relaxed a little before the daunting expression returned.

'How was it on this side of the river on Sunday night? Dundee was struck most terribly I hear, and what a shock to have had the bridge come down. It took me such a long time to cross the river this morning. Fortunately I was only in Tayport, so only five minutes from the ferry journey over the river to Broughty Ferry.'

'So were you not…'

'Do you recall me telling my nephew about the rumours that the ferry drivers used to race the train drivers over the river? They used to watch each other and see who would reach the north shore first. He never concurred, he said trains were always faster than boats. But I said the races were dangerous, the trains were only meant to travel at a slow pace on the bridge, but men do like to compete. However, my ferry today was slow and calm, respectful.' Lady Cruickshank paused for breath and Ann readied herself to ask a question, but her companion continued.

'And so there has been talk of the fact the train had been speeding over the bridge in such inclement weathers and that may have been what caused the terrible accident.'

A knock at the door brought a welcome interlude. Ann had forgotten how much her husband's aunt liked to talk, even though she was rather deaf and heard little of what others said. Mrs Baxter brought in a tray of tea and set it out on the table beside her.

'Thank you, Mrs Baxter.' Ann turned away, aware the housekeeper was still standing behind her. She had taken to doing that, trying to eavesdrop. Ann shot her a stern look. 'That will be all.'

Ann cut the cake and began to pour the tea.

'Aunt Euphemia, I presume you got my telegram?'

The older lady swivelled round, the taffeta of her black gown rustling. She had clearly not heard the question.

'Ann,' she said, sitting up in her chair. 'Where is my nephew?'

The delicate china cup Ann had been placing on its saucer clattered down, spilling some tea. 'What do you mean by that, Aunt Euphemia?' She raised her voice. 'Did you not receive my telegram? It was sent on Monday afternoon.'

Lady Cruickshank glared at her. 'I left Kirkmichael House on Monday after luncheon on hearing about the accident. Of course I had to be with Caroline in Tayport. My daughter was distraught and I had to be at her side. She is perfectly fine now, her confinement is still some three months hence, but she was anxious and I ordered bed rest until she is calmer. I shall return there tonight once I have done this dreadful thing I must do. Which is why I need Robert. Will he be back soon?'

Ann leant back against the chair, aghast.

'What ails you, child? Speak!'

Ann took a deep breath and sat up straight. 'Aunt
Euphemia, I had understood you were here as a result
of the telegram I sent you asking if Robert was indeed
on time for his usual train from Ladybank on Sunday
evening, after his afternoon visit to Kirkmichael House.
He had indicated you were unwell.' She paused. Aunt
Euphemia's expression was inscrutable. 'It seems now
that you never received the message, for, if you had, you
would be aware why I am in shock. Robert is – we must
presume – dead.' Ann's voice was raised. 'He was, again
we surmise, on that train and we know no one can have
survived.' She pressed her lips tight together. 'There,
now you have it.'

Lady Cruickshank tilted her head to one side and
swivelled in her chair to face Ann. 'First of all, I am
in full health and cannot imagine why Robert thought
otherwise. Also, I am unable to recall precisely when
Robert left on Sunday, but I feel sure it was not long
after luncheon. I had some letters to write so we said our
adieux directly after leaving the dining room. I believe
his custom was to walk round the estate before taking an
afternoon train back to Dundee. I am afraid I cannot help
you on his precise timing, but I am sure he was not on
that ill-fated train. Perhaps he had to travel to Edinburgh
for some business and has been unable to contact you.'

She paused to sip from her cup. 'But the reason I am
here today is to undertake the most frightful of duties.
My carriage is to take me now to the station where I
believe they have a makeshift mortuary. I must identify
the body of a young woman brought up from the waters
of the Tay on Monday afternoon.'

Ann picked up a small damask napkin from the tray

and began to fan herself with it. 'Why? Why have you been asked to do that?'

The old lady turned to look out the window where the branches on the magnolia were swaying in the wind. 'They believe she is – was – one of my housemaids. Janet Clark. They require me, as her employer, to attend to this. They have been unable to contact her father and her mother is dead. I had hoped Robert might accompany me on such an onerous task. But if he is not here...' She looked up at the clock. 'I must go soon. Shall you accompany me in his stead?'

Ann wiped her brow with the napkin and placed it on the tray. 'Yes, I shall accompany you. And if, as you believe, Robert was not on the train, then there is hope he might still be alive.'

'I cannot see why ever not.' Lady Cruickshank stood up. 'We must leave now. There is only one ferry sailing back to Tayport this afternoon, I cannot miss it for there will be none tomorrow. Henderson has the carriage waiting. Come along, and fetch your coat and bonnet, it is cold outside.'

Chapter 12
2015

'Hi, Doug, how're you doing?'

'Great thanks, you got time to chat?'

'Yeah, no worries, I'm driving but I've got you on speaker phone. What's new in Glenisla?'

'I've just had a phone call, Fiona. Had to let you know. It was kind of to do with the restaurant review from the weekend Pete disappeared.'

Fiona glanced at herself in the mirror. She was frowning, those increasingly obvious lines in her forehead furrowed.

'Restaurant been busy since, I presume?'

'Yes, it's really helped, though without Pete it's been tricky to keep the food as good. Tom had to really raise his game – and fast.'

'Well, let's hope they keep flocking to Glenisla. I miss it. We both do.'

'And we miss you, Fiona.' Doug coughed. 'Anyway, it was a phone call from somebody with an Australian accent.'

'Who from?'

'A woman, didn't give her name. But she said she'd been trying to find Pete for years and his name came up in the review on a Google search. When I said he'd upped sticks and left, she said something funny.'

Fiona turned into a lay-by on the ring road. She

couldn't concentrate while she was driving. 'What?'

'She said, "Oh, so he's gone and done it again, has he?"'

Fiona felt her stomach tighten.

'What else did she say?' Her voice was now a whisper.

'Nothing, she hung up. When I told Mrs C, she said I should have dialled 1471 and phoned her straight back, but the butcher phoned right afterwards about an order.'

'Did she sound young or old?'

'No idea. You think that was maybe his mum?'

'Maybe.' Fiona looked at the clock on the dashboard. 'I've got to get going, I'm picking up Jamie.'

She told him about Jamie's football lessons and about his new best friend Jack next door.

'And how about you, Fiona? How're you doing?'

'I was doing okay till just now.'

'I'm sorry, but Mrs C thought I should tell you and...'

'God, no, Doug, thanks for telling me. Really, I'm glad you did.' She turned the key in the ignition.

* * *

'Is there any more soup, Granny?'

'Jamie, I love feeding you. You have such a good appetite. Of course there's more soup. About a gallon.'

'What's a gallon?' Jamie held out his bowl.

'A lot!' Dorothy took the bowl and went to the cooker and picked up the ladle.

'So, tell us more about the football then. What position are you playing?'

'Well, I started off at centre midfield but now I'm playing centre forward and I've got to run even faster. I scored a goal.'

'What about Jack?'

Jamie giggled. 'They started him off in goal, he hated it.'

'But he's only a wee boy, what's that about?' Dorothy pushed the bread basket over the table.

Jamie helped himself to another roll. 'He's smaller than me but he's only ten and a quarter. I'm ten and a half. Anyway, they moved him to left back and he's cool with that.'

'Remember that day Pete and you played football all day long, the Easter weekend when I was doing a shift for Mrs C at the hotel?' asked Fiona.

'Yeah, he was ace at keepy-uppy.' Jamie rammed the roll into his mouth.

'And that training exercise you used to play too, what was it called again?'

Jamie swallowed. 'Dribbling Dingo Drills, Pete said he played it a lot at home. I loved playing that with him.'

Fiona grinned. 'Sounds a bit of a made-up name to me.'

'Said Sam taught him.'

'Who's Sam?'

Jamie shrugged then pushed his chair back. 'Pa and me fixed the chairs well, didn't we, Granny?'

'You certainly did, sweetheart.' Dorothy tickled the nape of his neck. 'Now, would you like a banana or an apple?'

'Can I take it outside? Said I'd meet Jack on the Green after lunch.'

'Okay,' said Fiona. 'You can play outside all afternoon, but don't forget to tell him we won't be around tomorrow morning. We're off to the museum, Martha's going to show you the pictures of the Tay Bridge disaster.'

'Cool.' Jamie went to the door and picked up the football. 'Oh, I've just remembered the other exercise Pete and I did. Starfish jumps. Look!'

Jamie threw the ball down and stood with his legs apart then stretched his arms out at his sides. He counted to three then jumped high in the air, arms wide. He did three then grinned and picked up the ball.

'Did Sam do those too?' Fiona asked.

'Yeah,' he said skipping out the door.

Chapter 13

Wednesday 31 December 1879

The door to the refreshments room on platform one was shut, a policeman standing at the door.

'Ladies, can I help you?'

Lady Cruickshank raised her chin.

'I have been asked to identify the body. Lady Cruickshank of Kirkmichael.'

Ann glanced at her. There was a rare tremor of emotion in her voice.

'If you would care to take a seat on the platform here, ladies. Dr Anderson is with the families in the waiting room, he said he would accompany you.'

'Thank you,' said Aunt Euphemia, heading along the platform for the bench.

Ann lingered to speak to the policeman. 'Excuse me, where are the passengers' possessions, the things washed ashore?'

'They've been taken to the first class waiting room. But you can only enter if you're a relative.'

She nodded. 'I am.'

'Sorry for your loss. Tell Donnie on the door.'

'Thank you. I shall first accompany my husband's aunt.'

Ann followed Lady Cruickshank down the platform and took a seat on the bench beside her.

'Have you ever seen a corpse, Ann?'

Ann darted a glance at her aunt. 'Yes, I have. Why?'

'Many ladies these days have not. Caroline and I were with dear Francis when he died at home.' She took out her handkerchief. 'So you know not to come too close. Besides, I am the one who must identify. Not you.'

'Lady Cruickshank.' A gentleman dressed in a black frock coat approached. He pulled off his tall hat as they stood up, stretching out his hand. 'I am Dr Anderson, from Broughty Ferry.'

Aunt Euphemia reached out her hand and inclined her head. 'This is my nephew's wife, Mrs Ann Craig.'

Ann inclined her head. 'You perhaps know our neighbour, Dr Archibald Donaldson?'

'Indeed I do. And in fact I have had occasion to visit their house on Magdalen Yard Road.'

'This is no time for pleasantries.' Lady Cruickshank interrupted. 'Tell me what to do, doctor.'

'Please follow me, ladies.'

★ ★ ★

The policeman unlocked the door of the refreshments room and stood aside. Ann was aware that her hands were shaking as she withdrew a handkerchief from her coat pocket. The room was cold, extremely cold. There stood a large oak ice box at the far end of the table, on which lay a body, covered in a rough woollen blanket. She stood at the door and watched Lady Cruickshank shuffle towards the table, her handkerchief over her nose.

The doctor pulled back the blanket and Aunt Euphemia peered over, grimacing as she caught sight of alabaster skin and blond ringlets.

'Is this Janet Clark of Kirkmichael House?'

The policeman had taken out a notebook and had his pencil poised.

Lady Cruickshank nodded and, just as the doctor was replacing the cover, blurted out, 'Wait, what are those wounds at her head?'

'The head injuries would have been caused as the body was buffeted about in the water, against rocks and so forth. It was nearly twenty-four hours after the accident till she was found.' He pulled the blanket over Janet's face. 'Might I have a moment with you in private, Lady Cruickshank?'

'Yes, of course.' She looked at Ann. 'Go and wait outside.'

Why did the woman treat everyone as a servant, thought Ann, shutting the door on the doctor and her husband's aunt, who were now deep in hushed conversation.

It was dreadful, being so close to the corpse. The girl had been pretty, no doubt about that, but those wounds on her forehead were gruesome. How terribly tragic it was; she was someone's child, sister, perhaps even wife. Someone somewhere must be grieving for the pretty girl with the flaxen curls.

'Please tell her ladyship I shall be with her presently,' she called back to the policeman, who was now standing at the door. 'I am going to the first class lounge.'

He nodded then tucked his notebook back in his pocket.

Ann walked away, feeling rather faint as she recalled the doctor's words about the head injuries. And this body was found only after a day… She couldn't bear to imagine what the others would be like after a week in the water.

★ ★ ★

Ann looked around at the dozen other people in the room, all of whom were dressed in black. They looked haggard, exhausted, as if they had not slept in days. They probably hadn't. Behind them were two long tables piled high with all sorts of items.

There was a cloying smell in the air, fetid and stale, and a reverential stillness. Ann stepped closer, to inspect the items. Here was a cap, possibly the headwear of an engine stoker. Here was a purse with shiny clasps and beside it a pair of spectacles, a pince-nez and a package of cards. She fingered these and saw they were temperance pledge cards for the suppression of drunkenness.

'Daft not taking a drink your whole life if you're going to end up at the bottom of the sea.'

Ann looked up to see a scruffy young man with a sullen expression, wrapped up in an oversized black overcoat; borrowed, she presumed.

'Who've you lost then?'

'My husband,' Ann said, putting her handkerchief to her nose. 'I think.'

He looked baffled.

'What I mean is, I think he is among the passengers lost.'

'See anything of his here then?'

'Not yet,' she said, turning away and walking round the table.

There was a woollen muff, a large wicker hamper and three large men's handkerchiefs. She stared at these then picked one up, holding her breath. The initials J. G. were embroidered at the edge. She sighed and moved on, taking in the packets of tea, a handbag, a woollen scarf and empty mailbags.

'They've took all the letters that were in them,' said the youth. 'Think they can post them out once they've all dried.' He moved towards Ann as he spoke, standing too close.

She moved away and glanced back at him. He was only young, his expression desperate.

'My apologies,' she said, aware that, like her husband's aunt, she too was treating others with disdain. 'I ought to have asked before. Who have you lost?'

For the first time, she took in his pasty complexion and watery brown eyes.

'Dad. And my two wee brothers, Jimmy and Bobby. They were all over at my Auntie Bessie's in Fife. My mother cannot come here, she cannot do anything, she just keeps crying and crying.'

He looked at her face, searching her dry eyes. 'You doing all your crying at home then?'

'Yes, yes, I suppose I am.' She pushed past him. 'Excuse me, I must leave.' She attempted a smile. 'I wish you and your mother well.'

She swept out of the room and gulped in the fresh cold air. She had never cried at all. Not once.

Chapter 14
2015

'Jamie, I've got a great idea.' Fiona climbed to the top of the stairs and peeked round the attic door. 'I thought it'd be nice to frame a couple of your pictures for Granny for her birthday next week.'

Jamie was kneeling on the window seat, binoculars in hand. 'You want me to do more pictures for her?'

'Well, let's see what you've got. Where did you put them all?'

Jamie placed his binoculars on the seat and jumped down.

'What were you watching?'

'The seals. Pa says the mum seals are going to be having their babies soon and that he'd give me a pound for each baby seal I see. He gave me a sheet of paper here to record them. So I'm keeping watch.'

Fiona chuckled. 'Yeah, well, good luck with that. Just make sure Pa pays up.'

Jamie opened the bottom drawer of his bedside table and pulled out a carrier bag, which he placed on his mum's lap, then returned to his seal watch.

Fiona sat down on the floor to empty out the bag of drawings. She looked through them, laying them out in front of her. There was Broughty Castle and the beach, there was Glenisla Hotel and the hills behind. There were drawings from years ago, when Jamie was little;

these were pretty basic, but he always had some sort of solid baseline, whether it was the sea or a road to give some sort of perspective. Fiona had some twenty laid out and was smiling at the memory of each when she noticed two that were smaller than the others.

She picked them up. One was of their little cottage in Glenisla, the other of sheep up the glen. Both sheets were creased in the middle and, as Fiona turned them over, she saw they were bank statements.

'Jamie, why did you draw on the back of these bank statements?'

And as she peered at one, she realised it was not hers, it was Pete's.

Jamie looked round from his binoculars. 'Must've been paper I found in the bin.'

'What bin?'

'Dunno, waste paper bin. I'd run out of paper so I used that.' He turned back to seal watch. 'Still can't see any babies, but a lot of those seals are really fat.'

'Doesn't necessarily mean they're about to have a baby, but who knows. Pa's usually right.' Fiona stood up. 'I'm just nipping down to get my specs, back in a minute.'

She ran down the stairs to her room, grabbed the glasses on her bedside table and scampered back upstairs. By the time she reached the top she was panting. God, she was unfit, she really had to get running again.

Now seeing clearly, she looked at the first statement, which was dated May 2011, carefully inspecting each transaction. There was his salary, some cash taken out, nothing unusual. Then she saw a withdrawal of three hundred pounds. The note beside it read D/D: Direct Debit. The recipient was Swansea.

She grabbed the other statement and turned it over. June 2011. Most transactions were the same but again there was this direct debit to Swansea for three hundred pounds. That was a lot of money, about a quarter of his salary in those days. What the hell was going on in Swansea? She couldn't recall Pete ever talking about having been in Wales. In fact, she remembered only recently a conversation in which they both decided they'd like to visit Wales, as neither had been before. Fiona peered at the two pieces of paper again as her mind raced. Pete had switched to online banking after they moved to Glenisla, and so presumably no longer received paper statements. He must have been clearing out his statements and presumed that no one in the house would rake in the bins. No one but a budding artist in desperate need of paper.

'Mum, there's a train on the bridge. It's the eleven o'clock from Edinburgh. Want to see through the binoculars? You can see the passengers inside, they're moving!'

'No, it's fine, sweetheart, thanks.' Fiona tucked her hair behind her ears and stared at the statements. Did those direct debits have something to do with why Pete suddenly disappeared? What had Swansea to do with anything?

'Can I just borrow these two, Jamie? I'd like them for my room.'

He turned round. 'If you want, but I could do you better ones now, I was only in P2 then.'

'No, thank you. I like these. And how about these two for Granny?' She pointed at one of the house that Jamie had drawn the previous summer. Its Ionic pillars were drawn much larger than they really were but it made the house look more symmetrical. The other picture was of the rail bridge, drawn from her mother's bedroom window below.

'Yeah, I think Granny'll like those. Mum, is it lunchtime yet?'

She looked at her watch. 'Another hour. Granny said one o'clock.' I'm going to go for a quick run along Riverside Drive, but tell Granny I'll be back for lunch. You can help her set the table.'

Fiona went downstairs and into her room where she opened the wardrobe to look for her running shoes. She sat down on the bed to peel off her jeans and pull on her tracksuit bottoms. As she bent down to tie her shoelaces, she thought how little she actually knew about Pete; what else had he been keeping from her?

Chapter 15

Thursday 1 January 1880

'You can carry the black bun, Lizzie. And James, take the bottle.'

'Is it the whisky Pappa bought for Dr Donaldson?'

'Yes, it is his usual Ne'erday gift, but today you must be the man and hand it over, James.' Ann gave it to her son. 'Hold it very carefully, please, two hands.'

'Will you be back for tea, Mrs Craig?' Mrs Baxter placed her hand on her lower back as she eased herself up from tying the ribbons of Lizzie's velvet bonnet.

'Is your back still sore, Mrs Baxter?'

The housekeeper shook her head and scowled. 'It's fine.'

Ann wondered why she bothered trying to be nice to the woman, she was always sullen. Baxter was definitely the more pleasant of the pair.

'Well, I imagine we shall be served tea at the Donaldsons', but I do not want to overstay our welcome. I cannot contemplate embarking on idle chatter, even though it's only our two families and Archibald's mother. They are holding their usual party tonight but I shall not attend.'

'Bye then,' said Mrs Baxter at the door. 'Oh, Lizzie, mind and tell Mrs Donaldson that black bun's different this year. I used more candied citron peel and some West Indian ginger, but the ginger's minced fine.'

'Lizzie cannot possibly remember those instructions, Mrs Baxter,' snapped Ann, ignoring low mutterings from her housekeeper as she marched out the door.

Outside, the branches of the magnolia tree were still swaying but the wind had abated a little.

'Mamma, I'm cold. I wanted to wear my muff, like you. Why do I have to carry this cake?'

'The Craigs have given the Donaldsons a black bun every January the first for years.'

'But why do I have to carry it?'

'Don't be lazy, my dear. You may wear my muff on the walk home.'

James stopped to look over the river towards the broken bridge. The water was grey, the waves rippling in the easterly wind. 'Mamma, do you think Pappa is out there in the sea?'

Ann came to a halt and stroked her son's head. 'I don't know, James. But I simply cannot think where else he might be. Until we have firm evidence though, we must continue to hope.'

'I was looking at the globe in the study this morning. I remembered Pappa used to tell me about someone he knew who had gone to Australia. He showed me on the globe where it is. I wonder if he has gone there and once he has a house for us, he will call us to live with him.'

'Mamma, the bun is too heavy.' Lizzie looked round from the Donaldsons' gate, whining.

'Wait there, Lizzie,' ordered Ann, tugging on her son's sleeve. 'Come, James, we will be late. I know of no one who went to Australia or indeed any of the dominions, what nonsense.' They joined Lizzie at the gate and Ann gave them each a kiss on their cheeks. Margaret would be watching from the window and she hated the affection Ann displayed in public towards her children. Well, let the cold fish see and judge.

Ann frowned as she pondered her son's comments. Australia? Robert had always been scathing when they read of people emigrating there, and he certainly never knew anyone personally who had gone.

'Now, best behaviour, both of you,' Ann whispered, as she pulled the polished brass door knocker. 'And be especially polite to old Mrs Donaldson.'

* * *

'Will you partake of another, Ann?' Archibald Donaldson lifted the crystal stopper from the decanter of Madeira.

'No, thank you, Archibald. We must leave soon, I must take the children home.'

'They are playing sweetly upstairs, Ann. They may stay even if you must leave,' Margaret said. 'Aggie will walk them round in an hour or so if that is suitable?'

Ann shook her head. 'I do not like to impose.'

Margaret stood up. 'Not at all. I shall go to the nursery myself and check they wish to stay.' She swept past Ann and out the door.

'This bun is terribly good, Ann. Tell that woman of yours, will you?' Old Mrs Donaldson's voice carried from the other side of the fireplace where she sat in a deep armchair.

'Thank you, I shall,' said Ann. This was the third time the old lady had told her this.

Archibald stepped away from the window and she noticed, not for the first time, how warm his brown eyes were, how kindly his expression. He must be such a wonderful doctor. She did not understand why Robert would not permit his family to attend his practice, right next door. Instead they had to go all the way up to Perth Road to ancient Dr Knox with his unpleasant bedside manner.

'Ann, will you come with me next door?'

He gave her his arm and, as they left the room and walked along the corridor, Ann could hear the old lady talking to herself. 'Terribly, terribly good. What a baker the woman is.'

Archibald unlocked the door to his medical practice and ushered Ann into the room.

'Please, sit down.'

Ann smiled. 'Am I to have a medical consultation?'

'I said to Margaret I would ask you in private if there is anything else we can do for you. It continues to grieve me that I was not available on the night of the storm to offer assistance, that long walk to the station and...'

'Please, Archibald, do not mention it again. You had to attend to that poor woman who lost those babies, how unpleasant that must have been.'

She looked around at the bookshelves, which were crammed full of medical texts. 'You have enough to contend yourself with, Archibald, thank you.'

'There is nothing pertaining to financial affairs for which you require my assistance?'

Ann shook her head. 'No, not at the moment. I must await more news before I consider my options. Whatever happens, I shall somehow provide for the children and the house.' She pursed her lips then leant forward to gaze into those kind eyes. 'Thank you for asking.'

The doctor lowered his head.

'Do you mind if I ask you something rather strange,' Ann continued. 'James was telling me Robert knew some people who had emigrated to Australia. Who could that have been?'

'I have no knowledge of anyone departing to the dominions, apart from one of my patients, rather a scoundrel. He went to Australia, but not through his own volition.'

Archibald went behind his desk and removed a tiny key from his mustard-coloured waistcoat pocket. Keeping his dark eyes on her, he opened his drawer. 'How are you sleeping, Ann?'

'I must admit that I am not sleeping as well as usual, though I am fine for the present,' said Ann, standing up as she heard noises on the stairs.

Archibald too heard the noise of voices approaching and slammed the drawer shut, turning the key in the lock and returning it to his pocket. He moved to open the door, passing close to Ann and breathing in deeply. Her heady perfume hung in the air. As he inhaled, he thought of Margaret's disapproval of her friend's use of perfume. 'Not for ladies,' she had said, commanding him to open the windows wide after Ann and Robert had left a dinner at their house.

Ann swept past in a rustle of silk and the hint of bergamot and jasmine floated after her.

Chapter 16
2015

'Remind me, what number are you in Magdalen Yard Road again?'

Fiona turned to her friend Martha, who had just pulled on a pair of white cotton gloves.

'Seventy-three. Why?'

Martha turned a page in the old document she was examining. 'Did you know that one of the passengers who died in 1879 lived along in number thirty-two?'

'Those are the tenements at the other end, I think,' said Fiona as she finished putting on her own gloves. 'Can I see?'

Martha pointed to a name and address in the yellowed document. 'Janette Ness, weaver, aged twenty-two. I suppose she worked in one of the jute mills.'

Fiona nodded and pored over the names. 'There's another weaver here, and a spinner, presumably mill workers too. All so young.'

'I know, I read that a fifth of all jute mill workers were under fifteen.' Fiona looked up. 'And the kids on that train, horrible. Look, one aged four, another five. The book said there would've been more children on the train but there's no record of them as they didn't need tickets.'

'I know, it's awful.' Martha pointed again to Janette Ness' address. 'Does number thirty-two still exist on your road?'

'Think so. I'm pretty sure it's the first tenement when you turn left onto our road from the Green. And I must ask Dad, but I'm sure one of his ancestors in our house was a mill owner in the nineteenth century. In fact, I think he might have been the one who had our house built. Wonder if he was there in 1879?'

'I thought you'd like this project. I'm glad the boss wants you to carry on researching for the exhibition.'

'God, yeah. I'm so pleased the interview went well.'

'I was speaking to her earlier, she said that you'd opted for four mornings a week instead of two full days?'

'Yeah, that'll be brilliant when Jamie starts school. Thanks for putting a word in, M, you're a star!'

'We can work together on some things – public outreach, papers, online and fliers – and I'll get in touch with other museums to see what they've got.'

Fiona nodded, grinning.

'Great, so I'm going to concentrate on details of the train, events on the actual day and so on, and at this stage you can look into Sir Thomas Bouch, the designer?'

'Deal.'

'He lived in Edinburgh, so you might have to nip down there.' Martha looked up at the clock on the wall. 'Only a couple of hours till home time. D'you have to dash back to Jamie or do you fancy a quick drink?'

'Mum's giving him an early tea then they're taking him to the cinema to see that new Disney film. Dad's more excited about it than Jamie, big child that he is.'

'Aw, your dad's great, he's so, well, different.'

'I know, he's a one-off. Still, he kept Jamie up till midnight playing on his ancient Scalextric set, way past bedtime. Think Jamie's just doing it to amuse the old man, to be honest.'

* * *

'Another bottle?' Fiona stood up and lifted the empty bottle from the bucket.

Martha glanced at her watch. 'Yeah, I'll text Allie to say I'll be late home.'

Fiona weaved her way through the tables to the bar and ordered another bottle. 'I love a sauv blanc, don't you?' she said, unscrewing the cap as she returned.

'Remember it was always gut-rot chardonnay we guzzled at college? Then I kind of got into Pinot Grigio with Pete, but this is delicious.'

'Gooseberries and elderflower!' Martha gave an exaggerated sniff over her glass. 'Cheers!'

'Cheers.' Fiona clinked glasses and sat back on the sofa. 'So, where was I?'

'Well, he did a runner, stole a car and wiped out all your combined savings. Bloody hell, there can't be more, Fi?'

'Oh, just you wait.' Fiona took a gulp of her wine and sat forward. 'Then I want to hear all about you and Allie. How're the parents taking it? Were her mum and dad not really weird about it all when you moved in together?'

Martha nodded. 'Yeah, more anon. Come on, spill.'

'So, Doug from Glenisla – remember the nice guy who owns the hotel, short, balding – well, he phoned me one day last week,' said Fiona, before telling Martha about the Australian woman who had been trying to track Pete down.

'Bloody hell, that's not good.' She frowned. 'Without wishing to sound like Allie with her psychotherapist hat on, "How does that make you feel?"'

'You really want to know?' There was a tremor in her voice. 'Fucking used, that's what. Used, abused, on the rubbish heap.' She took a swig from her glass. 'After all that time getting over Iain, at last I find my life's companion and then this. Don't think I'll ever trust a man again.'

Martha took her friend's hand and gave it a squeeze. 'There might be some explanation. What could that call have been about, Fi? You think she was his mother?'

'Who knows? Don't even know if he's even got a mother, looks now like he made everything up. I mean, he must've been from Australia, but Ross at the Old Chain Pier said he was from Tasmania, not Melbourne.' She stretched over to the bottle and topped their glasses up. 'I feel humiliated, M, embarrassed. I mean, who was he really? What else was he hiding from me? From us?'

'God, yeah, both of you. How's Jamie coping?'

Fiona shrugged. 'Good, kids are amazing, they just get on with it. And it's been brilliant having Mum and Dad around. I mean, if I didn't have them, where would I be?'

'Not in the palatial splendour of Magdalen Yard road,' said Martha, smiling.

'It always amazes me when I think about Dad's family owning that house for years. It looks so grand from the outside, but, well, you know what it's like inside – a tip!'

'I love the chaos. I used to think it was great, staying at your house with things all over the place. My mum's verging on the OCD, I'm sure of it. It was such a welcome contrast!'

'Anyway, one more thing about Pete then I'll shut up and you tell me about you two lovebirds.'

'Yeah, but wait a minute, let's go back to that woman's

phone call. So she hung up, no name, nothing. Could Doug not have tracked the call?'

'Too late, another call came in.'

'What about ringing the journalist who wrote the review? See if they'd had any calls at The Scotsman? Presume she was up at Glenisla recently?'

'Well, a couple of months ago. Yeah, could try that I suppose.' Fiona took a deep breath. 'So here's the final thing.'

She turned to face Martha and told her about the direct debits on Pete's old bank statements.

'But they were ages ago when you just moved to Glenisla?'

'Yeah, and he went online after that so I've no idea if he carried on with that direct debit every month. And why bloody Swansea?'

'We could always go to Swansea for a visit? Scour around for anyone with an Aussie accent?'

Fiona grinned. 'Better things to do with my weekends, M.'

'Yeah. I mean, Swansea. Doesn't sound like a happening place.' Martha pulled out her water bottle from her bag. 'I've got to sober up, I've just remembered I'm up really early tomorrow, got a meeting first thing in Perth. I hate driving there, I can never get parked anywhere near the museum.'

'Hang on.' Fiona was frowning. She raised a finger. 'Perth. There's one here, just along the A90, and one in Australia. What are the chances of...'

'Onto it,' said Martha, sitting up straight and delving into her bag again She took out her phone and started tapping.

'Genius, Fi, of course there won't be just one Swansea in the world, bet there's others… Here we go. Swansea is also a ghost town in Arizona, a community in Toronto, a winery in New Jersey, a cave in Jamaica and… Yes! A town in Australia. And guess where in Australia?'

Fiona shrugged. 'Give in.'

'Tasmania! Bingo.'

Chapter 17
Friday 2 January 1880

Ann Craig gazed out of the drawing room window. It was a clear, sunny morning, bitterly cold and crisp, the frost hard on the ground. There was barely a breath of wind. She surveyed this tranquil scene and cast her mind back to Sunday, when the worst storm for decades had hit Dundee. Was it only five days ago? So much had happened since then, but nothing, absolutely nothing, had been resolved. Donald Baxter said the city was still in shock, reeling from the accident, so many dead or presumed dead. It was the lack of knowledge that was the worst. And somewhere at the back of her mind, Ann nurtured a tiny inkling that Robert was still alive. Not that she was weak with worry about his actual loss; no, her worry was about their circumstances. She would not, whatever happened, allow her children to live in anything less than the luxury they now did. She had known poverty and would do anything to prevent the three of them ever being poor.

Ann turned her gaze towards the broken bridge and remembered the horror with which she had watched the train plummet into the water. She sniffed and dabbed her nose. She would not cry – that was something she had never done, even when she was little. She was strong and she would get through this, her children at her side.

She waved as she spotted her darling children playing on the Green. James and Lizzie were running together, a red kite trailing from the boy's hand. The Donaldson twins were just behind them, their kite white. All four children turned to look up and wave. And there, at the back of the racing children, strolled Archibald. Why was he not at work in his practice? But of course, she had lost track of the days – doctors, like other workers in the city, returned to work on the third. So he was still officially on holiday and taking the four children out with their kites. She tried to imagine Robert ever doing that – it simply would never happen, he would send Baxter out with them if their governess were away. Robert was not at ease with children, whether his own or others. He either treated them like his workers, imperious and authoritative, or like his servants, distant and aloof.

She picked up the binoculars and focused them on the doctor, who was wearing a dark brown frock coat and his mustard-yellow waistcoat. He ambled along, Bridie the dog scampering alongside. Robert was not even relaxed with dogs. One time Bridie had rushed into the Donaldsons' drawing room and Robert was aghast, with no idea how to react. It was she who ran to grab the dog's collar and dragged it to sit in front of her, taking the dog's head between her knees. She fondled its soft snout until an anguished servant arrived, apologetic and red-faced. Archibald and she had laughed as Margaret abjectly apologised, while Robert simpered in the corner.

Ann looked through the binoculars at the doctor's face, trying to see more closely those kind eyes, that rugged appearance. He was so very different from Margaret, with her dull complexion and tiny, bird-like eyes.

She soon became aware that he too was looking up at her window and waving. Goodness, what must she look like, examining him through the glasses? She hurried to replace the binoculars on the table and gave a little wave before retreating towards the fireplace to pick up her fan; she had become hot all of a sudden.

Ann left the drawing room and headed for Robert's study. She whirled the large globe on Robert's desk and clapped her hand down to stop it at Australia. She peered at the vastness of the territories. There was Victoria, New South Wales, Queensland... Why would Robert have been discussing Australia with his son and telling him he knew someone who had gone there? Both the occurrence of a father-and-son discussion and the subject were most unusual. Perhaps James was confused and the talk about overseas dominions had in fact taken place with Miss Graham. It seemed more likely since she often carried the globe into the nursery for geography lessons.

Ann turned to see Jessie standing at the open door. She bobbed and stretched out a silver tray upon which was a letter.

'I was led to believe there was no postal delivery until tomorrow?'

'There is not, Mrs Craig, but Mrs Baxter said this was handed in at the door the now.'

Ann lifted the letter from the tray and headed for the drawing room. 'Thank you, Jessie. That will be all.'

She returned next door and sat at the window seat, glancing down at the two kites billowing about in the breeze. The doctor was standing with his back to her, surveying the scene before him and the vast breadth of river. She looked beyond, to the wide gap in the iron structure where the rail bridge had collapsed.

She lifted up a paper knife from the table and slit open

the envelope.

Dear Mrs Craig, I do hope this finds you as well as can be expected.

Who was this from? She turned the page and read, With sincere regard, Alec Smith, Taybridge Station, Dundee. Why was he writing to her?

I had news last night which I believe may be of interest to you. My colleague Willie Robertson, the stationmaster at Leuchars Station, sent me news of an interesting incident on Sunday night past. When the Edinburgh train stopped there at 7 p.m., one first class passenger disembarked and stood waiting on the platform. When Robertson asked for whom he waited, he was told he had arranged for a coach to meet him.

The gentleman saw no coach and so got back on the train. Then, through the roaring wind, came the noise of the carriage. Robertson ran to open the first class compartment door, alerted the gentleman and proceeded to help him onto the platform with his luggage and to his coach.

He knows neither his name nor anything about his circumstances but he thought it might be of interest to any relative of any first class passengers awaiting news, for he was the last passenger to leave the train that night. With sincere...

Ann leant forward and pressed her forehead, now hot and clammy, against the cold windowpane. Had that been Robert? Did he get off the train at Leuchars? But why would he do that; how was that possible? And surely Robert had no luggage with him apart from his leather portmanteau? Why he even took that over to Kirkmichael each Sunday was a mystery. When confronted, he insisted it contained papers and writing material as his aunt usually required him to write letters and other such matters pertaining to the estate. She often wondered if he tried to emulate Archibald, who held essential medical equipment in his bag. What need did a jute mill owner have of such a capacious bag unless to simply portray grandeur?

Ann stood up, lifting a hand to her now cool brow, and sat at the writing desk. She opened the inkwell and dipped in her pen. There were questions to be asked. She must try to meet this Mr Robertson. She would ask Smith; he would do anything for her. Quickly, she finished her letter and rang the bell.

'Jessie, ask Mr Baxter to deliver this by hand to Mr Smith, the Dundee stationmaster. At once.'

The girl bounded away towards the stairs and Ann turned to the low table, lifting the stopper from the Madeira decanter to pour herself a glass. She brought it to her lips and then glanced round at the door, which the girl had left ajar in her rush. She tipped her head back and downed the drink in one draft, the tip of her tongue licking the last drop from the bottom. She sighed as she remembered how Robert would berate her every time she did that.

Out on the river, tiny waves were lapping against the shoreline. A light breeze was picking up.

Chapter 18
2015

Fiona sat at the kitchen table and pressed the palms of her hands to her temples. Her head was thudding. Very slowly, she turned to look out at the Green where Jamie was kicking the football around with Jack. He had settled in so well to life in Dundee. He did not say much about missing Pete, but she knew he did. Pete had been a combination of a cool uncle and an older brother, they had had so much fun together. She only wished she didn't feel such a huge loss whenever she thought about him; she was beginning to wonder if she had loved him more than her husband. Even though part of her hated him for the deceit, she still wanted him back. She tried to imagine what she'd say if he suddenly strolled in the door, grinning that cheeky smile. She thought of him taking her in his strong arms and kissing her. But then she remembered the deception, the fact he had removed all their savings, and the mysterious situation with his car.

She took a slug from her can of Diet Coke then turned back to her laptop and Googled The Scotsman. She picked up her phone.

'Yes, hi, is it possible to speak to Cressida Scott?'

'Oh, okay, yes, I'll leave a message on her voicemail, thanks.'

She cleared her voice then explained who she was and said that she was keen to meet up, leaving her phone number.

No way she'll phone back, she thought, looking back down at her to-do list.

Her head was aching, and it was another hour until she could take more paracetamol. Why did she drink so much last night? Martha had stopped knocking it back and was downing the water when Fiona had insisted they have one for the road. Why had she ordered a final large glass after they'd already guzzled two bottles? She hoped Martha was okay to drive to Perth.

Back to Google. Swansea, Tasmania was first settled in 1821 by a gentleman from South Wales and his family. He farmed the land around... arable, grazing crops... Established a tannery... A whaling station was built nearby and Swansea became the main port in Australia to export whale oil.

Why did that sound familiar? Of course, Dundee had links with whaling. She continued to scan. The final line read, Population of 553.

That's not many, Fiona thought. Surely everyone must know everyone there? Could she find someone else called Gibson?

The door swept open. 'Morning, party girl, how's your head?' Struan stood at the door, grinning. He had on a yellow sweater over long brown shorts, knee-length red socks and brown shoes.

'What on earth have you got on, Dad?'

Her father smiled again. 'Like it? Mum says I look ridiculous, but I think it's rather fetching. Meeting Mark for lunch today, thought I'd dress suitably.'

Fiona screwed up her face. 'Suitably? Has Mark become a twelve-year-old with a penchant for Noddy?'

'Always so amusing, Fi,' said Struan as he gave a twirl. 'I told you Mark's back for good? Remember he went to work in Bermuda straight from college, lived there all his life. Better bloody money designing beach houses than my tenement block conversions over here, I can tell you. Anyway, he's just retired and come home, poor bugger.' He flicked the kettle on. 'So, I thought I'd give Bermuda shorts a go in his honour.'

'But they're not Bermuda shorts, Dad, they're just big baggy shorts. And are you meant to wear long socks like that?'

'Yes. Remember Mum and I went to stay with them once? I found it so funny that they all went to work dressed in shorts with a jacket and tie. Thought I'd leave off the tie though. Coffee?' He peered at the coke. 'Or perhaps another can of death wish?'

'Needs must, Dad. Hangover cure.' She shook her head as she looked at his shorts again. 'Mum's my only hope for the sanity gene in this family. And yes please to coffee, make it strong.'

'So, presumably you had a good catch-up with Martha? How is she? Does she still think she prefers girls to boys?'

Fiona sighed. 'She's gay, of course she bloody does, Dad. She's coming round tomorrow, just behave yourself, will you?'

Struan put down a mug of steaming coffee in front of her and took his to the door.

'Thanks. Oh, Dad, before you go. Whaling, whale oil – why does that ring bells? Was Dundee into that?'

'Yes, Dundee was into that, Fi. What did they teach you at school? It was one of the most important centres of the industry in the world. If memory serves me right,

Dundee was the only whaling port left in Britain in the late nineteenth century. Whaling worked in a kind of symbiotic way with the jute industry – whale oil was used to soften the jute fibres before production.'

'Oh, yeah, it's all coming back. Thanks, Dad.'

Struan looked at his watch. 'Right, tutorial over. Got to finish a drawing before lunch.'

'You still working on that house for the Blacks?'

'Yes, I promised I'd do it even though I'm meant to be retired and enjoying a summer of fun and games with our lodgers.' He peered out the window. 'How fares the Little Prince today?'

Fiona smiled. 'Great, look at him, he's in heaven,' she said, watching him and Jack dribble their footballs along the Green.

She turned back to the laptop. How on earth could she find someone called Gibson in a town at the other side of the world? Was there a kind of database she could get into? Martha might know, she'd ask her later.

Her phone rang. Fiona peered at the screen; it was an Edinburgh number.

'Hello? Fiona Craig here. Yes, yes, thanks for calling back, Cressida. Well, that would be great to meet up. I've got to be in Edinburgh next week. Great, looking forward to it.'

She got out her diary and flicked through the pages to the following week.

Chapter 19

Saturday 3 January 1880

'So is Miss Graham coming back today, Mamma?'

'Yes, Lizzie, she is and about time too.' Ann Craig looked up at the clock. 'Although she ought to have been here half an hour ago, she's seldom late.' She continued untying the rags from her daughter's hair.

'Ow, Mamma, that hurt.'

'Sorry, darling.'

'Why do I have to have ringlets? Beatrice Donaldson does not have to have rags tied in every night. I asked her.'

'That is because you were not blessed with curly hair as she is. But your nose is far prettier than hers. There, that is the last one. Look how lovely you look now with these curls, dear child.' She kissed the top of her daughter's head.

'Do we have to have lessons today, Mamma, or will Miss Graham let us have a day off?'

'James, you have had several days off during this holiday. I am sure that, when she eventually arrives, she will be keen to have you straight back into lessons.'

'Even though we are still mourning?'

'James, we are not yet officially in mourning. Mamma is wearing dark clothes as a mark of respect for those whose loved ones are no longer here. We don't know what has happened to Pappa and, until we do, there will be no more discussion on the subject.' Ann stood up and glanced in the mirror at her stern expression. She tilted her chin up to the light then smiled. At least she did not need to use rags to curl her naturally wavy hair; she was blessed. It was little wonder she was often gazed at. She so hoped her daughter would be a beauty like her.

She turned at a noise at the door.

'Mrs Craig, there is a gentleman to see you. Mr Johnston, from the mill.'

Ann sighed. 'What is that man doing here? Are the mill workers not back at work today?'

Mrs Baxter shrugged. 'He says he wants to see you.'

'Very well, show him into the morning room.'

Mrs Baxter turned to go downstairs when Ann called after her, 'Do not bother with tea.'

She placed her hands at her daughter's shoulders and bobbed her curls up and down, then patted her son's head and headed for the stairs, wondering what might bring her husband's employee here.

Before she had even opened the door from the hall, she could smell it all around. The loathsome, putrid stench that was impossible to remove from clothes and hair. Whale oil.

'Good Morning, Mr Johnston.' Ann stretched her hand out, through habit, and immediately regretted it. She touched his hand lightly then pulled out her handkerchief and dabbed her nose. 'To what do I owe this pleasure?'

He blushed red. 'The mill opened this morning as usual, after the holidays. I called the workers together to speak about their fellow workers who had been on the train. We believe we lost one of our weavers, Eliza Lawson, and the husband of one of our best spinners, Margaret

Watson. While speaking to the workers, I informed them that Mr Craig had been on board the train too and they were keen for me to deliver their condolences in person.'

'Condolences?' Ann snapped. 'We know nothing yet. Until there is a body, we must presume otherwise.'

Alfred Johnston frowned. 'But we had all understood that Mr Craig was on the train last Sunday evening?'

'That is what we are led to believe but, until we know more, there is always hope.'

'Forgive me, but they have all said there are no survivors.' He began fidgeting with the cap in his hands before him.

Ann fixed him with a cold stare. 'I appreciate the sentiment, Mr Johnston, and do please convey my thanks to your workers.' She struggled to maintain her composure as she tried to be polite; she might need him in the future. 'Now, was there anything else?' She drew up her shoulders, so that she towered above him, and forced a smile.

'Yes, there was. It's something of a delicate nature, but it might be of use to you and the family as you wait for news. You remember that I meet with the whalers down at the port every couple of weeks? I get my barrels of whale oil there for the mill.'

'I recall my husband telling me, yes,' she said, evading his gaze.

'Well, I spoke to the whalers last night. There are fifteen whaleboats out searching at the mouth of the Firth. They said that the bodies would only come to the surface after a full seven days.'

'I had already heard such information from Alec Smith down at the station.'

'How's he doing? What a mess he's having to deal with.'

'Mr Smith is coping well, I believe.'

'Well, that's all I had to say. I'd better get back to the mill.'

He went towards her, hand outstretched, the pungent odour of whale oil hovering about him. 'Goodbye then, Annie.'

There was a sudden flush in her cheeks. 'Don't you ever call me that in my house,' she hissed, flicking his hand away. 'Or anywhere.'

She pointed to the door then turned her back on him and strode to open the window. A fresh blast of winter air entered and she took a long, deep breath.

Chapter 20

2015

Fiona heard the voices before she opened the kitchen door: guffaws and raucous shrieks. At the table sat Jamie, hands round a tumbler of orangey-brown juice. He was grinning.

'Ah, here she is.' Struan leant back on one of the no-longer-rickety chairs. In his hand was a large tumbler and his eyes were glazed. She sniffed the air. Whisky. God, her father was drunk.

She patted the top of Jamie's head.

'Sit down, Fi. You remember Mark, don't you?' Beside her father sat a tall, tanned man with a tartan scarf round his neck. He too had a dram in his hand.

'Yes, I do. Good to see you again, Mark.'

''Pa's been telling me some funny stories about when he and Mark were little.'

'That's Mr Thomson to you, Jamie!' said Fiona.

'Oh, don't be so Presbyterian. Mark's fine, isn't it?' said Struan. He turned to the other man and slapped him on the back. Some of the whisky in his full glass spilled and he brushed it off his trousers.

'What did you think about Dad's Bermuda shorts then, Mark?' Fiona smiled and looked under the table at them. She noticed that one of his long socks was down at his ankles.

'Good effort, that's for sure,' Mark said, taking a drink.

'Pa, tell Mum the story about when you two were up the glens with flat tyres on your bikes and...'

'Your mother doesn't want to hear those stories,' Struan said, grinning. 'Drink up now, lad. What do you think of it?'

'Well, it's quite nice but a bit sweet, Pa.'

'What is it?' Fiona snatched Jamie's glass and sniffed. 'Dad, what the hell are you giving him cider for? He's only ten.' She picked up the glass and tipped the contents down the sink.

'Good God, she gets so uppity,' Struan shook his head. 'My grandfather was giving me cider when I was half his age.'

'Yes, well, from what you tell me, he wasn't exactly the most conventional of men, maybe not a role model.'

'Certainly wasn't,' Mark chuckled. 'I used to love coming here; Stru's grandpa was so different, so unusual. And his parents were far more easy-going than other parents in those days. There was never any strict bedtime and it's true, Fiona, he was allowed to have cider with his meals.' He took another drink. 'Stru's grandpa told us some great stories. The best one was about a member of the family involved in something terrible, wasn't it a murder?'

'Murder, Pa?' Jamie's eyes were wide.

'They're just making up stories, Jamie don't listen.' Fiona said, glowering at her father and Mark. 'Right, enough now. Come on upstairs, Jamie. We've got to start that list of what you need for your new school uniform.' She pulled him to his feet and gave her father a dirty look as she dragged her son out to the hall, slamming the door behind her.

'But Mum, I don't want to do shopping lists, I want to stay and hear Pa's stories.'

'Tough,' Fiona said, wincing as she jerked her head to the side. Yes, the headache was still very much there.

★ ★ ★

A few hours later, Fiona sat at the kitchen table with a plate of pasta in front of her.

'Just a small portion for me, Dot, not hungry,' said Struan. He took out his pipe and laid it beside him.

'That's because you're still drunk. Get it down you, man.' Dorothy ladled her husband a huge bowl of pasta and thumped it on the table in front of him. 'And you can put the pipe away,' she said, pulling some loose hair up into the wooden clasp at the back of her head. She turned to Fiona. 'Jamie okay, Fi?'

'Yeah, fine, he's watching some action DVD at Jack's.' She turned back to her father. 'So, what're these family stories Mark was telling us about?'

'He's not been telling you about all that, has he?' Dorothy sat down with her bowl and shook her head. 'That boy does not need to hear anything about your family's disreputable past.' She looked at her husband. 'Remember Struan, you said we would never speak of it, gave me the heebie jeebies. I mean, this house has been in your family for generations, something could have happened right here.'

'What happened?'

Struan downed the glass of water Dorothy had placed in front of him and looked at his daughter. 'There was something that happened in the Craig family ages ago,

Victorian times. My grandfather used to tell me stories.'

'What stories? And why've you never told me about this?'

'Mum was convinced the house could be haunted or something. Utter bollocks.'

'What happened?' Fiona said, exasperated.

'There was a death, someone went to prison. I'm not sure of the details.'

Fiona's phone started to buzz. She scrabbled in her bag and found it. Unknown number. She put it on the table, ignoring it.

'Feel better after your afternoon nap, Struan?' asked Dorothy. 'Mark was always a bad influence on you. You'd think at your age, you'd know better.'

Struan tapped his pipe on the table, fumbled in his pocket and brought out his tobacco.

'Come on, Dad, you said you'd stop.'

'Needs must,' Struan said, getting to his feet with pipe and tobacco.

There was a ping as a text appeared. Fiona got out her glasses and peered.

> *Hi Fiona, it's Debs from the Old Chair Pier. Something I wanted to chat about. Let me know next time you're in Edinburgh and I can meet you for a coffee? Cheers. Debs.*

What now?

Chapter 21
Saturday 3 January 1880

Ann Craig slammed the window in the morning room shut. At last that vile smell had gone – she never wanted to be reminded of it again. Her mood was no better; it was already ten o'clock and the governess was not yet here. She would have to arrange activities in the nursery for the children, for she could not impose again on the Donaldsons.

She set them a task of drawing pictures in the nursery. As she left the room she noticed that James was drawing a long bridge with a train on it; she only hoped the governess would return the focus of his attention to other things, he was obsessed with the bridge.

There was a clank as the gate opened. Finally, there she was. Ann watched Miss Graham struggle along the path carrying her heavy bag. Her other hand was on her head, trying to keep her hat on over her frizzy grey hair. The magnolia branches were swaying in the strong breeze.

She waited. It was not up to her to let a servant in, so she took a seat on the chair by the door, ready to listen to Miss Graham's explanation.

The doorbell rang and Jessie scuttled along the corridor. She heard a thump as a bag was dropped on the floor.

'Jessie, please let Mrs Craig know I have arrived.'

Ann saw a blur as a figure swept past the door and headed for the stairs. Ann went to the door and called to her.

'Mrs Craig, I can only apologise for the hour of my arrival. Are the children being attended to?'

'They are in the nursery awaiting your return. Indeed they have been waiting for nearly two hours.'

The governess sighed and swept off her hat.

'Mrs Craig, I must offer my sincere condolences. My parents asked me also to convey their deepest sympathy. We heard about Mr Craig, I am so...'

'There is nothing more to say, Miss Graham. Until we have definite proof, we don't know if my husband was indeed on that train. I have an appointment this afternoon to meet the Leuchars stationmaster who might have some information for me.'

Ann glanced down at Miss Graham's crinkly hair and bulbous nose and, as so often happened, felt herself blessed to have not only height but beauty. Ann pulled out a handkerchief and lifted it to her own nose, pert and perfectly turned; celestial, Robert had once called it, a long time ago. 'Is there a valid reason for such a late arrival?'

'I am not sure if you have heard that a body of a woman was found on Monday night. She was a servant from Fife, I believe.'

'Janet Clark, housemaid to Lady Cruickshank, my husband's aunt. I believe you met her ladyship one day last summer?'

'Good Lord, was that who the girl was? I had no idea.'

Ann looked at the governess, expectant. Would she ever furnish her with an explanation?

'Mrs Craig, I left my house at the normal time. As you know it takes me about an hour and a half to walk, a perambulation I enjoy very much as it is a time when I can plan the lessons I shall take with the children. Two things prevented my usual precise timekeeping this morning, however.'

Was this going to take long? Perhaps she should ring for tea. She was still feeling weak after Johnston's visit.

'First of all, you may have heard the tragic news that debris and flotsam have been washed up onto the shore. As I have told you, the beach at Broughty Ferry is opposite my parents' house. There have been many crowds, foraging, as if searching for cockles and winkles.' She sighed and continued. 'Today, there were children there, very early. Bare-legged, these urchins were wading into the icy waters of the Tay and dragging out great planks of wood which were thickly clogged with pitch.'

Miss Graham shook her head. 'Those poor little waifs, they must have been freezing, they were shivering, but their mothers do not have the means to clothe them properly at the best of times.'

Ann pursed her lips. 'Pray continue, Miss Graham.'

'Oh, yes, so then one child, dirty, in ragged clothes, ran up to me and thrust something at me.' She looked down at her hands as if the thing were still there. 'It was a book with gold-edged pages and of course the child could not read. I saw at once it was a bible and I told them they must give it to the policemen. But that little boy asked me to read what was written inside. It read, "For David, On your twelfth birthday."'

She took out her handkerchief and dabbed her eyes. 'I found it so moving. That child, presumably now dead, was but a little older than James.' She shook her head and looked over at Ann. 'So then I continued on along the beach, noting that the children continued to drag planks of wood up the beach – I even saw two with a wooden door. These were, one must presume, all parts of the train. So I continued on and soon met a commotion.'

Ann sighed. Was she ever going to get to the point?

'I arrived at Dock Street and came across vast crowds of people. It was as if everyone in the city was out. No one could move.'

'What was the occasion?'

'That was why I mentioned earlier that poor woman, Jane?'

'Janet Clark'.

'Indeed. It was her funeral and it seems she was mourned by the whole of Dundee. A great crowd, perhaps a thousand people or more, followed the hearse. They were heading south, direct to the docks and so I was unable to pass. One simply could not, for fear of being trampled by the crowd, and besides, one would not, as a matter of respect. The hearse and horses were swathed in black crêpe and there were several ministers, perhaps six or seven, following behind. There was a band playing beside the cortège as it moved slowly over the cobbles to the docks and, according to the woman beside me, to the ferry and over to Fife.'

Ann rang the bell at her side. She was parched.

'And so that is why I am so late.'

'I see, well that was quite a morning, Miss Graham. But perhaps it is time to go up to the nursery? James and Lizzie are eager to see you again.'

Miss Graham lifted her hat from the table beside her.

'I shall go at once. Thank you for your understanding, Mrs Craig.' She swept out of the door, almost knocking into Jessie the maid.

'Bring tea, Jessie. As soon as possible,' Ann said. The maid bobbed then left, shutting the door behind her.

Ann went over to the window, pausing at the table. She lifted the stopper from the decanter and poured herself a glass. She downed it then tilted her head back. How long must all this last, she thought, gazing out over the swaying magnolia tree towards the dark rain clouds scudding over the river.

Chapter 22

2015

Dorothy ambled into the kitchen, her straggly hair more tousled than usual. 'Is there more coffee?' she said, sitting down with a thump.

'Plenty,' Fiona said, pouring a mug. She peered at her mother, whose eyes had dark bags under them. 'You have a bad night's sleep, Mum?'

'Terrible, tossed and turned all night. Not helped by your snoring father, mind you.' She took a large gulp of coffee. 'That's good, thanks.'

Dorothy swivelled round sharply to look at the wall clock. 'Good Lord, look at the time, I'm meant to pick Jamie up at his friend's in ten minutes. What number of Perth Road was it again?'

'510. Surname's Andrews.'

Dorothy lifted up three blackened bananas in the fruit bowl and retrieved the car keys from underneath. 'See you tonight. Have a good day in Edinburgh.'

Fiona opened the lid of her laptop again and continued to type.

Dear Sir/Madam,

Forgive this rather strange request out of the blue. My name is Fiona Craig and I live in Dundee, Scotland. I am trying to track down old family friends who live in Swansea. The name's Gibson. Sorry I don't have much more to go on.

With many thanks,

Fiona Craig

She reread it then clicked send. The librarian of the Swansea library in Tasmania would probably not have a clue, if they even replied.

★ ★ ★

She parked on the shore at Newhaven and locked her car. Debs had said she'd prefer not to meet at the Old Chair Pier so she had chosen a café, Porto and Fi, along the shore. It was her lunch hour in between two busy services. Fiona swung open the door and recognised Debs at once, her shocking turquoise hair obvious amongst the blonde yummy mummies and grey elderly ladies.

'Hi, Debs, how're you doing?'

'Good thanks, not too busy today.' She grabbed the menu and stared at it. 'I didn't tell him I was meeting you,' she said, not lifting her eyes from the menu.

'Oh, okay.' Fiona lifted the menu, but looked straight at Debs and smiled. 'So how are things at the Old Chain Pier then?'

'Fine, yeah, just fine,' she said, then turned away to look for the waitress. 'Excuse me? I'll have the sweet potato and coconut soup and a roll please.'

'The curried parsnip soup, please. And just water to drink, thanks.'

'I'll have Diet Coke.'

A silence followed then Fiona leant back in her chair and watched Debs, who was gazing at the scrubbed wooden table, biting her nails. 'How well did you know Pete?'

Debs's cheeks flushed and she tore the tab off the can in front of her, took a gulp then hiccupped.

'Pretty well.' Her pale grey eyes narrowed as she frowned. 'Christ, this is going to be bloody tricky.'

Fiona noticed a lady, dressed in perfect pastels, glower at Debs, who carried on, oblivious.

'Fiona, this is so difficult to say as I know how much you loved him.' She was concentrating intently on her soup bowl. She sniffed loudly. 'Oh, and he loved you. That was never in question.'

Fiona sipped her water. 'So, what do you want to tell me?'

'The thing is, Pete and I had a thing, not a big deal at all. But we slept together and...'

'What?' Fiona's heart was racing. 'When?'

'Well, it was before I left the pub and went down south for a couple of years, so maybe early on while you were up in Glenesk.'

'Glenisla,' Fiona snapped.

'Oh, right. Anyway, he'd come down to do something in Edinburgh – see the Australian Embassy about his passport or something?'

'You mean the consulate?'

Debs shrugged. 'Dunno, he told me embassy. Anyway, we met up after and had a drink. Then more drinks and, well, things got kind of out of hand and I asked him back to my place and...'

'Here we go, now who's having the sweet potato?' The smiling waitress placed down the bowls and Fiona leant back, gazing over the table at Debs as she did. What the hell did Pete see in her? She opened her mouth to speak then picked up her spoon instead. This must have happened in the first year they were living up in Glenisla. She remembered Pete getting the train down and staying overnight in Edinburgh, said he had to meet a mate from home. When she queried him about it the next day, he said it had gone okay, they had got drunk then crashed at some room in the Premier Inn in the Grassmarket. She'd had no reason not to believe him.

'The thing is, Fiona, it all ended badly.' Debs glanced at her then looked down at her soup. 'In the morning, I realised I didn't have any money for the bus so, when he was in the shower, I shouted through to ask if I could borrow money for the fare. He said yes so I took out his wallet and got out £1.50. That's all I took, it's what I needed to get to work.'

She lifted her spoon and dipped into the large bowl. She looked at Fiona, her eyes moist. 'So then I don't know why I did it but I looked in the backflap thing in the wallet where he had his passport. I love having a laugh at folk's passport photos. Anyway, I pulled it out and a photo fell out.' She paused to take a swig from her can.

'That was when he came back into the bedroom. He was smiling, happy – well, you know guys after a night of rampant sex...'

Fiona glowered at her. Was she really so stupid? Could this slut really not be aware of her feelings?

'Sorry, it's all coming out wrong,' Debs muttered. 'Anyway, he was smiling, then when he saw me with his passport his face changed immediately. Suddenly he had this dark angry look, his eyes were full of, well, hate. He came towards me and ripped it out of my hands. Then he swung at me with his fist but I just jumped backwards and fell on the bed. Then he called me a fucking whore and other stuff I couldn't even begin to tell you. He started ramming his clothes on and I just kept saying sorry. Then he was gone, out of my flat in two minutes. Slammed the door so hard I thought it was going to splinter.'

She swallowed. 'I tell you, I was actually terrified, thought he was going to kill me. That look on his face was so scary.'

'Did you see him again?' Fiona pursed her lips tight together.

'No, never heard a thing. Well, till you came in last month.' She tore a hunk of bread off her roll and started slathering it with butter. 'Sorry, Fiona, the whole sex thing meant nothing. But I thought I should tell you, as I was really, really scared.'

She delved into her bag. 'Thought you might like to have this though.'

'What is it?'

'The photo that dropped out of his passport.'

Fiona took it from Debs and noticed her sore, bitten nails. She gazed down at it. A little boy smiled out at her. She felt her stomach tighten. His blond curls framed a freckled face with the same shape of eyes as... And the nose, hell, the nose was the giveaway. There was no doubt about it. This must be Pete's son. She slumped back in her chair.

'Did he know you had this?'

Debs shrugged. 'Must've worked it out, but I never heard from him again. Never mentioned a thing to Ross either.' She leant across the table. 'Fiona, I was so scared that night, I thought he was going to kill me.'

'Can I keep this, please?' Fiona tried to stem the tremor in her voice.

'Sure, no good to me.' She looked at her phone and sniffed again. 'Got to get back, I said I'd only be half an hour. She stood up and rummaged in her bag for her purse, slapping a fiver down on the table.

'Sorry to have to tell you all that, but I reckoned you needed to know. He was a grade-one bastard so if I were you I'd just forget him. I think he was one of those people you could never really get to know.'

She pulled her coat on. 'Oh, and when there was the fire, when the pub burned down, I thought of him. Obviously impossible really as he was up in Glen Whatever with you but…'

'What are you talking about?' Fiona stood up, her legs trembling.

'It was arson, Fiona. They never found out who did it.'

Chapter 23
Saturday 3 January 1880

The horse's hooves clattered up the cobbles of Roseangle and turned right along Perth Road. Ann Craig pulled her cape tight round her. The wind had got up and she shivered inside the hackney carriage. She pulled back the curtain and saw people rushing along the street, heads down against the biting wind. As the carriage passed tall tenement blocks, she thought of the hovels inside, housing large families in one filthy room. Since women outnumbered men three to one in the jute mills, many men stayed at home. Kettle-boilers they were called; they brought up the kids and took their turn to clean the stairhead cludgie, the communal toilet on the landing. She shuddered at the thought.

Ann let the curtain go and looked inside her bag for the note she had received from Willie Robertson, stationmaster at Leuchars. He had said he would be at Dundee's train station for a meeting at two o'clock then would have half an hour before he went for his ferry across the Tay. She was to ask for him at the ticket office.

She adjusted the ribbons in her bonnet, a splendid black hat with a broad dark grey satin ribbon. She had removed the blue-and-copper peacock feather before departing, for fear of appearing less than respectful of those in mourning. She herself still did not feel as if she was in mourning. According to the Baxters, everyone in the town was shedding tears; where were hers?

She heard a 'whoah!' from the driver and felt the carriage slow. She pulled back the curtain to reveal Dundee station. The carriage driver helped her descend and she looked up at the large clock over the entrance. 'Wait here for me. I should be no longer than twenty minutes.' He lifted a finger to his hat then plunged his hand into his pocket and retrieved a morsel to feed the horse.

She went down the steps, thinking that this was the third time she had done so in less than a week. Usually she only went to the station once a year for the family's summer outing to the beach at Monifeith.

'Good afternoon, I am here to see Mr William Robertson from Leuchars.'

The man at the ticket office pointed towards the platforms. 'Second class waiting room.'

'Thank you.'

She knocked on the door and it was opened by a small man with a large moustache. He carried his hat in his hand.

'Ah, Mrs Craig,' he said, gesturing for her to enter. 'I find I only have ten minutes until I must leave for my ferry. My apologies, but the timings are all muddled up today, even though this is the first day of the regular timetable. Please take a seat.'

Ann sat down and angled her head up. She knew he was looking at her face; she was used to men giving her admiring glances. She brought her fingers to the jet brooch at her neck and smiled.

'So, Mr Robertson, what can you tell me about Sunday night and the first class passenger who alighted at your station?'

'Well, Alec here told me it might have been your husband, so I know how keen you are for more information. But I have to be honest with you and say that I have no idea who he was.'

'Do you not have a record of passengers' names? In first class surely?'

He shook his head. 'No, it's all just a question of collecting tickets, we've no record of their names.'

'So could you see him at all? How would you describe his figure?'

'It was so terribly stormy, as you know, and the wind was howling so much we both kept our heads firmly down, me holding onto my work cap, him onto his top hat.'

'How was the hat?'

'I couldn't say, it was pitch black, the only lights were from inside the train itself and the one light inside the station waiting room. The two that usually hang at each end of the platform were blown away in the gale.'

'His face. Did you see that?'

'Again, I only caught the glimpse of some dark whiskers and that was all. He was in such a hurry once he saw the carriage approach.'

'What did his bag look like?'

'He didn't have much with him, that I can tell you. That's what made me think he had perhaps been away for a day and not overnight. I believe the bag was more a small valise; it certainly was not a large trunk, I'd have remembered that.'

He glanced up at the clock by the window.

'And there is nothing else you can recall that might help me to know whether this gentleman was indeed my husband? His voice?'

Willie Robertson shook his head. 'I'm sorry, Mrs Craig. I heard nothing in that gale. Mr Smith has invited you here under false pretences. All that's certain is that a gentleman got out of first class at Leuchars. No one knows who he was. But we must pray it was indeed your husband.'

Ann glowered at him. 'Surely there is something else. Was he, for example, tall, short, lean, fat?'

'I recall he looked tall, but that was perhaps the appearance from his hat. We were both bent double against the wind.'

Ann nodded, recalling how she and Baxter were also bowed over, heads down, as they struggled against the wind whipping across the Green on Sunday night.

'I am so sorry but I must leave now for the ferry. I told my wife I would be home for tea. She's been in such a state all week, worrying.'

Ann got to her feet and stretched out her hand. 'Thank you for your time, Mr Robertson. If there should be any other fact you recall, please let me know.'

She strode along the platform and headed up the steps. Near the top she sniffed and detected a familiar smell. Pipe tobacco. She had always loved the smell, it reminded her of home. She walked out the entrance and saw her driver beside the carriage. From her right drifted the strong smell of pipe smoke. She turned and saw a beggar place her pipe on the ground and pick up her melodeon. She began to play and as she pulled the instrument out and in, Ann stopped and stared. The tune was so familiar, the strains of the music evoked vivid memories in her, memories she did not want to surface.

She stepped forward to see the player better. The woman was middle-aged and wore ragged clothes. Her boots were scuffed and her grey plaid shawl threadbare. As Ann stared at her, the woman turned to face her; her eyes were empty, glazed. It was then Ann realised who she was and turned away towards the carriage. As she stepped inside, she risked another look back towards the melodeon player.

'That's Blind Mattie,' said the driver. 'She's not usually this side of town, normally in Lochee. Someone must've took her down here for the afternoon. Grand song she's playing. What's it called again?'

Ann opened her mouth to reply then pressed her lips firmly together.

'Oh, I ken now,' he said, smiling. 'It's "To the Weaver's Gin Ye Go". Fine song, one from the mills.'

'If you say so. Now drive on. Home to Magdalen Yard Road.'

The driver continued to stand, listening. 'What a grand instrument that is. I love a melodeon.'

Ann shuffled in her seat and pulled her cloak round her.

'She cannot see a thing yet, did you ken, she's got a gift, sees things no one else can.' He shook his head. 'It's a gift, but she's still a poor soul.'

'Drive on!' Ann commanded. As the horse began to trot off, she pulled back the curtain a fraction to see Blind Mattie put down her melodeon, pick up her pipe and put it in her mouth. Ann watched as she put her other hand behind her onto the window ledge where she felt for the tin can, placing it on the ground in front of her. The woman looked up, towards the street, as if searching for someone. Her dead eyes met Ann's gaze and she felt a chill penetrate her soul. She slumped back into the seat and pulled the curtain shut.

Chapter 24
2015

'Sounds to me like that Debs woman made it all up. She seems like a psycho. Mind you, where would she have got the photo.'

Martha was pulling on her white gloves in the archives room the following morning. 'At least Cressida told you how madly in love he was with you though.'

'Yes, I suppose that was something. She kept saying she couldn't believe he'd done a runner as he'd told her how blissfully happy he was at his work and at home; he said we were good together. Though why he poured his heart out to her I have no idea.'

'Maybe just because they were both into food? Allie's always telling me about the great chats she has with Claire, that woman she works with. Makes me feel quite jealous sometimes.'

'Yeah, suppose you're right. She was actually really nice, much nicer than slutty Debs.' Fiona sat down at her desk and turned on her laptop. 'Right, I'm going to get all the stuff out on Sir Thomas Bouch today. Did you know there'd been a gale, about the same intensity, in 1853 that sank boats and wrecked houses? Must have been gale force nine or ten, just like in 1879. So there was history of bad storms, but he still paid little attention to wind pressure when he designed the bridge. Got to find out if he was just plain incompetent or if he was trying some new technique.'

'He certainly doesn't come out of the tale well, does he?'

'Definitely not, there were a lot of Dundonians who wanted his knighthood stripped, but then he died only a few months after the public inquiry.'

Fiona went over to the bookshelf. 'Oh, where can I find out about Dad's ancestors, M? In the nineteenth century. According to Dad, there was something that went on in the family, a murder or something.'

Martha looked up from her screen. 'Wow, amazing. What sort of date?'

'I'm not sure. Dad's grandpa told him the story, so the late nineteenth century at some point?'

'The Dundee Courier and Argus was the main paper in the city then. You'll find the back copies in the archives room along the hall.'

'Thanks. I'll see if I've got time to nip along in the lunch break. I don't need to go out, Mum's made me one of her famous cabbage and peanut butter sandwiches.'

'Your mum's a hoot.'

'Hmm… Anyway, it's her birthday tomorrow, sixty-five. Big tea party once Jamie's home from football. Why not pop in for cake and a glass of bubbly if you want. Bring Allie?'

'Thanks, Fi. We're out for dinner tomorrow night, our fifth anniversary. But I'll nip out and get a card at lunch.'

A couple of hours later, Fiona's blackberry pinged with an email.

Dear Ms Craig,

Thank you for your enquiry. I am in fact from New

Zealand and new in this post so not familiar with local knowledge. My colleague is currently away but he is due back tomorrow so I will try and find out more then. Swansea's not that big, so I'm sure it won't be difficult. In the meantime, wishing you all the best from Swansea.

Yours sincerely,

Joanna Coles, Librarian, Swansea Library.

★ ★ ★

Dorothy Craig sat at the kitchen table in front of a pile of presents.

'Open them, Granny. This one first!' Jamie thrust forwards a large present from the top of the pile.

Dorothy smiled and put it on her lap. 'Jamie, the wrapping's lovely. I don't really want to open it. Did you wrap it yourself?'

Jamie nodded, grinning...

'Takes after his artistic dad, of course he did, Mum.'

Dorothy peeled off the paper and lifted out two pictures, both with purple wooden frames. She gazed at them and sighed. 'Jamie, these are beautiful, I love them. What a talented boy!'

Jamie pointed to one of them. 'I did this ages ago, but Mum thought you'd like one of the bridge from your bedroom. If I did it now, I'd do Fife better, it looks all flat. I'd draw more hills now.'

'But it's great, you've drawn the old columns where the old bridge stood too.' Dorothy looked up at her husband, who was peering over her shoulder. 'What d'you think, Pa? Look at the detail.'

'I think it's his grandfather as well as his father he takes after, what a hugely talented artist. Look at the precise lines of that bridge!' He poured more bubbly into the glasses on the table.

'And this picture of the house is amazing. Look, you've got the gravel path and the gate and the windows all just right.'

'And the pillars, Jamie. Remember I told you what they're called?'

'Iconic, Pa.'

Struan guffawed. 'Nearly, Jamie. Ionic.' He patted Jamie's head. 'The lad's learning well.'

Dorothy peered closer. 'Goodness, you've even got the magnolia tree in it, with the flowers out. And what's that behind the tree?'

'A summer house. Pa said there used to be one there and there was a gap in the picture so I put it in.'

Dorothy frowned. 'What?'

Struan took a gulp from his glass. 'The original plans for the house from 1871 showed a small stone structure in the garden. It was a little summer house, behind the magnolia.'

'So when was it taken down?'

'Don't know. I can't remember my grandfather mentioning it and he was born in 1880.'

'It must've been lovely in the summer,' Fiona said, going to the window and looking out to the magnolia tree. 'Would it have had large windows like Jamie's drawn?'

'Definitely, they would have had lovely views over the river but complete privacy inside as it's high up on the lawn. Maybe they wanted to sunbathe naked in there?'

Jamie stared up at his grandfather, eyes wide. 'Would they have done that, Pa?'

'Who knows, young man. The Victorians were a funny lot, all prim and proper on the outside, but a den of iniquity inside.'

'What's iniqu...'

'Moving on,' said Fiona, grinning at her dad. 'Open your other presents, Mum.'

Dorothy was staring out at the magnolia tree. 'You must have some idea of when it was demolished?'

'End of the nineteenth century, maybe.' Struan pushed his present towards Dorothy. 'Mine next, Dottie.' He downed his drink. 'Now, who's ready for another glass?'

★ ★ ★

Fiona turned on her laptop and clicked onto her emails. Another one from Swansea Library.

Dear Ms Craig,

As promised, some more information. Sadly it is not good news. My colleague says there was a Hilary Gibson who worked in Woolworths in the town for some time, but she has sadly died. He says he thought there was something in the local press about the death, but cannot recall what. However, since the graveyard is only next door, he took a picture for you, which might be of help. I am so sorry that this news is not what you had hoped for.

Yours sincerely,

Joanna Coles

Fiona opened the attachment and looked at a photo of a gravestone. She zoomed in and stared. It was a simple black stone, with two names engraved on it and picked out in gold. It read, *In memory of Hilary Jean Gibson, 24/6/1952–3/5/2004.*

Below this was, *And her son Peter Gibson.* But there was no date.

Fiona leant back in her chair and let out a long sigh. What the hell did that mean?

Chapter 25

Sunday 4 January 1880

James and Lizzie ran to the window and jumped up onto the seat.

'Mamma, come and see, snow!'

Ann crossed the room and joined her children on the window seat. The snow was falling steadily, thick flakes descending in great flurries. The branches on the magnolia tree were bending under the weight of the heavy snow lying along their length. The lawn was covered in a blanket of pure white, dotted by tiny black holes where birds had landed.

'Can we go out, Mamma?'

'No, James, you cannot, I'm sorry. It is Sunday and we must all go to church. But you can sit here and look out, while I go and complete my toilette. Miss Graham needs you in the nursery shortly for your Bible lessons then we'll all leave at half past nine. In the meantime, I intend to find those boots you both had last winter although I fear yours will be too tight, Lizzie.'

'And the toboggan!' James said. 'Pappa put it in the summer house after the last snow. I could go with Mr Baxter and get it?'

'As I said, Sundays are not for playing, even after church, but perhaps, if we see the Donaldson children out on the Green this afternoon, you might join them briefly.'

'Pappa would have let us out,' James muttered, scowling.

'Pappa would most certainly not have let you children out.' Ann scolded. 'He is the one who obsesses about Sunday rules.' She stood up. 'And now I must attend to things upstairs.' She ruffled her daughter's hair then swept out of the room.

At half past nine, the family left the house for the walk up to Roseangle and to St John's Kirk on Perth Road. The snow had stopped but there was a thick slushy layer on the ground. Ann Craig walked with her two children by her side. James started to run ahead then slid and fell onto his bottom.

'James,' Ann hissed, stretching out a hand to her son. 'Get up and stop walking so fast.'

James lingered, sulking, until Miss Graham arrived. She brushed the snow from his coat and nodded for him to walk on, which he did, snivelling.

'Big baby!' shouted Lizzie.

Ann wagged her finger at her daughter then burrowed her hands deeply into her fur muff.

Mrs Baxter, struggling to keep her footing in the slush, clamped onto her husband's arm. 'Why could she not have called a carriage on a day like today,' she whispered.

'You heard her, there are none available. If you walk slowly, you'll be fine,' Baxter replied, patting her arm.

Ann looked round and chided their slowness. 'Oh, do hurry up, it's not so bad.'

They arrived at the top of Roseangle and Ann looked towards the tenement buildings at the other side of Perth Road. Four storeys high, they had solid stone fronts dotted with long narrow windows.

'Mamma, what is it like inside those houses?'

'Dark.'

'How do they get to the top floor? Is there a big stair like in our house?'

Ann pointed at a close entrance. 'There's stairs inside that go up to the very top floor.'

A couple of boys ran out of the close of one of the tenements and jumped into a pile of snow that had been cleared to the side of the road. They laughed as they emerged, covered in wet snow. James and Lizzie both stared at the boys, who had no shoes on. They wore ragged trousers and dirty shirts.

'Where are those boys' coats and boots, Mamma?' James asked.

'They have none, dearest boy.' Ann stopped near the entrance to the church. 'Come along now, it's time to enter the kirk. 'Best behaviour and no looking round from the pew, Lizzie, like you did last week.'

'Last week Pappa was with us. Shall I take his seat, Mamma?' James looked up to his mother and pushed his shoulders up high.

'That would be good, yes, you might enter the pew last, James.' Ann said, drawing her dark grey cloak round her. She pushed her black bonnet down a little over her forehead at an angle she knew suited her profile. She would walk down the aisle slowly as usual, knowing the other members of the congregation would be looking at her statuesque figure.

'Hat, James!' she whispered to her son, who was still gazing at the two boys frolicking in the snow over the road. He swept it off and put it under his arm, as he had seen his father do on countless occasions.

They proceeded down the aisle, Ann taking the lead, then the children and Miss Graham behind. The Baxters headed upstairs to their usual place in the gallery. As she walked towards their pew near the front, she took in the dark cloaks and hats. There were many ladies wearing full black veils, she noticed. Goodness, would they think her disrespectful not wearing a mourning veil? Jeannie Baxter had suggested that very morning she could fetch it from its box in the attic.

'I am not mourning my husband until we have proof he has gone, Mrs Baxter,' she had retorted. 'And from what Lady Cruickshank said, and the lack of firm evidence, there is hope.'

But after her housekeeper had left, muttering about Ann's behaviour being 'unseemly', Ann took the fur wrap from the bed and put it back into the wardrobe. Fur and velvet were inappropriate for a lady in mourning and, at least in church, she ought to comply. The whole city was still grieving, or so it seemed by the even more sombre tone of the congregation this morning.

They took their seats on the hard wooden benches in the third row. Once Ann had arranged herself in a favourable pose, she tilted her head slightly forward and looked over to the other side where the Donaldsons sat. Margaret was dressed in black with a grey bonnet and her twins were both in dark colours. Only Dr Donaldson had a splash of colour – a hint of his mustard waistcoat emerged from the top of his coat. She inclined her head a little in acknowledgement of his nod. He was beaming, a smile she knew was directed at her, even though he took in the entire family.

'Let us pray,' intoned the Reverent Arbuthnot from

the high pulpit and the entire congregation bent their heads low.

* * *

Outside the church after the service, Ann and the children watched the Baxters and Miss Graham walk gingerly down the hill. Ann looked round to see the Donaldsons approaching.

'Oh, Ann, my dear, how did you feel when the minister said those special prayers for those drowned?' Margaret whispered in her friend's ear.

'It needed to be done,' said Ann, turning to face Archibald, who was chatting to the children.

He smiled, showing his dimples. 'The sermon was tasteful, do you not think, Ann?'

'Indeed, although I do wonder about the choice of hymns. Surely *Eternal Father* was unwise, since its theme is saving those in peril upon the sea.'

'Oh, my dear,' said Margaret, 'you are of course right. I had not thought.'

Ann stopped abruptly as something white whizzed past. A snowball landed with a thud on James's shoulder. She spiralled round to see the two boys from the tenement, laughing. Without thinking, she bent to scoop a handful of snow from the railings. She squeezed it tight and then, her eyes screwed up in concentration, threw it across the road with an unladylike grunt. It reached the other side and landed with a thunk on the pavement. The boys fled back inside the dark close as Archibald marched towards them.

'That was some shot, Mrs Craig.' Alec Smith stood at

her side, hat in his hand.

'Yes, well, perhaps I should not...' said Ann, flustered. She removed her kid gloves and beat them against each other to shake off the snow.

Margaret was standing open mouthed, aghast at the sight of a lady throwing a snowball. And on a Sunday.

Archibald returned and said, grinning, 'Well then, yet another sign that Mrs Craig is an unusual lady. Snowball rolling is to be added to her long list of talents!'

'I will have no one hurt my children.' She spat out the words. 'Ever!'

Margaret raised an eyebrow. She was always telling Ann she was too over-protective and affectionate towards the children, which did them no good at all.

There was silence until Archibald chuckled. 'Quite right, these urchins need to be kept in their place.' He turned to Alec Smith, extending his hand to the stationmaster.

'Good morning, Mr Smith, how is the knee?'

'Better, thank you, doctor.'

'Good. What news from the station?'

'Not good, I am sorry to say. Yesterday afternoon, a mesmerist was taken out onto the river by a fishing boat and they stopped the boat, as she commanded, to the east of the high girders. She stood up in the boat as it sailed north-east and muttered some things and after an hour or so on the water, she gave her prediction. She said that many bodies would be found that day and the next two, delivered up from the depths. She said she saw three clearly and that one had a watch on his body and she saw silver in his pocket.'

Ann and the Donaldsons leant in towards him.

'Well, this very morning, in the midst of the snow

shower, three bodies were washed ashore at Broughty Ferry beach. Of those three bodies, one gentleman had a silver pocket watch on him. The time said a quarter past seven, the time the train fell into the Tay. The mesmerist's prediction was true. So we await the other bodies.'

Ann fanned herself with her gloves.

Margaret looked horrified. 'A mesmerist? What nonsense. What does a mesmerist have to do with it?'

'She has second sight, gets herself into a trance and can see all sorts of things. Which is surprising as she's blind.'

Ann Craig put her hands up to her face. 'Was it Blind Mattie?'

'Indeed it was, Mrs Craig. They went to Lochee yesterday to take her down to the harbour.'

'So, there will be other bodies in the next few days,' Ann whispered.

'If you believe the rantings of some mad woman,' Margaret tutted.

'She will be right, she always is.'

'Mamma, the twins are going onto the Green this afternoon to build a snowman. Please say we can go too?'

Ann Craig looked at her son, who was jumping up and down beside her. She shivered and seemed to spring back into life. 'We shall see, but let us all walk home now. Lizzie, James, come along please.'

She grasped her children's hands and began to walk down the hill.

'Good day,' she said. The Donaldsons and Alec Smith watched as she strode away over the slippery cobbles, sure-footed.

Chapter 26
2015

Fiona and Jamie walked along Perth Road and headed down Roseangle towards the river.

'Right, it's your turn to carry the bag, Jamie. It's heavy.'

Jamie grabbed the carrier bag from her, saying nothing. He stomped on ahead.

'Stop being so grumpy,' Fiona called after him. 'You should be excited about going to a new school tomorrow and with a nice uniform.'

'I don't see why I can't go to Jack's school. His blazer's black. This one's a silly colour. Purple's for girls.' He scowled. 'And I won't know anyone.'

'Stop sulking. We've been through this. Jack's mum and dad have saved money to send him to the High School. I don't have any so you're going to the local school, which is really good. It's a brand new building and it'll only take you five minutes to walk there. Jack'll have to get a bus.'

'No he won't, his dad's going to drive him every morning on his way to work.'

Fiona sighed and stopped walking. She nabbed her son's collar to get him to stop.

'Listen, I'm sorry about all this, I really am, but it's not my fault Pete left us. I'm still trying to make sense of it so what I need right now is for you to accept that we don't have much money and we're lucky Granny and

Pa have a big enough house for us to live with them. My job's not paying much right now, but things'll get better, you'll see.'

'It's not fair.'

'Life's not fair. About time you learnt that.'

She leant down and lifted her son's chin up. He had tears in his eyes. 'Oh, Jamie, it'll all be fine, you'll see.' She knelt beside him and gave him a hug. 'Bet you make nice new friends on day one. Look at Pa and his friend Mark. They met on the very first day of primary one and they're still best friends all these years later.'

Jamie wiped his eyes with his sleeve and started walking again. 'What's Granny got for lunch?'

'Soup, she said it'd be your favourite. Come on, nearly there.'

* * *

Fiona was helping clear up after lunch as Jamie was getting ready to go and play with Jack.

'There's the three thirty Edinburgh train,' said Jamie, pointing at a train going over the bridge.

'Don't know how you can remember all the train times, Jamie. Anyway, off you go then, but back for tea at six. Remember you've got to have an early night before school tomorrow.'

He slammed the door and Fiona watched him run down the path onto the road, pausing to take another look at the train, and head for Jack's house.

She went to flick on the kettle. 'Coffee, Mum?'

'Thanks.'

Fiona brought two mugs to the table and sat down.

'Mum, have you ever heard of a person's name being inscribed on a gravestone without dates? Just the person's name without saying when they were born or when they died?'

Dorothy took a sip. 'Seems strange, have you seen one like that?'

'Yeah, just seems like a weird thing to do.'

Dorothy leant back against the chair and frowned. 'Hang on, I do remember something like that. My Auntie Mabel's husband David was from Wales somewhere, the south I think. And I remember one of my cousins telling me that when they went to their grandfather's funeral in Wales, their dad's name was already on the gravestone.'

'What d'you mean?'

'So, it would've said something like, "In loving memory of Whoever", then the dates he was born and died and then underneath that were both his children's names, but no dates as they were still living, obviously. They were both there, at the funeral.'

'But why would you do that?'

'Don't know, seems mighty peculiar to me. Could be a way to save money I suppose? Engraving's not cheap. But you'd still have to engrave the dates later anyway, so, really, no idea. It's just maybe something they did in that part of Wales.'

'So, a name with no dates could mean the person's still alive.'

'Presume so. Anyway, enough morbid talk. How's my grandson really feeling about school tomorrow? He's trying to be brave, but I can tell he's not that enamoured.'

'He'll be fine, best if none of us make a fuss.' She glanced at her watch then downed her coffee. 'Right,

I've got to head for the museum now. Be back at six.'
She kissed her mum on the cheek then delved under the
oranges in the fruit bowl for her car keys.

★ ★ ★

'Listen, Fi, I had this new idea about Pete,' Martha said,
sitting down beside Fiona in the archives room at the
museum.

Fiona pushed aside her pile of books.

'Last night Allie and I watched a brilliantly trashy
movie, *Madea's Witness Protection*. You heard of it?'

'Nope.'

'It's about this guy who's a Wall Street banker and
he's been set up to run the company's mob-backed Ponzi
scheme. Then he's nearly killed by a hit man who's been
sent by the boss so he goes to the FBI to trade what he
knows for a new identity. He and his wife and two kids
are coached in completely new identities and they go to
another state and live there. Doesn't end well.'

'So?'

'So, we were chatting about witness protection and
Allie said what if Pete was under a witness protection
scheme and then, when the newspaper review came out,
his cover was blown and he had to leave. At once, for fear
of being detected.' Martha smiled and raised an eyebrow.

'But you just said they give them new identities and
names so how on earth would that tally?'

'Well, yeah, but maybe enough was written about him,
like the fact he was an Aussie and a chef. Oh, maybe
he had a kind of signature dish that was recognisable or
something.'

Fiona scratched her head. 'Well, that's some theory. I'm trying to remember what was in the review. What was it Cressida mentioned again?'

She looked up at the ceiling. 'I think she wrote about his crab dish and the venison and what the hell was the pudding? Oh, I know, rhubarb syllabub with ginger macadamia shortbread. That was one of his classics, I'm pretty sure he used to cook it when he worked in Australia – in Melbourne I thought but who knows, could have been anywhere.'

'See, that could be it. Just one little clue and you've got someone onto you.'

Fiona smiled. 'It seems a bit unlikely. And do countries have agreements where they can exchange witnesses? Say from Australia to the UK?'

Martha shrugged.

'Well, as I said, it's a theory. I'd love to think that Pete has some amazing excuse like that for just up and leaving, but... I think we're clutching at straws.'

'I know, I suppose it's a bit far-fetched. It's just that I sometimes felt that there was something about him, like he was hiding something.'

'What do you mean?'

'Well, that Saturday morning in Glenisla, when we'd stayed the night, you left to run Jamie to football in Alyth. I noticed Pete was shaking, quite badly. I asked him if he was cold and he just suddenly lost it. Shouted at me that it was none of my fucking business, stormed out and I never saw him till you came back and he was all sweetness and light.'

'Why didn't you tell me?'

Martha shrugged. 'I'm not sure, really. You were so loved

up, and when I saw him next he was back to normal, and nothing was said. I thought maybe he was just hungover – remember that was the night of the Baileys.' She looked up at the clock. 'Sorry, I've got to go in a minute, meeting the boss. How's Sir Thomas Bouch going?'

'Pretty good, though the more I find out about him, the more I'm amazed he even got the contract to build the bridge in the first place. I just came across this poem written by William McGonagall after it was finished in 1877. Check it out, it was a couple of years before the disaster, mentions my man Bouch.' She pointed to a poem in the book at the top of the pile. 'Look at the last two verses.'

Beautiful Railway Bridge of the Silvery Tay!
I hope that God will protect all passengers
By night and by day,
And that no accident will befall them while crossing
The Bridge of the Silvery Tay,
For that would be most awful to be seen
Near by Dundee and the Magdalen Green.

Beautiful Railway Bridge of the Silvery Tay!
And prosperity to Messrs Bouche and Grothe,
The famous engineers of the present day,
Who have succeeded in erecting
The Railway Bridge of the Silvery Tay,
Which stands unequalled to be seen
Near by Dundee and the Magdalen Green.

'Great, isn't it!' said Fiona.

'Only because it's got your address on it! Some poem!'

Fiona laughed. 'Not sure it's so much a poem as a piece of doggerel.'

'You are such a pedant, Fiona Craig.' Martha headed for the door. 'See you tomorrow, hope Jamie gets on okay at his new school.'

'Thanks, M, so do I.'

Chapter 27

Sunday 4 January 1880

Ann stood at the door of the kitchen. 'Will your husband be back soon?'

'He left over an hour ago, Mrs Craig.' Mrs Baxter looked round from the sink. 'I would think he will be back soon.'

'I shall wait.'

'Are the children in the nursery?'

'Yes, Miss Graham is about to take them to the Green to make a snowman. She is a daughter of the manse so if she says it is suitable for a Sunday, then so be it.'

Both women looked round as the back door opened.

'Baxter, what news?'

Baxter shut the door behind him and walked towards Ann. 'I did as you requested and asked Mr Smith to see the three bodies in the mortuary at the station. Two were women, one a man. He was indeed a gentleman but he was short and his hair white. I looked no more than I had to.' He let out a sigh and shook his head. 'That wasn't Mr Craig, that's for sure.'

Ann pursed her lips together and stood up tall. 'Thank you for doing that, Baxter. There will be more bodies soon.'

'Aye, they said they are going to use grappling irons to fetch any more up.'

'It is simply too awful. But now there is an errand I

must attend to this afternoon. Call me a carriage, will you, as soon as possible. And Mrs Baxter, ask Miss Graham to keep the children occupied until I return.'

'Do you need to be accompanied? You're not usually out on a Sunday afternoon.'

'No, Baxter, I shall be fine alone.' Ann saw Mrs Baxter raise an eyebrow at her husband as she turned and headed for the stairs.

* * *

'Lochee? Where about?' The driver stood at the carriage door, his cap in hand.

'Just drive towards Lochee Road. I shall tell you when to stop.'

'Are you sure it's Lochee you want to go? Not a usual place for a lady.'

'That is where I wish you to take me. Now drive on!'

Ann sat back and arranged her moss-green cloak. She wore a modest black felt hat; nothing fancy was required for this outing. Pulling back the curtain, she peered out through the frosted glass. They turned left onto Perth Road then right along the Hawkhill. Though a mere ten minutes' drive from her splendid house, the tenement buildings here were some of the worst in the city. Those with two storeys still had rickety outside stairs leading to the top floor. The newer tenements were taller, with dark inner staircases and dingy passages that were filthy.

The carriage turned a corner and trundled along West Henderson Wynd. On the right was a jute mill, then another, and then Ann could see her husband's mill. Built in creamy grey stone from the Angus quarries, there was a hint of red in it when the sun shone. The snow-capped roofs were peaked and the windows long and rectangular. She shivered as she passed it, thinking of the last time she had been up this road, only a couple of months ago, when that poor mill worker was killed. Robert had insisted she accompany him to inform the girl's parents. When she protested, he had told her that his manager, Alfred Johnston, was off that day burying his mother and that he expected her, as his wife, to attend to her charitable duties.

The girl had been one of the many Irish workers in the mill and their home was even more of a hovel than those of the locals. On entering the room, Ann had noticed, apart from the odour of bodies, that there were at least eight people there. They all looked at Robert, standing incongruously in his frock coat and top hat at his side, as he explained that the girl, who was only fourteen, had become entangled in a carding machine and sustained such terrible injuries that she had died. He was socially ill at ease at the best of times but this had tested him and so Ann had tried to comfort the mother while he watched from the door.

What a terrible death the girl had suffered, but of course life for most of the workers was short. Living in overcrowded squalor, disease was still rife, even though the council had tried to improve the health of the community by introducing cleaner water. She recalled Archibald saying that the life expectancy of a Dundee worker was just twenty-four years. Ann shuddered as she thought of the dire poverty all around. Thank the Lord her own children would never know such deprivation. Of that she was sure.

'Where are you wanting to go now?' the driver shouted to her as he turned out of Smellies Lane onto Lochee Road.

'Go up to the Market Cross and stop when you see someone on the street for me to ask.'

'Whoah!' he called and drew the horse to a halt.

She leant forward and saw a couple standing by the road, both dressed in black. The man whipped off his cloth cap when he saw the carriage stop.

'Excuse me,' Ann said, leaning out. 'Can you tell me where Blind Mattie is today?'

They stared at her then the woman spoke. 'Who's wanting her? No trouble, is there?'

'No, there's no trouble, just someone who seeks her company for a moment.'

They looked at each other then the man said, 'She's not out on the streets the day, she'll be at home. She bides in the next close from us. Round the corner at Logie Street then up to Paddy's Brae. Ask there.'

Ann gave the driver instructions and, once the carriage had halted at the close, she alighted. 'Wait here. I shall not be long.' As she started to walk off, she saw two small boys, barefoot, running towards the horse. She heard the driver tell them to hold their hands out flat so they could help feed the horse.

She stood at the entrance to the close and removed her handkerchief from her pocket. The offensive stench all around was strong. She lifted her skirts a little so that they did not touch the rubbish at her feet. When she emerged at the other end of the close she looked up at the greenie, the wooden pole from which a multitude of washing lines was strung. Today being the Sabbath, the lines were bare. Ann took a deep breath, grabbed the rail of the outside stair and started to climb, the smell of pipe smoke strengthening with each step.

Chapter 28
2015

Fiona glanced in her rear-view mirror to see the janitor locking the gate to the playground. The first morning at school had gone much better than she'd expected. Jamie had bumped into two of the boys from his football club in the playground as they went towards the school entrance. Once he had found his classroom and the teacher had welcomed him as the new boy, Fiona had slipped out the door, looking over her shoulder at him. He was setting out the pencils from his pencil case on the desk.

She was sure he would settle well; he was a robust boy, even after losing both his dad and Pete within a few years. Thank God for the stability of Granny and Pa, Fiona thought, as she drove onto the ring road and headed north. She had texted Mrs C and Doug to say she'd pop up for coffee and, though they were disappointed Jamie wouldn't be with her, they were looking forward to seeing her again after two months.

Fiona turned left for Alyth and thought about all the threads she still hadn't tied up. She was keen to continue the research into her dad's family but thus far had found nothing in the archives room. And since she didn't have specific dates, it was taking too long. She had to concentrate on her research for the Tay Bridge project.

She thought again of the photo of the grave. She didn't like to email the Swansea librarian again, but the gravestone inscription had freaked her out, even though her mum had said there might be a plausible reason. And she still had no idea how she could find out more about the photo, and whether the boy on it was actually Pete's son. He looked so like him, she felt sure it was. Did he have another family on the other side of the world?

She parked the car in Alyth and went into the florist's to get flowers for Mrs C. She had been emailing Fiona every now and then with news of kitchen calamities since Pete had left, telling her how much she missed Jamie and his drawings. Fiona put the flowers in the car, checked her watch and saw she had some time to kill; there was no use getting up to the hotel before ten when they'd still be in the middle of breakfasts and check-outs. She walked along Commercial Street, pausing to look over the road at a large stone building. Though it was now an antique car restorer, it had formerly been a jute mill. A couple of years ago she had volunteered to help on a school trip from Glenisla and they had taken a tour of the building.

She had found it fascinating, finding out about the hardships of the jute workers in the nineteenth century. Linen, made in part from local flax, had originally been the main textile produced, but after flax imported from the Baltic states became too expensive, the supply of Angus flax was insufficient, and cheaper jute was imported from India. By the 1880s over a million bales of raw jute were unloaded in Dundee for the mills all over the county.

On the school trip, the children had been told how the coarse jute fibres were wetted and mangled, then spun and woven. Then there had been the major discovery that whale oil softened the harsh jute strands. From then, the entire process became easier and Dundee's whaling industry expanded alongside the jute. Why had she not remembered that before, when she'd had to ask her dad? He was so dippy in daily life but what an amazing memory he had for history – well, apart from specifics about his own family history.

Fiona got back to the car and drove north to Glenisla. As she neared the hills, she stopped her car and got out, looking back down the glen at the rolling hills and the sheep and the scattering of tiny cottages along the river. She breathed in deep; she missed living here. It had been such a good three years, the best time since Iain had died.

★ ★ ★

'Fiona, how are you?' Mrs C ran to the car and hugged her as if she had been away for years.

'Good, thanks. Lovely to see you. Nice hair!'

'Yes, well that new girl at the hairdresser's asked if I wanted a wee rinse so I said why not. It was a bit too purple at first but it's calmed down. More lavender now.' She took Fiona's arm in hers. 'Come away in.'

Fiona turned to look across the road at the cottage. 'Looks just the same, is it being well looked after?'

'Yes, though she doesn't keep it as nice as you did, Fiona.'

They walked inside and into the kitchen.

'I'll get us some coffee and we can sit in the lounge. Doug'll be back in a few minutes.'

A portly chef appeared from the larder. 'Hello,' he said. 'You must be Fiona. Mrs C's told me all about you.'

'This is Billie, he used to work here years ago but then

he went to Gleneagles. Now he's back here, just had his first weekend with us. Tom couldn't handle it all, he left and went to Glasgow.' Mrs C clattered about setting the tray with mugs and a plate of shortbread.

'Scones'll be out in two minutes if you want to wait for those?' Billie pointed at the oven door.

'Yes, please,' Fiona said, looking around. 'The kitchen looks different, really organised. Did you see it when Pete was in charge?'

Billie shook his head. 'Nope, but I know I had a hard act to follow. Customers are still talking about that review.'

Fiona smiled. 'Can I take that for you?' She lifted the tray from Mrs C. They went through to the lounge, followed by Doug.

'So tell me all about Dundee and Jamie,' said Mrs C. 'How's school going?'

Fiona told them about Jamie's first morning, and chatted about what they had been doing during the summer holidays.

The door opened and Billie appeared with a plate of steaming scones. He handed a folder to Fiona. 'When I was doing a big clear-up on Sunday, I found these in the kitchen office, tucked away under the huge volume of environmental health regulations. I presume it's Pete's.'

Fiona frowned and reached for the folder. When she opened it up she found pages of recipes. 'I've never seen this before, but it's his handwriting.'

She stopped at a page that said Mum's Scones. Then on the back was Hilary Gibson's Macadamia Ginger Shortbread and lots of scribbles annotating the recipe. She forced herself to shut the folder and return to coffee and chat as Billie went back into the kitchen.

After an hour or so, Fiona said she had to leave and there were hugs at the door. She waved and drove off down the road then, when out of sight of the hotel, stopped on the roadside and reached for the folder, inspecting every page. Some were handwritten recipes, some cut out of magazines, and there were three more recipes from either Hilary or Mum. And then, on the final page, she felt her stomach tighten as she read the words Sam's Flapjacks. Fiona scrutinised the recipe and realised it was the same one he used to make for Jamie, a regular flapjack recipe but with generous helpings of chopped apricots and white chocolate chips. Not for the first time she found herself thinking, who the hell is Sam?

Chapter 29

Sunday 4 January 1880

Ann took a deep breath and rapped on the door. There was the scraping of a chair and the scuff of footsteps before the door opened. A girl, about eight years old, peered out at Ann through greasy, tangled hair. She had bare feet and a ragged plaid shawl round her shoulders. Underneath she wore a baggy dress that was far too big for her.

'Aye?'

'Is Mattie in?'

'Aye.'

The girl continued to stand.

'Who's there, Elspet?' a voice boomed out from inside.

'A lady, Auntie Mattie, wants to see you.'

'Let her in.'

Ann pushed the door and entered the room. She had seen worse, and smelled worse. Perhaps it was simply the pervasive odour of pipe tobacco. The walls were bare stone and a piece of jute hessian hung from an open window. She looked towards the empty fireplace to where Blind Mattie sat sucking on her pipe, her melodeon by her side.

'Draw closer, will you,' she said and Ann remembered the country lilt to her soft voice. She smiled as she looked at the old woman but then steeled herself; she must not give herself away.

The girl came to stand beside her aunt and stared at Ann as if she had never seen a lady at close quarters. Ann looked more closely at the girl and realised she was wearing a dress similar to those that Lizzie wore; in fact, it may have been one of the items that Ann gave annually to the church for the poor.

Ann stood up tall and looked down at the woman, her face enveloped in puffs of smoke. Could she not do without tobacco and buy kindling for the fire?

'I've come to ask you about the train, Mattie. I heard you were on the water yesterday.'

'Aye and what's it to you?' Her opaque, dead eyes swivelled up towards Ann.

'My husband was probably on board and I need to know if he is in the water.'

'Come near, let me have your hand.' Mattie reached out one of hers and Ann removed one of her dark green kid gloves.

The woman felt all over her hand then said, 'I can tell you are a lady, but I know you, don't I?'

Ann withdrew her hand. 'From Glenisla, you know me from there,' she whispered. 'Can you tell me if my husband, Robert, is in the river?'

The girl crouched next to Ann and rubbed her fingers along the scalloped edges of her woollen cloak. Her hands were filthy, the nails caked in dirt.

'What colour does the lady wear, Elspet?'

'Green, Auntie Mattie, dark green like moss on the stones.'

Ann drew her cloak around her and watched the child's breath condensing in the cold room. 'Do you have no money for kindling for the fire?'

'Not till I gang out the morrow with my melodeon,' said Mattie. 'Nothing till then.'

Ann pulled a small purse from her pocket and took out a sixpence. She put it in Mattie's hand and tried to pull away but the woman held fast.

'Where did you stay in Glenisla? The big house? The manse?'

'It was a long time ago, Mattie.' Ann managed to retract her hand and watched as Mattie turned the sixpence round and round in her fingers. 'So, can you say if my husband is there?'

Blind Mattie pocketed the coin and extended both hands. 'Give me them again, both this time. Elspet, go to the door and stand still, I don't want your spirit to get in the way.'

Slowly, Ann reached forwards with both hands.

'Look straight at my eyes. Nowhere else.'

Ann felt her hands being gripped tight then loosened then gripped once more, the bony fingers playing up and down her palms in an increasingly frantic rhythm. This went on for some time as Mattie's head moved from side to side, her dead eyes glazed. Her lips moved but no noise emerged.

After what seemed an interminable time, Ann's hands were released and she sat back. Mattie stopped rocking and spoke. 'Your husband is not in the water; he is not one of those poor bodies floating to the surface. There are so many, down in the icy depths, but I can see nothing of yours down there.'

Ann took a deep breath.

'Elspet, fetch my melodeon.'

'It is by your side, Auntie Mattie.'

The woman patted her hand around her until she found the instrument. When she played, the haunting melody filled the air and a deep, visceral ache swept over Ann. The tune was once more 'To the Weaver's Gin Ye Go' and for the first time in years, Ann felt tears begin to trickle down her face. The music continued and she began to shake as she sobbed silently. The past came flooding back and she felt she was in a place she did not want to be.

Mattie finished the tune and placed the melodeon at her feet. Ann sat up straight, pulled a handkerchief from her pocket and dabbed her eyes.

Mattie pulled the sixpence from her pocket and stretched out her hand. 'Elspet, gang out for some kindling. And get a wee poke of meal from Janet Smith. We'll have porridge today.'

Ann, now more composed, got to her feet. She looked down at Mattie who was picking up her pipe.

'Thank you, Mattie. I hope you enjoy your porridge.'

Mattie put her pipe to one side of her mouth and turned her head up towards Ann. She beckoned with a finger and Ann drew closer.

'It is a good thing you are not wearing mourning. For he is not dead, but sleeping.'

Ann went towards the door and turned as Mattie called to her.

'You are not as you seem, young lady. The past has a hold on you. Do not ignore it, you might need people from back then.'

She puffed on her pipe then turned back towards the empty hearth.

Chapter 30
2015

Fiona watched Jamie saunter along the path, his knee socks as usual down at his ankles. He stepped onto the grass, kicking the autumn leaves into a golden flurry. Beneath the magnolia tree, he picked up a stick and started jabbing around on the ground.

He was several weeks into the first term at his new school, and seemed to have settled in well. Fiona was so relieved, the guilt she had felt at uprooting her son somewhat abated.

She knocked on the window and beckoned him inside.

'What were you digging for with that stick, Jamie?'

'The summer house. Remember, Pa said it used to be at the back of that tree. There must be foundations or something.' He shrugged off his blazer and dropped it over the back of a chair. 'Pa's going to give me a spade from round the back and I'm going to dig. Ben Conti said his grandpa found treasure in their garden back home.'

'I'm not sure Granny'll be too pleased if you start digging up her lawn while she's away, so make sure you don't make a mess.' Fiona poured him a cup of tea. 'Come and have a drink. Granny's left some rock buns. D'you want one?'

Jamie nodded and sat down at the table.

'Here you go. She placed a plate in front of him. 'How was the school trip today then?'

'It was cool. We saw where the train fell into the sea!'

'I'm not sure that's cool, there were a lot of people killed that day.'

'Yeah, they've got this memorial thing – well, it's three slabs of stone – on the riverside.'

Jamie ran over towards the kitchen dresser, opened the drawer and brought a pad of paper and his coloured pencils over.

'I'm going to draw the Tay bridge.'

Fiona helped herself to a rock bun from the cake tin, grateful that her mum had baked them before they had left for their holiday up north.

'So, this is the other side, Fife it's called. And the train started here,' said Jamie, drawing an outline of a bridge and a river. 'And it got this far, here where I've drawn these tall pillar things, and then it just fell off. Amazing. Everyone drowned!' His eyes lit up.

'I know why you find it so fascinating, Jamie, but there were a lot of people dead that night. There was something on the news recently when the memorial was put up – there's about sixty names on it. That's pretty sad, isn't it?'

Jamie nodded. 'What do drowned people look like, Mum?'

'I don't know. Bloated, I suppose, with all the water.'

'Bit like that sheep we saw up the glen, remember?'

'Why are you so fascinated with dead things, Jamie!'

She pointed to his picture. 'And, by the way, those pillar things are called high girders.'

'Yeah, so they are.' He nodded then looked at her over his mug. 'Thing is, I know it was a disaster and all that, but it was a big deal at the time. It was the longest rail bridge in the whole world, imagine!'

Fiona nodded.

'Why did they not have the other people's names up on the memorial again? Mr Syme said there were maybe twenty more.'

'Well, many bodies were never found, they'd have been washed out to sea.'

'Could they still find one of the bodies now then, Mum? Would they carry on getting more and more swollen and huge and...'

'I really doubt that. Far too late.'

Jamie got out a blue pencil and used wide strokes to colour in the river.

'Did Mr Syme say what time of the day it happened? I thought it was night-time, so the river can't have been blue, can it?'

Jamie looked up, perplexed. 'Yeah, think he said seven o'clock. Blue's for daytime, isn't it?' He got out a black pencil and started to shade in the river. 'There, that looks more like night-time now.'

He pushed the picture towards Fiona and put his pencil down. 'We're getting ready for the Halloween party on Friday before half term. Can you make me a pumpkin lantern?'

'I could have a go.'

Jamie picked up the mug and took a loud slurp.

'Don't be so noisy, Jamie. Any homework?'

'Yes.' He rammed in a large mouthful of rock bun then mumbled something, his mouth full. 'Saw a man today who looked just like Pete.'

'What?'

'He was standing at the railings, with all the mums and dads.' Jamie swallowed then took a gulp of tea. 'They're a bit dry, aren't they?'

Fiona nodded, distracted.

'What did he look like?'

Jamie shrugged. 'Like Pete. He was tall like him, but more skinny. His face looked like his too. He had a cap on so I couldn't see his hair.'

'Who was he picking up?' Fiona realised she was trembling.

'Dunno. I turned round to say bye to Josh then when I turned back he'd gone.' He pushed his plate away. 'If I do my homework just now, can I go round to Jack's for a game of football before tea?' He ran over to the window and peered out. 'There's the four o'clock Edinburgh train coming over the bridge, Mum.'

Fiona was gazing at her son, deep in thought.

'Okay, but this is Wednesday, doesn't Jack have rugby after school today?'

Jamie's shoulders fell. 'So he does.' He stood up. 'Can I watch Robotboy instead then?'

'Yeah.' Fiona picked up the mugs. 'Jamie, what else was this man wearing?'

'Dunno.' He shrugged. 'Blue fleece and jeans?'

Fiona began to load the dishwasher and looked up at the calendar on the wall. The twenty-ninth of October, the anniversary of the day she had met Pete five years before.

★ ★ ★

'So are Granny and Pa home next week?'

'Yes, they're in Lewis this week then Skye at the weekend, home on Tuesday.'

'It's funny without them in the house. Quiet. D'you think there's a ghost that comes out when they're away?'

'Don't be daft, of course there's not.'

They were sitting at the kitchen table, eating macaroni cheese and looking out at the pouring rain.

'Can I have some more tomato sauce, Mum?'

'No, you put far too much on. Your plate's all pink, it looks disgusting.'

Jamie continued forking up the pasta. 'Ben Conti said his granny found a ghost once. Somewhere in Italy at her house there. He calls her Nonna, funny really.'

'What, the ghost?'

'No, his granny. She told him it was a friendly one. How d'you know if ghosts are friendly?'

Fiona splashed some more wine into her glass. 'I have no idea. Now eat up if you want to see Robotboy.'

The phone rang and she stretched over to the counter for it.

'Oh, hi, Mum. Yeah, everything's grand thanks. Yes, he's right here, want a word?'

Fiona picked at her pasta as Jamie chatted, smiling as he nattered on about football and Halloween and macaroni. She took the phone back once he was done.

'Yes, everything's good here thanks. House hasn't burned down yet.'

Jamie frowned at her. 'Joking!' she mouthed.

'Wait!' said Jamie, reaching over to grab the phone back. 'Forgot to tell you, Granny. Guess what, I saw someone today who looked like...'

Fiona snatched the phone, scowling at her son. 'Mum, me again, sorry, we've got to go now, love to you and Dad. Bye!' She clunked the phone down and looked at Jamie, who had a puzzled look.

'Jamie, it's fine for you to tell me these things, but you

mustn't share them with Granny and Pa. They wouldn't understand.'

'Understand what?'

Fiona sighed. 'The fact that you and I miss Pete so much we really believe we're seeing him, dreaming of him and...'

'But I did see him, Mum. Then he went away. He'll be back to see us soon.'

Fiona leant over and gave Jamie a hug. 'Why don't I get out some old photos and you can draw me a picture of him on your new drawing pad?'

'Okay.' Jamie shrugged. 'But Mum, he wasn't a ghost like Ben's Nonna's ghost. It was a real man!'

Chapter 31
Monday 5 January 1880

Ann mopped her brow of sweat and took a deep breath. She picked up the bundle of jute from the batching and softening area and lugged it over to the carding machine. The stench of whale oil hit her nostrils and she tried to hold the bale away from her but it was hopeless. Again, she would have oily patches all over her dress. She dumped the bundle by the carding machine and looked over to Alf for her instructions.

'Take this lot over to the drawing frames, Annie. Then go and see the spinning girls over yon. It's time you learned more about winding the yarn onto the bobbins.'

She looked up at him, her blue eyes imploring.

'And don't give me that look, Annie. You're thirteen, it's time you were doing a proper job, not just helping your Ma. We've got to get Alyth mill producing as much as Dundee. Get a move on.'

She walked towards the spinning frames and looked up. Peering over the railings on the gallery was a young man, gazing down at her. She tilted her head up a little and smiled a coy smile. She knew he had been watching her and he had even spoken to her outside the mill the day before. She had tried to speak proper, like Ma told her. Keep in with Robert Craig, she had said. Even though he's a peelie wallie sprauchle, he's the boss's son. Never know what might happen. And so Ann stood up tall and nodded in acknowledgement of his gaze.

'Get on with your work, lass!' came a cry from behind her. The stench of the oil began to stifle her; she thought she might fall down if she didn't get some air. She ran to the door, ignoring the manager's shouts. At the foot of the stairs, the boss's son met her and extended his arms. She put up her hands to try to stop him embracing her because of the stench, but he pulled her into his arms and then the dust and stour of the mill was choking her, and then they were in the water together and the sea was suffocating her and...

Ann woke with a start and opened her eyes wide. What a horrid dream. She sat up and reached in the early morning light for her water, shaking her hair from side to side to get rid of all vestiges of the nightmare.

Did the dream mean her husband was still alive? If only she had had the dream before visiting Blind Mattie, she might have explained what it meant.

Ann remembered walking barefoot with her mother every day from Glenisla to the mill in Alyth and at the end of the village passing Mattie's cottage, a wisp of smoke coming out of the chimney. Ann used to be scared when she saw her standing at the door, pipe in hand, facing them with her dead, blank eyes. Everyone in the village knew the story of how Mattie had started in the Alyth mill at twelve and soon became better than everyone else at stitching the jute bags. Then when she was only sixteen she became ill with a fever and, though she eventually recovered, it left her blind. The minister had said the doctors in Dundee might have done something to save her sight if she'd been taken there quickly. Her parents believed it was God's will and so she stayed home to look after the family. Now everyone else was gone, she lived with her only relative, a young niece, in Dundee. Ann's mother had told her to be kind to her, that although she could now see nothing in their world of hills and glens and streams, she had an inner sight.

Ann was thankful Mattie had not remembered more about her from the village. When Ann's mother had died and Ann was only fifteen, she had been taken into the care of Robert's aunt in Perth and groomed to become a lady. Aunt Ethel had doted on her only nephew and said she would help provide him with a perfect bride. When he told her that he was infatuated with one of the mill workers, she had been shocked. But she soon realised that nothing would change his mind.

Aunt Ethel taught Ann everything about being a lady. Ann twisted her wedding ring round and round her finger as she recalled their wedding. She was just eighteen. It was a splendid affair and she looked beautiful, everyone told her. So tall with such clear, pale skin. All Robert's family and friends had marvelled at this flower who had been hidden away for three long years. Where had this divine young woman come from?

Only Robert knew the truth, as his father and aunt were both long dead. He had told her one night that had his mother been alive she would have sent him abroad to get over his foolishness: how could a jute mill owner's son have become infatuated with one of the workers? Aunt Euphemia, his mother's sister, was never told. Thankfully for Ann, those relatives who knew were gone; indeed, until eight days ago, her future had been secure. Even though she had never loved her husband, she had a big house with servants and had felt confident that her past would never be revealed. And she had her two wonderful children. She loved them so much; she would kill to protect them. The relationship she had with them, mother to child, unknown in her childhood, was something they would always remember.

Ann got out of bed and wrapped her shawl around her shoulders. She tiptoed to the window and looked out towards the River Tay. To the east, a pearly light shone through a thick layer of murky grey clouds. Straight ahead was the silhouette of the bridge, at the far end of which was the dark, twisted structure, a reminder of how transient life could be. She stood by the chill of the window and resolved that, whatever had happened to her husband, she would not suffer; she would not put James and Lizzie through what she had gone through as a child, the deprivation and hardship. The three of them would survive. She was proud, but also pragmatic; perhaps she might need to call in some favours. She must ensure the money from the mill continued to come to her, whatever happened. She went back to bed and rang the bell for tea.

★ ★ ★

'Mrs Craig, there is more news this morning,' Mrs Baxter said, as she served her luncheon in the dining room.

Ann had just placed her fish knife at the head end of the sole, ready to fillet it with a deft hand. She loved doing this in front of her housekeeper – who evidently believed she had had such exquisite table manners all her life.

Ann placed her cutlery down and looked up, expectant.

'First of all, you might ken this from the newspaper, but there is a court of inquiry beginning today.'

Ann nodded.

'But the other thing is, you ken how Jessie's pa has that wee job at the post office? Well, she says that they found a bag with bank notes. Completely intact, you'd never even ken they'd been in the water. How's that possible?'

Ann shook her head. 'Some things are too much to comprehend.'

'So, they're saying at the post office that yon mailbags they found on the shore might have letters that can still be sent out. Imagine that!'

Ann nodded. 'Did you hear how many bodies have been recovered today?'

'Donald is away the now. We heard another dozen or so. He'll let us know later.'

Ann dabbed at her lips delicately with her napkin, lifted up her cutlery and began to fillet the fish on her plate. 'That will be all.'

★ ★ ★

Ann looked into the cheval glass, tilting the mirror so she could see her face at its best angle in the dim late afternoon light. She leant forward and pouted, her full lips soft and pink. She fixed the tortoiseshell comb into her hair at the back then admired her dark grey taffeta gown, shot through with a silver thread. It was perfect for this evening. She had invited the Donaldsons for their New Year drink, and although they had remonstrated that it was unnecessary this year, she had insisted and persuaded them by saying that things must continue as usual, if only for the children's sake. James and Lizzie had been in the kitchen all afternoon helping Mrs Baxter prepare special shortbread for the guests.

Ann turned a little and smiled as her skirt caught the light and the metallic threads sparkled. Her smile broadened as she thought of Margaret, who would no doubt be wearing her usual heavily brocaded gown in dark colours that did nothing for her pale skin.

A knock at the door.

'Enter!' she commanded, turning away from the mirror.

'Might I have a wee word please, Mrs Craig?' Baxter stood at the door, cap in hand. 'As you know, I was down at the station this morning and went to the morgue, checking everything for you. It's not a pleasant task, that's for sure.'

Ann swallowed and looked at him, expectant.

'There were ten men's bodies there, none of them Mr Craig.'

'You are sure?'

'Yes, none of them was a gentleman.'

She nodded and touched Baxter's arm. 'Thank you, I appreciate you doing this for me.'

'They're moving the morgue to the main hospital tonight. Did you ken?'

'No, I did not, but it makes sense.'

There was a crashing noise downstairs and they both ran out of the room and looked down from the balcony to see Miss Graham pulling the little hall table upright; she had evidently knocked it over as she flung open the front door. She is so clumsy, thought Ann. The governess looked up and picked up her vast carpetbag from the floor.

'Mrs Craig, I have news. Such news!'

Ann and Baxter watched as Miss Graham bounded

up the stairs. She dumped the bag on the floor and bent down to prise its shiny clasps open. She took out a package, tipped it up at one end then carefully pulled out a letter.

'As you know I had many errands to do this afternoon, one of which was to visit the post office. While there, I heard talk of the mailbags that had been on the train last Sunday. Even though the bags were in the water for several days, they were tightly sealed, so some of the addresses were legible. I enquired if there was anything for Magdalen Yard Road and the postmaster returned with this package. It feels heavy, from having been in the water. He said it might still be damp inside so to dry it out fully, but the address is fully legible. Look, Mrs Craig, it's for you.'

Ann took the letter and stared at it. It was Robert's writing. She turned it over and looked at the sender's name. She bit her lip; it was from her husband.

Chapter 32
2015

'Want to come and give me a hand with this stuff, Fi?'

'Yeah, what is it?'

'Bit gruesome,' said Martha. 'Working on the post-mortems today. Need to rake through all the records and see if anything's suitable for the exhibition.'

Martha and Fiona sat down in front of piles of folders on the table and put on their white gloves. 'Where did they take place?' asked Fiona.

'Well, at first they had a makeshift mortuary in the station, in one of the waiting rooms.'

'Wow, that must have been weird.'

'Yes, but that was just for the first few days when Dundee was a city in shock. No one was using trains at first, then they moved everything to the Dundee Royal Infirmary in Barrack Road.'

'So did they have enough doctors specialising in pathology to carry out the post-mortems?'

Martha shrugged. 'Dunno. There was no university then, so no professors of forensic medicine. They'd have had to use just regular doctors, I guess. Main man here seems to be a Dr Donald Anderson, he's signed off most of them but there are some other signatories.' She flicked through the pages and pointed at signatures.

'How could they tell a body had actually been involved in the disaster and not just drowned?'

'They used rectal temperature to assess the length of time since death and the state of rigor mortis.'

Fiona squirmed. 'God, what a job. Presume it's all a bit less grim nowadays?'

'It's certainly more precise.'

'Right, so how accurate could the doctors have been in 1880?'

Martha shrugged. 'Well, they must've had so many bodies all at once, it would have been a sort of production line. The body would first have to be identified by family, desperate for news. Then, once it had a name, they'd have examined it and written the report.'

'So, any injuries not caused by just drowning would have been noted too?'

'Yeah, some had injuries caused by boat hooks or grappling irons used to recover the bodies from the water. Not all of them were conveniently washed ashore.'

Fiona sat down and pulled a pile towards her.

Martha pointed to the one on the top. 'They're all done to a standard formula, so they have the cause of death at the top under "Disease". Then the doctor's name, name of patient, age, when they died. We can cross-reference them to the list from the Tay Bridge Memorial.'

'Okay, so what are we looking for, M?'

'Anything that gives basic facts about the dead but nothing too gruesome, we're hoping loads of school kids will be coming to the exhibition.'

'Oh, I wouldn't worry about kids and gruesome. Jamie loves grisly detail, he asked me what the drowned bodies looked like!'

'Okay, so more a matter of dignity.'

'God, yes. Of course.' Fiona looked upwards, eyes

screwed tight in concentration. 'So, let me think, the great-grandchildren of those who died are all middle-aged now?'

'Yeah.'

'We won't be putting the names with the post-mortems on display though, will we?'

'No, just relevant snippets from the causes of death. No names.'

★ ★ ★

An hour later, Fiona pointed to one of the post-mortems. 'This one's not too bad, gives details but not too much. Name's John Mitchel. I've cross-referenced him, says he's an engine driver.'

'Wonder if he was the actual train's driver. No way of knowing as we don't have any records of the working crew's names. Apparently lots of off-duty train personnel travelled free on Sundays, so he could have just been a passenger.'

'The memorial list says his address was 18 Peddie Street, Dundee. That's the other side of the Hawkhill.'

Fiona's finger hovered over the page and pointed. 'Here's what it says. Death by drowning. Dr Anderson was the doctor. John Mitchel, aged thirty-six, died twenty-eight of December, 1879. Post-mortem fifth of January, 1880. It says he was washed ashore at Broughty Ferry beach and taken to Tay Bridge Station for examination. Presumed drowned in the River Tay. It says he was five foot nine inches, shoulder circumference forty-one inches, and then it goes on to describe the state of his heart, kidneys and so on. But it's the lungs that are most important.' She pointed at the paper. 'Left lung over-inflated with fluid and congested. Right lung over-inflated and contains considerable quantities of serous fluid.' She traced her finger down the page. 'Then look here, torso bloated... consistent with methane gas produced and trapped inside body... considerable quantities of water and debris in stomach... changes related to decomposition delayed by the temperatures of the deep water of the River Tay.'

'So the methane gas build-up while they were submerged eventually caused the bodies to rise to the surface. Then they'd have been washed ashore, many at Broughty Ferry,' Martha said, nodding.

'My God, can you imagine if you arrived at the beach one morning and just saw all these bodies strewn on the sand. Horrible.' Fiona shivered. 'Dad told me about a beached whale there once, when he was a boy. The entire city was out in force, trying to get it back into the water. Pretty sure they managed.'

Fiona pointed to the paper in front of her. 'Anyway, what d'you think? Does this one seem suitable for the exhibition?'

'Yeah, could be. This one here's similar.' Martha read aloud. 'Name Annie Smart, says aged mid-twenties. She was twenty-four and from 52 Union Street. She was a weaver. Death by drowning, but this one also mentions hypothermia. Again, there's mention of lungs over-inflated, filled with water, serous fluid in the pleural cavity. Also mentions white froth in the airways.' Martha grimaced. 'Bloody hell, what a way to die, they must have struggled under the water, but I suppose the water was so cold, it can't have taken long.'

'Horrible. I noticed another one had lesions on the forehead, presumably from being bashed against the rocks. Or against something in the train – crashing into the carriage or part of the engine or something.'

'Thanks for helping, Fi. I'll take our selection to the boss once we've done them all, see what she says. She might think we can't display any of them, but at least without names it's just representative of the disaster, not of any specific family. Thankfully there were no photos in those days in morgues.'

Fiona looked at her watch. 'I'd better clock off now, if that's okay. D'you want me to do more work on these tomorrow?'

'Might need you to, but I'll see how I get on.'

She shuffled the papers and put them into a neat pile. 'We've done up till the ninth of January. I'll carry on with the post-mortems from the rest of January this afternoon and see what's left.'

Fiona peeled off her gloves. 'Thank God we've not come across anyone named Craig!' She laughed and headed for the door.

Chapter 33

Monday 5 January 1880

'You smell nice, Mamma,' said Lizzie, putting her arms around Ann. They were sitting on the window seat in the drawing room awaiting their guests.

'Thank you, sweetheart. A lady must always smell delicious.' Ann turned as she heard the crunch of feet on the gravel. 'Here they are!'

Ann and Lizzie went down to meet the Donaldsons and, with each step, Ann was thinking of the letter upstairs in her room, drying off in front of the fire. Hopefully she would be able to unfold it and read it later.

'Please would you do the honours with the Madeira, Archibald.' Ann smiled and turned to Margaret who, as predicted, wore a black gown, buttoned tightly up to the neck and with a pearl brooch at her throat. 'That is a pretty brooch, Margaret. How well it offsets the black.'

Margaret smiled at her friend and placed her hand on Ann's sleeve. 'I presume there is no more news?' She looked Ann up and down, as if to ask if she would ever wear full mourning.

'Nothing. Baxter continues to seek out information each day. Until then we must have hope.'

'Here we are, ladies,' said Archibald, handing his wife and Ann a glass of Madeira each.

'Thank you.' Ann turned to the four children at the window. 'James and Lizzie, before you go to the nursery with the twins, you may hand round your shortbread.'

Lizzie ran to the table and picked up the plate of shortbread. James sat at the window seat, scowling.

'James, go and help your sister, please!' Ann turned to Margaret. 'The children have helped Mrs Baxter in the kitchen this afternoon.'

James slouched across the room. He took the second plate of shortbread and handed it to Margaret.

'This looks excellent. What an unusual idea having the children help in the kitchen. How terribly novel.'

'It's not for boys,' James mumbled.

'Nonsense, young man.' Archibald said, wiping sugar from his lips. 'I used to adore helping Cook with her baking. Nanny used to help too. We loved it. I used to help make bannocks and pancakes. My mamma said I made them better than Cook in fact.'

'Is that old Mrs Donaldson?'

'Lizzie, it is impolite to mention a lady's age.' Ann looked sternly at her daughter. 'Yes, it is Dr Donaldson's mother.'

James looked up at Archibald. 'Pappa used to say cooking was for girls.'

'Not at all. Girls are doing all sorts of things now. Good God, there is even a woman doctor practising in Edinburgh these days.'

'Is there really?' Ann's eyes widened. 'Lizzie, did you hear that? You might become a doctor one day, like Dr Donaldson.'

Lizzie ran over to them and beamed. 'I'd like that.'

'And so should I,' Ann said, hugging her daughter. 'Now off you children go upstairs. Take some shortbread up with you, if you like. Miss Graham is up there waiting with a new game.' She caught James's arm and drew him towards her to kiss him on the top of his head.

Margaret pursed her lips.

'Ann, do you really think it a good idea for ladies to become doctors?'

'Of course. If both my children ended up in medicine, I should be delighted.'

Margaret raised an eyebrow.

'Dr Jex-Blake is not only the first lady doctor in Scotland, she also does something which more of my profession ought to,' said Archibald. 'She concentrates on helping the poor.'

'A cause near Ann's heart,' Margaret said, twirling round her Madeira glass and smiling sweetly.

'What do you mean?' Ann snapped.

'All those clothes you give to the children in the hovels. That is most charitable.'

'Yes, yes, I do help take them to the tenements to be distributed, but what else is there to do with one's children's clothes?'

'Make rags. That is what my Aggie does. It does not behove us to become too close to such people, Ann, they will get ideas above their station. They are content with their lot.'

'Content?' Ann felt a surge of anger. 'How do you know? How do any of us, in our fine houses, know?' She pointed to the table with the Madeira. 'Archibald, would you be so kind.'

Archibald came over to top up their glasses then sat down beside the ladies. 'Let us change the subject,' he said, noting Ann's flushed cheeks. 'Ann, now the children are gone, might I ask if there is anything you need help with?'

'It is most kind of you to enquire, thank you. I was wondering whether, since there is still no news of poor Robert, I might have to begin looking at financial matters. But the entire business of finance is all a mystery to me. I am, however, aware I shall need some...' She paused to fan herself. 'I, or rather we, shall require funds soon.' Ann turned away and took a delicate sip from her glass.

'Ann my dear, Archibald and I were discussing this very matter. Of course you must have some assistance.'

'Indeed we were. Ann, come and see me tomorrow morning in my study and we shall arrange something.'

Ann nodded demurely. 'I am most grateful.'

'Did you hear the news that the court of inquiry has been adjourned?' Margaret asked. 'They had the key people called in – eyewitnesses, construction workers, divers and so on – but have had to adjourn for a couple of weeks until more information is gathered.'

Ann nodded. 'I had heard. '

'One imagines they also await more bodies,' said Archibald. 'My colleague Dr Anderson has been attending to things along at the mortuary. A most unpleasant task.' He glanced at Ann's rigid expression. 'But Ann, do you still believe that, until there is firm evidence that Robert was on the train, there might still be some explanation to account for his absence?'

Ann gazed out the window at the dark night and listened to the wind howling round the trees. 'All things are possible.'

Chapter 34
2015

'What perfume's that you're wearing, M?'

Martha looked up from a large document spread on the table in front of her. 'Jo Malone, honeysuckle and jasmine. It was a present from Allie, she gave me the body lotion too. Took me a while to take to it, but she loves it so thought I'd force myself to like it by full immersion! And it's worked.'

'I should try that with Mum. She always witters on about how she hates the smell of jasmine, associates it with those big white lilies at funerals. God knows why.' She leant in towards Martha and inhaled. 'That's lovely, give me a skoosh, please?' Martha reached down to her bag, lifted out her perfume and sprayed it onto Fiona's wrist.

She breathed in deep and rubbed her wrists together. 'I'm still keen to find out now about Dad's family, whether there was anything in the papers in the early 1880s. Is the archives room open over the weekend?'

'Yeah, all Saturday.'

'Thanks. Though not sure that's Jamie's idea of a fun day out. Mum and Dad are still away in the Hebrides.'

'Well, why don't we take him to the football? You know how Allie likes any excuse to see Dundee United play.'

'That'd be great, he'd love that. Pete kept promising he'd take him to Tannadice Park.'

'Okay, it's a plan.'

'Great. He's having tea at his friend Josh's tonight and then we're making his pumpkin lantern for the Halloween madness tomorrow night.'

'Is he going out guising?'

'Yeah, going with his pal Jack next door. They won't go far.'

'Remember that year you and I were guising and got lost and had to ask some big scary man the way home. So your mum opened the door to see two little witches with hats and broomsticks and a random giant of a man wearing all black.'

'Yeah, she wasn't too pleased. We were meant to stay with Penny Farquhar's big brother, weren't we, but we decided to do our own thing.' Fiona turned a page in her book. 'Did you realise Sir Thomas Bouch died in October 1880, only months after the disaster? Probably just as well, given the feeling of the locals.'

'Possibly the most unpopular man in Dundee's recent history.'

Fiona sat back in her chair. 'Yeah, the entire city must have been in mourning.'

'Terrible, I mean, everyone must've been affected.'

'What was the population?'

Martha flicked through a couple of pages in the book. 'It was only 45,000 in 1841 but the jute industry meant a huge increase. By the 1881 census it was 140,000.'

'Wow.' Fiona scribbled on her notebook. 'When was the last body discovered?'

'Most bodies came ashore during January 1880. But even four months later, one was washed up somewhere in Caithness. Many were never found, obviously washed out to sea.'

'Imagine waiting for months and months to find out what had happened to your loved one. Or never finding out at all.' Fiona sighed. 'Oh, remember that McGonagall poem from before the disaster? Well, look at the last verse of this one written after the disaster. Like everyone in Dundee, he blamed Thomas Bouch and his faulty bridge design.'

'It must have been an awful sight,
To witness in the dusky moonlight,
While the Storm Fiend did laugh, and angry did bray,
Along the Railway Bridge of the Silv'ry Tay,
Oh! ill-fated Bridge of the Silv'ry Tay,
I must now conclude my lay
By telling the world fearlessly without the least dismay,
That your central girders would not have given way,
At least many sensible men do say,
Had they been supported on each side with buttresses,
At least many sensible men confesses,
For the stronger we our houses do build,
The less chance we have of being killed.'

Chapter 35
Monday 5 January 1880

Ann pulled the clasp from her hair and shook her tresses loose. She buttoned up her nightdress and threw a shawl round her shoulders. Taking a deep breath, she moved towards the fireplace. She lifted up the letter; it definitely felt drier. She could wait no longer. She cleared her hairpins, combs and brushes aside and laid it on the dressing table. Slowly she opened the envelope and pulled out the crisp paper. Hopefully she had not dried it too much. It was brittle, but as she unfolded the letter with a delicate hand, she could already see words. The ink had remained clear. She took a large slurp of Madeira she had poured after her guests had left, drew the lamp nearer and began to read.

My dear Ann,
By the time you receive this in Tuesday's morning post, I will be gone.

Gone? What on earth did he mean? How could he have foretold the accident?

And it is here in this missive I want to tell you my reasons. I know you will find this difficult reading, but I feel I owe a full explanation, to our children at least.

And not to me, the wife who has put up with your foibles and moods for the past twelve years?

I do not feel I owe you anything, Ann, having taken you from the deprived life you lived up in Glenisla, from the misery and hardship of work at my father's jute mill in Alyth, to a life of grandeur and...

Here the ink bled over the page. She thought it read opulence. Ann sighed deeply. Was he to bring up his Master Bountiful once more? Had she not been grateful enough when she stayed at his Aunt's house in Perth for three long years then married him, ugly wee sprauchle though he was. Another sip.

But I digress. I like to think we had a happy marriage at the start. When we lived in our first house on Perth Road and the children were but babies, we were just fine. Then you wanted more, bigger, better and so I had the Magdalen Yard house built. You had everything you wished for – staff, a large house and garden and two beautiful children. That is when I began to feel an outsider. I was only included in your life when you needed me for social reasons, when we saw the Donaldsons, for example, or when we went to other jute mill owners' homes for dinner. You dressed in your finery and, dear God, the bills I have had from Dundee's finest couturiers, furriers and haberdashers have made my blood boil. But did I remonstrate? Seldom, as you well know. I have only ever reproached you when you have not attended to your wifely duties in the bedroom. And that was not infrequent.

Ann turned to look at the wide bed, where the pillows were all stacked up in the middle, suitable for one person to sleep. 'What must Mrs Baxter think,' he'd often say.

'I do not think she lies awake at night worrying about whether her employers are sleeping together,' she would retort.

> *As you know, I have been paying visits to Aunt Euphemia in Fife over the past year. This began on your recommendation and at first I thought it was some hitherto undiscovered kindness in you towards my elderly aunt. But no. For although she is healthy (yes, I lied about her ill health recently), she is ageing fast and I know you had hopes to inherit some of her wealth. Her daughter, my cousin Caroline, would undoubtedly be left the house, but you had alluded to the fact there were many jewels and other items such as her antique furniture. So I began Sunday visits, usually arriving for luncheon, following which I would tour her estate to see if there was anything I could be of assistance with. Then, ten months ago I met someone there, a young woman whom I hold in high regard. With each visit to Kirkmichael we got to know each other more and the relationship grew.*

Ann's stomach lurched. Good God, what sort of woman was he talking about here. Young? What did that mean? Was she sixteen, seventeen? She turned the page over. The ink had bled again and she could barely read the words. She peered at each smudge but little was legible. She hoped the name of the girl would be written but it was difficult to read, though she could make out some individual letters. She moved on to the final page.

...so she and I are leaving for Tasmania on Tuesday from Liverpool. I have been in close contact with my whale-oil dealer there and he has arranged a house, overlooking the sea.

Ann felt her breath becoming short. She was panting now. She leant forward over the page, her eyes open wide.

Once everything is settled, I shall send word to the children and shall arrange for them to be sent over to join me.

Over my dead body!

There is talk of a university being established in Hobart so perhaps James could attend there for further study.

And what about your daughter? thought Ann.

I do not imagine I shall see you again, Ann, but I feel I owe you nothing. Your life would have been so different had I not rescued you from the gutter. In the meantime, there is a trust fund set up for the children. The mill shall continue as it is and you will have a share of the proceeds.

She skimmed over some lines on the mill ownership.

You may keep the house. Money will be placed in the

bank account each month for the upkeep and the staff.
Yours,
Robert.

Ann collapsed back against the chair and stared at the heavy velvet drapes before her. She felt light-headed, as if drunk. What had he done to her, to them? What would she do? She felt tears starting to prick her eyes but she shook her head and sat up, pushing her shoulders back. How dare he. She wiped her eyes with the back of her hand and made her decision there and then. She resolved that no one would ever know the contents of the letter. Why should they? And as for his suggestion that he would take her children to some God-forsaken land at the other side of the world, well that would never happen. Not ever, she thought, strumming her fingers on the dressing table.

No, what would happen was this: she would become the grieving widow, it was the only solution. She would mourn outwards, while inwards she hoped the sense of injustice, the feeling of anger would one day dissipate.

Ann picked up all the pages, rushed over towards the fire and threw them in. She would tell Miss Graham and the Baxters that the letter was illegible, and now was the time to begin to grieve, for there was obviously no hope, her husband must have perished. She would say that even if a body was never found, she was to be alone, alone now with her children and together they would survive. She always did. She grasped the poker and prodded the paper in the grate, watching the last fragments of letter blacken then shrivel into ash.

Chapter 36
2015

Fiona was going through the sequence of events at her desk. By the Sunday after the accident, three more bodies had been washed ashore, the first was that of the woman who had been fished out of the river early on. Her funeral was celebrated as if she had been nobility, though she was only a humble servant in some big house in Fife. Those not washed ashore were pulled onto boats with grappling irons that caused the injuries noted in the post-mortems. The mussel dredgers carried out much of the recovery work, with divers continuing to go down under the bridge. The whalers' prediction on the timing of bodies surfacing was correct. By Tuesday the sixth of January, there were another eleven bodies and by the end of January thirty-seven bodies had been recovered altogether.

Fiona leant back on her chair and thought about how the families must have felt. At least those whose loved ones' bodies were recovered could grieve properly. There was a specific Victorian mourning etiquette she had read about; widows were meant to dress in mourning clothes for between one and four years. Indeed, some followed Queen Victoria's lead and remained in black for the rest of their lives. Half-mourning was introduced for younger widows, who were permitted grey and lavender. That seemed all well and good for the wealthy, but what about the vast majority of Dundee's population, the poor? They might already have black or grey clothes, but lavender?

And what about those many families who could never grieve? Only fifty-nine bodies were ever recovered, some washed ashore months after the accident. Though the specific passenger list was unknown, it was believed that up to twenty bodies were never found.

Fiona turned to the following chapter in her book, entitled 'Relief Fund'. Most of the passengers were poor, travelling in the three third class carriages, and money was given where needed. McGonagall was right: Sir Thomas Bouch had a lot to answer for. Why the hell had he not been up for trial? He was certainly blamed throughout Scotland for his lack of knowledge on structural engineering but he died soon after the court of inquiry report had absolved him of guilt. It concluded that the collapse of the bridge 'was occasioned by the insufficiency of the cross bracing and its fastenings to sustain the force of the gale. If the piers had been properly constructed and maintained, the bridge could have withstood the storm that night.' Though according to McGonagall, the girders needed sturdy buttresses to support them.

Fiona looked up at the clock. She had to go, it was an early pick-up from school and then an hour to get Jamie ready for guising. The pumpkin lantern was looking pretty good; it had taken hours to make. And they would be eating a great deal of pumpkin soup for the next few days.

★ ★ ★

'Mum, this looks silly. Why have I got a black bin bag for my wizard outfit when Jack's got a proper cloak?'

'Because Jack's mum is a natural seamstress and I'm hopeless. Granny was going to do it before she left but then she didn't have time. But it looks great, Jamie!' Fiona leant back and looked her son up and down. 'And I bet Jack doesn't have a brilliant broomstick like this one!'

Jamie turned the old-fashioned broom round in his hand. 'What are these spiky bits called again?'

'Bristles. They're made from long birch twigs. I think the handle's made from hazel wood. Pa said it's been in the shed for decades.'

Fiona opened the box of face paints. 'So, do you want to look really scary? All white with only big black eyebrows?'

'Yeah.'

'Okay, close your eyes.' Fiona daubed white paint across Jamie's face, ignoring his cries that it tickled. Once she was finished, she gave his brow one last thick black line and smiled. 'There we are, go check yourself out in the mirror. I think you'll find your cloak's just as good as Jack's!'

Jamie ran upstairs and she tidied away the scissors and black bags. What a palaver guising was. She couldn't remember everything taking so long when she was a girl.

Jamie ran back downstairs, beaming. 'So, what do I take to put the treats in?'

'That other bin bag. You can take yours and Jack's things. I presume the bigger boys'll have their own bags.'

Jamie nodded.

'So, you've remembered your jokes?'

Jamie giggled. 'Yes.'

'And the song?'

'Yeah, I hope we don't have to do that though. Jack's rubbish at singing.'

He skipped to the door, turned around and gave a sudden lunge at Fiona with the broomstick. She jumped back and laughed. 'Looking good, Jamie, looking good.'

She bent down to kiss his cheek then crouched down so they were face to face. 'Now remember,' she said, staring into his eyes. 'It is really, really important to stay with the big boys. Jack's cousins are old enough to keep you right. You have to stick with them all the time. Any nonsense and you won't be going to the football with Martha tomorrow, and you certainly won't ever go guising again!'

Jamie nodded then rushed to fling the door open before setting off down the path. She watched him running towards the gate, his broomstick held up high like a trophy. Fiona shut the door behind him and sat down at the table. She picked up the face paints and arranged them back in their box then sniffed. What a horrible smell, why had she not noticed before. It was a kind of musky, off smell. She slammed the lid down and headed for the fridge to pour herself a well-earned glass of wine.

Chapter 37
Tuesday 6 January 1880

Ann was about to push open the door to the kitchen when she heard voices.

'I don't care what you say, I'm fed up with her airs and graces, she treats us like dirt.'

'You can't say that, fair enough she gets sulky if she doesn't get her own way but...'

Ann flung open the door and swept into the kitchen, head held high.

'Mrs Baxter, I need your help to fetch my mourning clothes from the attic. All of them.'

Baxter got to his feet and grabbed his cap from the table then headed for the door. His wife was making a production of untying her grubby apron and did not look up at Ann. How dare they talk about her like that.

'Come along. We need to get down my other black gowns and the heavy black veil and that dark hat with the lace.' She was fingering the jet brooch at her throat. 'There should also be a black fur muff up there.'

Mrs Baxter folded her apron, placed it on the table and came towards her. 'Very well, Mrs Craig.' She frowned. 'Have you had any more news?'

Ann drew herself up even taller so that she towered over the rotund little housekeeper. 'No, but I have decided that, since I now know my husband was on the train, he is, sadly, deceased.'

'Did the letter say that?'

Ann glared at the housekeeper. 'The letter was illegible. We must all now accept the situation.' She marched towards the stairs, the black silk crêpe of her gown rustling. Mrs Baxter huffed along behind.

'And I need you to ask Jessie to go to Bruce the milliner's on Perth Road, to purchase a mourning cap. Ask her to take one of my other hats to size it. One made of tulle, perhaps with a little black lace. And with long silk streamers, of course.'

Jeannie Baxter nodded. 'I'll go with her. Just so she buys what's required.'

'Good,' Ann said, walking up the stairs. 'I shall be going out presently to the Donaldsons, but Miss Graham is busy with the children in the nursery all day. I have asked her to don black attire. And I should be grateful if you and Mr Baxter and Jessie wear black armbands. I do not, however, want the children to alter their appearance. I think children in mourning outfits are morbid and sad.' She looked at Mrs Baxter whose mouth was open.

'And of course the children are sad. But they must continue their lives. Do you not agree?'

Jeannie Baxter puffed up the stairs then hung onto the banister to catch her breath. 'It's not for me to say, Mrs Craig.'

'Very well then. Let us get up there and open those trunks.'

★ ★ ★

'Ann, my dear. I am glad to see you.' Margaret looked her friend up and down, trying to conceal her surprise.

Last night she had been wearing a shimmering evening gown that would grace a ball; now she wore widow's weeds. 'You are in full mourning. Is there a particular reason? Any evidence?' Margaret's face was pinched as she showed Ann into the morning room.

'I now have definite knowledge he was on the train.' Ann sat down with a thump and looked out towards the sea. She lifted the black veil from her forehead and swept it back over the crown of her bonnet.

'Did you hear from the doctors at the mortuary? Did they find—'

'I should prefer not to discuss this further at the moment, Margaret,' Ann said, removing a handkerchief from her bag and dabbing at her eyes.

'Of course, Ann. Of course. How are the children?'

Ann nodded. 'As children always are. Sturdy and robust. They will recover from the loss of their father.' She sniffed and glanced up at her friend. 'Far more quickly than I should recover from the loss of a husband.'

'Ann, my dear, how are you?' Archibald swept into the room and took her hand. He looked puzzled. 'I see you are in full mourning today. Have you had news?'

'I just explained to Margaret, I should prefer not to discuss this until I am feeling stronger. But I now know for sure that Robert was on the train. There is absolutely no doubt. And so now, nine days after the tragedy, I must begin to grieve as a widow.'

The Donaldsons both looked solicitous.

'Will it be appropriate for you to begin to plan the funeral, Ann?'

She snuffled and delicately wiped her nose. 'I think not yet, we shall wait and see... Perhaps some sort of memorial service, in time.'

'That is a fine idea. And you must permit us to assist in anything with regards to a service.'

Ann turned to Archibald and looked into his kind brown eyes. 'Thank you.'

'Archibald has been asked by Dr Anderson to assist at the mortuary all this week. They expect many more bodies now.'

Ann nodded and looked down. 'Yes, I have heard.'

'Might you wish to…' The doctor paused and cleared his throat. 'Might you wish to see if there is any possibility of identification, Ann? Shall I send for you should I discover anything?'

'Oh, I don't think I would be able to withstand any more anguish. No, thank you, Archibald. I should be most grateful if you can attend to any formalities at the mortuary for me.' She swallowed. 'As and when that might occur. They say some poor souls will never be found, some may be washed many hundreds, indeed thousands of miles away. Perhaps they might even end up ashore in Australia.'

The clock struck eleven. 'Will you take tea, Ann?'

'No, thank you, Margaret. There is much to be done at home.'

'Of course, of course.' Margaret nodded.

'Would you please accompany me to my study?'

Ann stood. 'Thank you, Archibald.'

He gestured towards the door and she followed him, crossing the corridor to the study. Archibald shut the door behind them and pointed at the seat in front of the desk, which he went behind and waited for Ann to sit.

He sat down then leant over the desk, clutching both

hands together. He had an expression she had not noticed before. One of compassion, yes, of deep sorrow. But there was something else, something hidden.

'Ann, we alluded to this before but now I must be frank and tell you that whatever financial assistance you require is yours.'

He removed a tiny key from his pocket and unlocked the drawer in front of him. He pushed aside some pills and small phials and stretched in towards the back, removing some bank notes.

'Are you in need of much in terms of cash, Ann?'

Ann began to fan herself with a black fan. 'I am sure that, once things are settled, I shall be able to speak to Robert's lawyer in Union Street. There is surely some way that I can access the money in his account, but for now, I should be most grateful if I might have a small loan.'

'Think nothing more of it.' Archibald began to count out notes in front of him and looked up at her, expectant. She said nothing, just continued to gaze into his warm brown eyes. He continued counting until a substantial pile sat there.

'Thank you, Robert, that is most kind. I shall repay it just as soon as...'

'Do not worry at all. You have enough to consider at this moment. All in good time.' He replaced the few remaining notes at the back of his drawer and hesitated. 'Are you sleeping better, Ann?'

'I must confess that I am not. Indeed, not well at all.'

He withdrew a phial of dark brown liquid from the drawer and handed it to her. 'Take only a couple of drops of this tincture at night. No more than three drops, in water. You will sleep like a baby.'

Ann pushed the phial into her bag and stood. 'Thank you. I do not know how I would manage without such devoted neighbours.'

Archibald locked the drawer then came round the desk to stand in front of her. 'Not just neighbours, Ann, but friends, dear friends.' He leant down towards her. He was very close to her face. She felt his warm breath as she gazed up at him, her ice-blue eyes shining. He withdrew a little and inhaled deeply.

'What is your perfume, Ann? It is intoxicating.'

Ann stood up. She flicked the veil back down over her face and smiled. Now she knew what his hidden expression was. Desire.

'Jasmine. Do you like it, Archibald?'

★ ★ ★

That night, Ann lay in bed, the phial on her bedside table. She unstopped the stopper and sniffed – the smell was horrid. She would take only one drop tonight; she wanted to sleep well, but not too deeply. If it worked, she could try more the following night. She thought of the children; would they have nightmares or indeed be sad at all? She had sat them down at suppertime and told them that Pappa would not be coming home and that they must not be sad for he was in Heaven now. That had been difficult to say, since she now knew he was on his way to Australia with some serving maid. She loathed him so much, she hoped he would burn in Hell some day. But now her priority was the children; she would do anything to protect them.

She took the tincture – just one little shake in the water glass – then blew out the candle by her bed and soon fell into a deep sleep. Some time during the night, she shivered and pulled the blanket round her. Then she became aware of something; she felt there was someone in the room, she was sure of it. She clasped her hands tight together under the sheets. How had she woken, had the sleeping potion not worked? It was still the middle of the night, it was pitch black.

Ann looked around as her eyes adjusted to the dark. She saw nothing at all, but she felt a presence. And there was an icy draft. She looked towards the door and could just make out the gleam of the brass handle; the door was ajar. She looked down the bedclothes, without moving her head, and made out something at the end of the bed. Terrified, she did not move but watched as something – was it a figure? – moved in the dark towards the door.

In the morning, she awoke and looked around in the dim light. She turned towards the door which was firmly shut and shuddered as she recalled her dream. It had been horrid, she had truly believed someone had been in her bedroom. Perhaps she would not take the sleeping potion any more. She had enough to worry about without also having nightmares.

Chapter 38
2015

Fiona rushed to pick up the phone, knowing who it would be.

'Hi, Mum.'

'How did you know it was me?'

'I'm psychic!'

The conversation followed the same pattern every time Dorothy phoned Fiona out of the blue.

'How's the holiday going?'

'Not bad, we're still on Harris but heading for Skye tomorrow. That's unless you need me home. Sure everything's okay? Jamie fine?'

Fiona could hear a noise of muttering in the background. 'Ignore your father, he thinks I'm mad. I've got this feeling, sweetheart, I just feel something's going to happen.'

'What are you talking about, Mum?'

Her dad took the phone. 'For God's sake woman, stop blethering. Fi, it's me. Your mother is becoming more insane by the minute. She somehow has got into her dippy head that something bad's about to happen. I think it's all the cheese she had at lunch with, I might add, most of a bottle of claret.'

Fiona heard a yelp of indignation.

Her father continued. 'But just to put you in the picture, Fi, we are okay. Beautiful weather, unseasonably mild. And we've only had one heavy shower.'

'Great. Everything's fine here, house still in one piece.'

'Is the Little Prince out doing the rounds with my broomstick?'

'Yeah, he went out with Jack and his two cousins.' Fiona glanced at the clock. 'Nearly an hour ago. I'm expecting him to ring our bell soon.'

'Give me the phone, Stru!' Dorothy was strident. 'Fi, take care, will you. I can feel it in my waters, there's something...'

'Hell's teeth, woman. Will you stop worrying the girl. She's not a child.'

'Mum, Dad, I'm fine.' She grinned. 'There's a howling gale outside but we're nice and snug here and – oh, and I've had the heating on all day and all night in case of frost.'

'What? That's bloody ridiculous!'

'Ha, got you, Dad. Don't worry I've not had to move the timer from your three stingy hours morning and night. Yet.'

'You should see our heating bills, Fi. Anyway, got to go, but we'll speak tomorrow. Christ, stop trying to grab the phone, Dot. Here she is, Fi.'

'Can you phone the surgery tomorrow please, darling. Your dad's actually not been great – tired, bit breathless. I want him to see Dr Stobie on Wednesday afternoon when we're back. The last appointment if you can.'

Fiona could hear muttering in the background. 'You don't need to top up your dram, Stru! Sorry, Fi. Is that all right, sweetheart? That busybody receptionist's there for a couple of hours on a Saturday morning.'

'Okay, will do.'

The doorbell rang. 'That'll be the guisers at the door now,' said Fiona. 'Got to go.'

★ ★ ★

'So, Jamie, time for your joke please.' Four boys stood at the door, under the front light. It was pitch dark outside and the wind had got up. The boys were all holding on to their hats and Jamie's bin-bag costume flapped around him. Jack's cousins were dressed as ghouls, with impressive face painting, and Jack was another wizard. Fiona had to admit, he was wearing a wonderful outfit. Why could she not sew like the other mums? The other three boys had done a poem and a couple of songs.

'Okay, here goes.' Jamie stepped forward and grinned broadly. 'Why was six afraid of seven?'

'I don't know, Jamie. Why was six afraid of seven?'

'Because seven eight nine!'

Fi shook her head as Jamie chuckled. 'And the other one?'

'What did one toilet say to the other?'

'I don't know, what did one toilet say to the other?'

Jamie's shoulders began to shake with mirth. 'You look a bit flushed!'

All four boys stood grinning, waiting.

'Okay, you've all done your party pieces. Let me go and get something for your swag bags.' Fiona went into the house and returned with four tangerines, a bag of nuts, four chocolate bars and four pound coins.

'Wow, thanks Mum, it's more than we got at the other houses.'

'Yes, that lady at the end of the street only gave us one

Rolo each, not even a packet!'

Fiona looked at her watch. 'Right boys, you've only got another hour. Remember Jack and Jamie have to be back by seven thirty.'

They set off down the drive, Jamie running ahead, brandishing his broom above his head.

★ ★ ★

About an hour and a half later, Fiona had just topped up her glass and looked up at the clock again. Where the hell were they? She went to the window and looked out. The wind was now blowing in squalls of fury. The branches on the magnolia tree were swaying and the leaves billowing all over the lawn.

The phone rang.

'Yes?' Her voice was urgent.

'Just me, Fi.'

'Oh, hi, Martha. How's things?'

'Good, just checking Jamie's still on for the football tomorrow?'

'Yeah, fine, he's really excited.'

'You okay? You sound weird.'

'They're late back, he was due home half an hour ago.'

'For God's sake, Fi, don't you remember our mums used to have near panic attacks with us? We always dawdled on our way home after the last house. In fact we used to go home via the swings and sit there chomping on all the sweeties and things. Felt sick when we eventually got home.'

Fiona leant back against the kitchen chair and sighed. 'Of course, that's what they'll be doing. Thanks, M. I had him kidnapped by some crazy child-snatchers.'

'That was Chitty Chitty Bang Bang, Fi. Got to rein in that imagination of yours. Right, see you tomorrow at one.'

The doorbell rang.

'Oh, that's the bell. See you tomorrow!'

Fiona flung open the door. Two ghouls stood there.

'We're really sorry but we've lost Jamie, we've looked everywhere but...'

There was a noise behind them. Two figures crunched up the drive, Jack with his dad at his side.

Fiona had only met Chris a couple of times but she did not recognise his grave expression.

'What d'you mean, you've lost him? How is that possible?'

'Fiona, they came to us about twenty minutes ago and I've been out on the Green with them just now, can't see him anywhere. Three of the lampposts are out and it's really dark down there so we can't see. I just got a big torch from home.'

Fiona felt her heart lurch. She yanked her coat off a peg and struggled to put it on. She was about to shut the door when she stopped then ran back to the kitchen table to grab her phone. She pulled the door to, leaving it slightly ajar, then stomped off after the boys. As she walked down the drive, she felt like a puppet. It was as if someone else was controlling her voice and the scream that wanted to escape did not. Instead she said, in a composed voice, 'Right, where did you last see him?'

Chapter 39
Wednesday 7 January 1880

Ann Craig sat at the window seat in her black gown and gazed out at Magdalen Green. The wind had got up and the trees along the shore were swaying. She was watching Miss Graham walk over the grass, stopping every now and then to point something out to James and Lizzie. The governess was holding onto her hat and her skirts were swirling around her. Ann lifted the field glasses and noticed that she was wearing grey. She had apologised that she had no more black clothes, but had asked for leave to go to her home in Broughty Ferry to fetch more. Ann swung the glasses east a little and noticed someone standing under a lamppost, as if watching them. The thin figure – and as she peered through the glasses she could see it was a man – was huddled, as if trying to obscure his face and body. She got to her feet and turned up the focus on the lenses. The man was holding onto a top hat and wore a long dark frock coat. She could see nothing else as his face was turned towards the sea and the children on the Green.

James ran along the grass, his hoop and stick beside him. She smiled as she watched him stop and lift the stick in the air, as if brandishing a sword, and the hoop wend its way, wobbling, in front of him. He ran after it, stooped down to pick it up then set it off once more, sprinting beside it. Lizzie was slower, she was skipping with the new skipping ropes with beautiful wooden handles she had been given for Christmas. She'd been thrilled when she had unwrapped them. This was only the second time she had been out with it as the weather had been so bad and then of course there was the accident. Ann shifted the glasses back onto the lamppost: there was no one there now, the figure had gone. She continued to watch the children at play, wishing she could be out with them, but it was unseemly for a lady in mourning to do anything other than stay at home and grieve. For months. Besides, even if she were not in mourning, it would be frowned upon for a lady to run along the Green with a skipping rope.

She sighed, remembering her own childhood up the glen. All the children would take the washing lines down when the mothers had gone to fetch water from the spring and use them as skipping ropes. They raced along the road, skipping as fast as they could, until the women came back down the hill, tight-lipped and scowling, demanding the ropes back. Most of the children would get a skelp around the lug; James and Lizzie would not even know what a skelp or a lug was.

Her children were about to come home to a table laid formally with china cups and saucers and silver teapots, with hot scones served on silver ashets. When she was a child, after playing in the filthy streets, she would go into her mother's tiny croft, which was invariably cold, and find little more than a chipped cup of sour milk if her mother had been to beg some milk from Bessie who worked at the big house. She shivered at the memory.

What was it Blind Mattie had said about her past? Do not ignore it. But why ever not? She lived in a different world now. She looked around the room to remind herself that this was now where she belonged. There was the tall oak grandfather clock, handmade by the best clockmaker in the city. There was the crystal decanter filled with the finest Madeira wine, with cut glasses on the silver tray. There was the chandelier, resplendent and sparkling above her even in the dim afternoon light. She turned back to the window and saw the children running across the Green towards home, Miss Graham struggling along behind them, clutching James's hoop and stick under her ample arms.

★ ★ ★

'Mamma, there was someone on the Green today who looked like Pappa,' James said through a mouthful of scone.

'Manners, James, my darling. Do not speak with your mouth full.' Ann swivelled round. 'Where was this person?'

James swallowed. 'Standing under the lamppost at the far end, you know where we go with the Donaldsons and their dog?'

Ann nodded. It was the man she had seen. 'Why did you believe he resembled Pappa?'

Lizzie was peering at her scone as she slowly and methodically spread it with butter and then jam. 'Is this strawberry jam, Mamma?'

'Yes.' Ann stroked her daughter's hair and looked at her son once more.

'Well, he had the same hat as Pappa wears and though I could not see his face, I saw him looking at us.'

'James.' Ann put down her bone china cup. 'Do you recall what I told you the other night? Pappa is, sadly, never coming back. He is in heaven and...'

'But Mamma,' said Lizzie, sitting up straight. 'Maybe he swam to the shore and got dried off and he has been getting better and drier since then and now he is returning to...'

'Your father is dead!' Ann snapped, immediately regretting it. She kissed her daughter's plump cheek. She rubbed the nape of James's neck then kissed him too. 'Sorry, my dears, but you have to try to accept that. He will not be back. Never ever.'

She looked at Lizzie, whose head was bent low over her plate. She tilted her daughter's sweet little chin up and saw tears fill her eyes. Lizzie blinked and swallowed then took a large bite of her perfectly buttered scone.

James nodded. 'I am the man of the house now, Mamma. I shall take care of you and Lizzie.'

'Thank you, James, dear. Now, let us never talk of it again.'

She lifted the lid off the silver salver. 'Another scone, while they are warm?'

* * *

Ann poured herself a glass of water from the pitcher beside her bed. Lifting the phial from the bedside table she shook one drop carefully into the glass. She had wanted to take more of the potion tonight but since Miss Graham was away, collecting her black clothes, she did not want to sleep too deeply, in case Lizzie awoke and needed her. James she knew would never wake and even if he did, she felt sure he would never come to seek comfort. Robert had been telling him for the past year or so that he was no longer a little boy and that he must be strong and stoical, like a man, no tears, no whining. James was still her baby, Robert had never understood that.

She turned out the little lamp by her bed, lay down and shut her eyes. Sleep came fast. She was lying still, breathing deeply, when all of a sudden she opened her eyes. The room was still dark. What had woken her? It was a pity she had not slept through till the morning.

Then she heard something, a rustle, and looked towards the noise. There was a figure standing at the end of the bed, just like in her nightmare. The sleeping draught obviously did not agree with her, she was having bad dreams again. She shut her eyes and turned onto her side. Then she half-opened one eye and looked towards the door. Once more it was ajar, she saw the gleam of the handle in the dark. She sat up, felt for the lamp, struck a match and lit it. She turned towards the end of the bed and gasped. Standing there, in a dark coat and with a top hat by his side, was Robert.

Chapter 40
2015

'So you last saw him under the lamppost, then you three went up the slope towards home and presumed he was following?'

The boys nodded in unison.

'And there's no way he'd have gone down to the funfair on Riverside Drive by himself?'

'Mum and you both told us a million times we weren't allowed. He wouldn't have,' Jack said.

The three boys, Fiona and Chris strode down the sloping grass towards the lamppost, their torches flashing. When they got there they stopped and looked around. It was deserted, as if the wind had blown everyone away.

'Why on earth did you come here?' asked Fiona.

'None of the other lampposts are working so it was the only place we could see properly. We emptied our swag bags out onto the grass to divide up the money and we were eating those funny chews that lady at number ten gave us and no one could speak, remember?' said Tom, the tall cousin.

'Yeah, then we went back up the slope. We thought he was behind us but he must've been picking up the sweeties and putting them back in the bag.' Andrew, the shorter cousin, looked at the other boys. 'Remember we ran up the slope, to see who could get to the top first, thought he was with us.'

'But obviously he wasn't.' Fiona spoke through clenched teeth. She sighed and looked south towards the river and the bright lights of the funfair.

'Jack, did you and Jamie talk about going to the funfair at all?'

Jack shook his head and screwed up his eyes.

Fiona knelt down so she was face to face with him. 'Are you sure? Listen, we're not going to be angry with anyone, are we, Chris?' She glanced up at Jack's dad. 'But we just need to find him.'

Jack shook his head and she could see tears in his eyes. 'No, we didn't.'

Fiona patted his head and started to get up.

'I called him a name,' Jack blurted out, tears now running down his face. 'I said his jokes were for babies and that he couldn't run as fast as us and I think he got in a huff.'

'What did you call him, Jack?' Chris shouted at his son.

Fiona put up her hand and shook her head. 'Leave it, not important.'

There was a whisper from Jack who was now blubbing. 'A schemie, I called him a schemie.'

'A what?' Chris barked.

'I didn't mean it, he's not, but some boys in his class are and...'

Fiona got to her feet. 'Forget it. Right now, we need to find out where he went from here.'

'We still thought he was with us though, really we did,' Andrew said. 'Why don't we all go along in lines towards the far end, like you see on the telly, see if we can see any of his sweetie wrappers or anything, then get back to the house and...'

'Phone the police.' Fiona snapped.

Chris put an arm gently on Fiona's. 'I'm sure it'll be fine, Fiona, really. But why don't you head home with the boys and I'll nip down to the funfair, just in case?'

Fiona nodded 'Okay, have you got your mobile?'

Chris nodded and set off towards Riverside Drive, marching with his arms by his side. A beam of light from his torch flashed up and down as he headed for the river.

Watching him, a lone figure in the dark, Fiona's thoughts turned to something horrible she had read in the papers recently about a child molester who hung around school gates during the day and funfairs at night. And hadn't Jamie said he had seen someone who looked like Pete at the school gates? Surely not.

* * *

About twenty minutes later, she and the three boys crunched up the gravel path and she pushed open the back door to hear the noise of the television. She was sure she had not left it on. She ran through to the lounge and flung the door open. In front of the television, his Halloween costume in disarray, sat Jamie, chomping on something chewy. His broom lay on the floor in front of him.

'Hi, Mum, sorry I was late.' He poked a bit of toffee from a tooth with his finger.

Fiona rushed to her son and hugged him. She drew back, looked at his face, smudged with paints, and shouted, 'Where the hell have you been? We've been looking everywhere for you!'

Jamie looked round at the three boys who had come

into the room. He said nothing but put the volume up on the television.

'Where have you been?' Fiona blinked her tears away and grabbed the remote control from her son. She stabbed the off button and threw it onto a chair.

Jamie glared at the boys then whispered, 'Tell you once they've gone.' He picked up the swag bag beside him and flung it over towards them. It landed at Jack's feet. 'It's all just my stuff in there, you can check.'

'Stop being petty, Jamie,' said Fiona, flushed. She turned towards Tom and Andrew. 'You can go home now. Jack, can you phone your dad and thank him for going to the funfair for us, but say Jamie's safely home.'

Andrew and Tom headed for the door. Jack turned to go then stopped. 'Sorry, Jamie, I didn't mean what I said.' He slunk out the door, his head hung low.

Fiona watched him go then sat down on the sofa beside her son. 'So?'

Jamie frowned, his brow furrowed. Fiona smiled; he looked so like his father, he used to make that same face while poring over drawings in his studio, his forehead a mass of lines as he concentrated.

'Well, Jack called me a schemie, said all the boys in my class were schemies, and...'

'Is that what it was all about?' Fiona shook her head. 'Just leave it, ignore him Jamie, not worth it.'

Jamie shrugged. 'He's called me that before but he thought it was big to call me that in front of the big boys. Think he forgot they don't go to his posh school either.'

'So where did you go?'

Jamie bit his lip. 'I wanted to get back at him so I ran along to Ben Conti's house in Step Row but there was no one in. House was all dark. So I hung around that end of the Green for a bit, eating my sweeties and watching the trains from Fife on the bridge. Saw the seven forty-five and the eight ten, then I just came home.' He gave her a forlorn look. 'Sorry, mum.'

Fiona gave her son a tight hug and patted his hair. 'Never ever do that again, Jamie. I thought something horrible had happened. I was so worried. Thank goodness Granny and Pa weren't here, they'd have had at least one heart attack between them.'

She turned and stroked her son's hair then kissed his cheek. 'Remember, Jamie, you've got to ignore stupid remarks like Jack's. It really is more grown-up not to rise to it. Try laughing at him next time he says it or even better, just ignore it.'

Jamie nodded and popped another sweet into his mouth.

'And that's enough of the sweeties, Jamie. Come on, upstairs and let's get your teeth brushed.'

'Can I take some of the toffees to the football tomorrow? I think Martha likes them.'

'Good idea. Right, come on, let's get that face paint scrubbed off.'

Chapter 41

Thursday 8 January 1880

'Robert, is that you?' Ann croaked, holding the lamp in front of her as she peered into the gloom. She sat upright, the bedcovers pulled around her shoulders.

'Good evening, Ann, forgive the intrusion.'

He approached the bed and sat down at the end. 'How are you?'

Ann glared at him, taking in the unshaven face and gaunt body in the dim light. It was most definitely her husband; he had a rugged look, but still the haughty sneer.

'Fine.' She pulled her knees up to her chest. 'But what on earth are you doing here in the middle of the night?'

He was staring at her and then looked all around the room. 'I see nothing has changed apart from your apparel. Instead of frivolous lilac, you now wear black, even in bed. Is that a new nightgown?'

Ann looked down at her gown, flustered. She pulled the collar up higher. 'No, it is not. Robert, tell me where you have been?' She looked up at him, her eyes round. 'We have been so worried. We have been grieving, mourning a husband and father who was lost in the Tay.'

He shook his head. 'Ah, what a tragedy, so many lost. Up to fifty they think?'

'Or more, the bodies are still being washed ashore.' She tried to move her legs down the bed but his body blocked them. She must remain calm, considerate, attentive. She looked at him again and attempted a smile.

'The children look well.' He smiled as he shifted his weight further towards her.

'When did you see them?' she snapped.

'I saw them last night in their beds and today on the Green.'

'So you have been watching us. Why did you not make yourself known? Why are you resorting to subterfuge, visiting in the middle of the night?'

Robert shrugged and continued to stare at Ann, as if taking in every feature anew.

'What happened to you, Robert?' Her voice was almost a wail.

He tilted his head back and looked up at the ceiling. 'Before I tell you, I must ask you something important.'

'Yes, dear husband, ask.' Contrite and humble, that is what she must be. But she must remain in control.

He turned back to her, his dull grey eyes looking into hers. 'I sent a letter. I do not suppose it was delivered? I know the mailbags on the train must have been in the river so they would be sodden and...'

'A letter? What letter?'

He sat up straight. 'Nothing important, Ann. It was simply some financial matters I had to attend to. But it is not a problem if it is at the bottom of the Tay.'

Her heart was thumping against her ribs, but she attempted another smile. 'No, Robert. No letters have been delivered here since the accident.' She reached out for his hand and looked up at his stern face framed by his bristly beard. 'What happened? Did you get off the train at Leuchars? I heard there was a gentleman who did. But why did you not come home?'

'Why indeed.' He pulled away his hand, stood up and began to pace up and down, by the side of the bed. He stroked his beard then sat down on the chair next to her bed. Good, less threatening, thought Ann. She could run to the door if necessary.

'As you know, Ann, our marriage has been a sham, an unhappy union with only two happy consequences. Our children. I have been thinking for some time that I would venture far afield to start a new life and Australia was often in my mind. Tasmania is where I have contacts through the whale oil business.'

Ann began folding and unfolding the hem of her bed sheet with her fingers, nimble as the jute spinner she had been.

'My intention was to travel there and begin a new life.'

'A new life without your family?' Ann attempted to sound calm though she wanted to shout and scream.

'Well, of course I would have sent for you and the children later.'

Ann nodded, her icy blue eyes narrowing at this blatant lie.

'What happened, however, was most unfortunate. I had never intended to travel on that ill-fated train and was horrified when I heard what had happened. I took the train from Ladybank after visiting Aunt Euphemia and thence to Edinburgh where I began the long journey to Liverpool, where I was meant to board the ship to Australia, to prepare a home and establish my work before sending for my family.'

'Why did you not tell me?'

'I wanted it to remain my little secret, to have everything

ready for you over there then send for you.'

Liar, liar, liar! She continued twisting the hem of the sheet with increasing speed. 'But that would have meant weeks with no word from you, Robert. Even if the train had not crashed, I would have believed you dead, the children too.'

'Do not question me!' he snapped, his voice loud.

'Hush, Robert, you will disturb the children,' said Ann, scolding herself for inflaming Robert's temper. Though his excuses made no sense, she must go along with his lies.

'So what happened, Robert? Why are you not on your way to Australia at this moment?'

'During my journey south, I was taken hostage by some brigands and kept captive for three days until I eventually gave them all the money I had hidden in my portmanteau. Then, since I had nothing left, I had to wait there till I was able to secure funds for my return journey.'

Ann was aware her mouth was wide open. How could he lie so? She swallowed. 'What a terrible time you have had, Robert. We have been so worried that you were at the bottom of the Tay. You should have communicated with us, any word at all would have helped alleviate our pain.' She must overplay the grieving widow.

'I am sorry for the children's sake. They must have missed their Pappa. I missed them too, but I look forward to taking them to Australia soon.'

'That will not be possible, Robert.'

'Why ever not? I am their father, you have no rights to them.'

Ann took a deep breath and began to smile as a thought occurred. 'Robert, let us not argue. Whatever you desire is of course your command. But first, let me tell you about how things have been here in your absence. Everyone else is well. Your cousin Caroline was distressed about the news of the bridge but she is resting, all is well with her lying-in.' Ann glanced over at Robert. 'Aunt Euphemia came to visit us one day. She informed me that you had been for luncheon that day of the tragedy as usual and so I had presumed you would be on your regular train, the six fifty from Ladybank. We watched the train go over the bridge and then fall, tumbling into the depths.'

Robert removed his pocket watch from his waistcoat and peered at it in the dim light as she continued.

'But Robert, this is not the time to talk about the future. I would prefer if we do not inform the children until everything is settled.'

'And you will not tell anyone of my visit until I return from Glasgow, where I plan to go tomorrow to set about securing passages for us all on the next boat to Tasmania.'

Oh, the deceit of the man. Why would he insist on keeping his return a secret unless his intentions were dubious? She knew fine that his plan was to snatch her children from her and set up in Australia, where he would no doubt find someone else he could call a wife.

'And I have many things to attend to in the next two days before we can sail.'

'As you wish.' She nodded then breathed deeply. She needed time to think, to plan. She would not let him see the children, ever. They were hers. She looked directly into his dull eyes and forced herself to continue calmly. 'Then why do we not meet somewhere to discuss further, once you are returned. Does three nights hence suit you? You cannot return here, in case the children waken and see you. I suggest we meet down at the shore, you remember our favourite place, where we used to sit on that bench above the river. Is midnight suitable?'

'That seems rather late.'

'Sunday will be quiet, we will not be disturbed. And until we decide what to do, I shall not reveal that you are back, especially if it is only temporary.'

'Very well.' He sat forward and muttered, feigning disinterest. 'What else did Aunt Euphemia say?'

A smile played around Ann's lips as she recalled the letter. 'She was in a most frightful state for she had an unpleasant task to perform. She had to go to the mortuary at the station and identify a body.'

'Whose?'

Ann sat up straight. 'One of her servants. Now, what was her name?' She shook her head then yawned widely.

His eyes opened wide. 'Can you not recall, woman?' As he raised his voice, a sound was heard.

They both looked towards the door.

'Is Lizzie still speaking in her sleep?'

Yes.' They waited until the heavy silence had resumed.

'I repeat, woman, can you remember the servant's name?'

'Let me think. Yes, I know now. But it would be of no interest to you, Robert. She was a maid, her name was Janet Clark. Terrible head injuries, bashed about on the rocks.'

'Janet? Dead?' He sat stock-still, his face pinched.

'Dead,' she nodded. 'Now, Robert, please leave before the children waken. We shall meet on Sunday evening.'

He staggered to his feet and headed towards the door, stumbling as he knocked against the side of the dressing table in the semi-darkness. When she saw he had shut the door tight, she blew out the light and laid her head down on the pillow. So, it was as she had thought, he had intended to run away with the maid. He would deem it another conquest of the lower class.

She had regretted burning the letter but the more she thought about it, she was convinced there were the letters J and C at the start of the names which were otherwise illegible. A fling with a maid; well, he would pay for his stupidity. The ignominy of it all. She uttered a long sigh as she shut her eyes tight. She had seen the woman that day in the station, the body of her husband's lover. She shivered and pulled the blankets up around her.

As her mind played over every word he had just said, she became convinced that, even though he could not run away with the serving maid, he was after the children. Her children. He had come back to remove them from her. Well, that would never happen, not over her dead body. So, he wanted to steal her precious children? There was no doubt about it, he would pay for this.

Chapter 42
2015

'Oh, hi, Doug, how are things in Glenisla?'

'Doing away fine, thanks, Fiona. Had a busy season and the new chef's settled in better now.'

'Good, any other news?'

'Remember that issue with Pete's car, the one you thought was stolen?'

Fiona swallowed. She regretted having told Mrs C and Doug about that. 'Yes, have the police been?'

'No, but there's a piece in the Alyth Voice today about Lawsons, the car dealer in Main Street.'

'Is that where Pete bought his car?'

'Yes, you said his mate from Dundee got him onto it but he can't have known.'

'Known what?'

'They're crooks, all crooks, just been rumbled. First of all, one of the ghillies from the Glen Clova estate shopped Bill Lawson. Wait till you hear what he'd been doing.'

Fiona took a sip of coffee as Doug cleared his throat.

'He was storing body parts of deer that the ghillie gave him, fresh carcasses, all bloody and full of gore. And he staged accidents, made it look like a driver had hit a deer, took loads of photos then got half the insurance money from the driver. Got the guys who worked for him to get weeds and stuff from down at the river to make it look real.'

'What? That's ridiculous!' Fiona typed 'the Alyth Voice' into her Google search.

'Strange but true. He was only found out when the ghillie shopped him as he got fed up delivering the deer that he'd shot – legally – to Lawsons whenever a gullible enough driver arrived. So, once they started investigating Old Billy Lawson, there was a lot else wrong with his books. He'd been selling stolen cars for years apparently. Thought he could get away with it in sleepy Alyth.'

Fiona gasped. 'So Pete had no idea his car was stolen, he bought it thinking it was just a second-hand car?'

'Certainly looks like it. The other two guys who worked for him are also up for charges as they were all in cahoots. Now they've just got to find out how many drivers got fraudulent insurance claims. Amazing to think there are so many dishonest folk nearby!'

'Wow, amazing, Doug. Thanks,' she said, clicking on the story online.

'Mrs C said you'd be dying to hear that news. Well, I'd better go, say hi to the wee guy.'

Fiona was still beaming when she put down the phone and read the whole article. So, Pete hadn't broken the law, he'd been duped by some criminal, in Alyth of all places. She frowned – he had taken all their savings though and there were other things unexplained, including her conversation with Debs. But at least she could delete 'car thief' from the list of attributes of 'My Boyfriend the Bastard'.

* * *

Fiona put the ironing board away in the cupboard

and looked up at the clock. Half past three. They'd have just blown the whistle for half time at the football. She couldn't wait to hear how he enjoyed it. Jamie had been so excited all morning before Martha and Allie picked him up, he could hardly even eat his lunch. She was feeling upbeat, having had that phone call from Doug. She knew Pete wouldn't have bought a stolen car if he'd known. She was still incredulous that there were so many alleged criminals near Alyth willing to go along with Lawson's insurance scam involving dead deer.

She chuckled and headed for the larder, having decided she'd bake some scones for Martha and Jamie coming home. She had meant to go into work to research the Craigs, but decided she'd stay at home instead.

She was just weighing out the flour when the phone rang.

'Fi, it's me.'

Dorothy's voice was soft, breathless.

'You all right, mum?'

'Not really, there's been…'

'Speak up, Mum, I can hardly hear you.'

'I'm in an ambulance, on the way to hospital.'

'What? What's happened? Are you okay?'

'It's Dad, he's had a heart attack, they're trying to stabilise him, they need to put a stent in and…'

'Where are you, Mum?'

'Not sure, I can't say. I'll give you over to…'

'Mum!' Fiona shouted. 'Mum, speak to me!'

'Hello, you must be Mrs Craig's daughter.' It was a softly spoken voice; a lilting accent.

'Yes, it's Fiona Craig here. Can you tell me what's going on, please? My mum sounds really strange. Did she say my dad had had a heart attack?'

'Yes, I'm afraid so. She's a bit upset.'

Fiona leant against the back of the chair.

'He'll be all right, won't he?'

'Early days, still early days.'

'What happened?'

'Well, they were on the Tarbert to Uig ferry. It takes only about an hour and forty-five, but unfortunately the attack happened just about half an hour from arrival, so not near enough to the shore to get immediate help.'

'Can't Mum speak to me?'

The voice had softened to a whisper. 'Your mother is in a state as she said they'd had a blazing row. And Mr Craig had just shouted something at her when he collapsed. She seems to think the heart attack was her fault, that's also why she's so upset. Obviously it wasn't, but that's not important right now. They gave him CPR on board while the captain got emergency procedures in place, managed to get the ambulance waiting at Uig harbour and we got him in twenty minutes ago and we are off now to Portree Hospital.'

Fiona let out a long sigh. 'He'll be all right, won't he? He's not that old, only sixty-eight and fit as a flea.'

'Are you in a position to find your way to Portree, Fiona?' The paramedic sounded calm and steady.

'Yes, yes of course.'

'That's good. I think it would do your mother good to have your company. Now, I'd better go now as we're nearly there.'

'Give Mum a big hug please!' Fiona swallowed. 'And Dad too!'

The phone clicked off.

Fiona stared at the phone as she replaced the receiver. How was that possible? How on earth could her healthy father have had a heart attack? He was never ill. The only thing Mum said was ever wrong with him were 'the Grumps', as she called them.

She tapped into her laptop and Googled 'AA route finder' then ran to the study to attach the laptop to the printer. As it whirred into action, she wondered why the hell she had always refused to buy a sat nav. She'd always insisted she didn't need one, she could read a map. Martha had one, she could borrow that. God, Martha. She had to tell her what she was doing, she couldn't just leave her with Jamie.

Fiona grabbed the sheets of paper from the printer then ran back to the kitchen, picked up her mobile and tapped in Martha's number. She didn't answer. She tried Allie's number next, but didn't get a response either. They would be concentrating on the game. Her eyes darted to the clock. Just four o clock, the game wouldn't be over for another half hour. But she couldn't wait that long. She ran upstairs to her room, dragged out a wheelie suitcase and started shoving things in. Then she stopped and sat on her bed. No, she couldn't go anywhere, let alone Skye, without Jamie knowing what was going on. Also, she remembered Martha and Allie were out at some ball later, she couldn't presume they'd cancel everything.

She ran downstairs and flung the satsumas out of the fruit bowl to find her car keys. She was at the back door when she stopped. What would be the point of driving to Tannadice as the fans emerged? She'd never find them. She had to wait. She delved in her bag for her phone and texted Martha and Allie.

Please phone as soon as game over. Emergency! x

Then she hurried towards the stairs. She would pack a bag for herself and one for Jamie, they would leave the minute he was home.

At the foot of the stairs, she sniffed; what was that smell? She peeked into her dad's study and noticed the vase of flowers her mum had been sent for her birthday. They were almost dead; she'd forgotten Dorothy had told her to throw them out once the pollen started dropping on the floor. She went over and inhaled. It was the smell from the night before, which she thought was the face paints. The smell was sickly, almost musky. It was the smell of jasmine, the scent her mum associated with death.

Chapter 43
Thursday 8 January 1880

'Mrs Donaldson to see you, Mrs Craig.'

'Good morning Ann,' said Margaret, as she swept past Jessie and went to take her friend's hand. 'How are you?'

'Fine, thank you, Margaret. Please take a seat.'

Margaret tucked her dark grey skirt around her legs and peered at Ann. 'You do not look well. Are you sleeping?'

'Sleeping? Oh yes, like a baby.' Ann forced a smile. 'I have a bout of melancholy, but it will go. It is all this black.'

'Ah yes, I recall my mother feeling the same when she was in mourning for my father. She told me that simply putting on her black clothes every day sent her into a deep depression. She told me it was like sitting under a heavy black rain cloud.'

Ann nodded and brushed at her black silk gown.

'Did your mother mourn your father's death in such a way, my dear?'

Ann suppressed the urge to laugh. 'Of course, just as one is duty-bound to.' She remembered her mother rushing into the kitchen where ten-year-old Annie had been scrubbing tatties. Her mother was beaming. 'He is gone, gone at last!' she had shouted. 'The prison just sent me the news. Now we are free.' Ann then remembered vividly how her mother drank herself into the sort of stupor her father had been prone to, the drunkenness that caused him to kill a man and put him in prison for life. Her mother's spree, in contrast, meant they had no money left and had to exist on porridge, made from oatmeal handed in by Mattie across the street.

She turned back to Margaret, trying to dismiss the feeling of jealousy bubbling within. Her childhood had been hard, every day a struggle, whereas this woman opposite had been brought up in the lap of luxury. 'Will you take some tea?'

Margaret shook her head. 'I have no time to linger, Ann. I simply came to see you to let you know I shall be away for a few days. I think you might recall me telling you my sister in Glamis was having problems with her health. And so now it seems that, although she is most definitely out of danger and is becoming stronger every day, she is in need of my company, for we are close. I intend to read some novels to her and perhaps play some Chopin, her favourite composer.' Margaret smiled. 'We loved doing these things together as children.'

Again, Ann could not help but feel resentment. She did not have a sister, but even if she had, she could never imagine finding pleasure over a book or music. Their memories would be of the dust and stour in the jute mills clogging their eyes and noses, and of the fatigue of having to get up at dawn each day, from the age of eleven, to set off for the mills.

'I am sorry she is still not strong but what good news that she is recovering well.'

Margaret continued speaking about what she would do at her sister's house and Ann's mind began to whirr. When her companion had stopped talking, she said, 'So how many days do you anticipate you must be away?'

'I hope not more than four days but if the weather sets in, it might be longer.'

'Might we assist with the children in any way?'

'Oh, how kind, Ann. But that will not be necessary. They are coming with me. Helena has the most wonderful governess for her two children and she insisted the twins come too and join classes there.'

Ann smiled, perhaps too eagerly. 'That is wonderful, what a pleasant trip that will be, Margaret.' She felt round the back of her head to pin up a stray lock of hair into her loose bun. 'And Archibald? Will his mother move in again to take care of him?'

Margaret got to her feet. 'Goodness me, no. He has in fact stated that he will only visit her for tea, he would never have time for his patients if she were at the house all day and night. No, he will be alone, he says it will be a chance for him to catch up with work. As you know, he is still assisting at the mortuary and there is much to be done there. Have you heard there are now many more bodies recovered? Archibald said last night the count was twenty-two.'

Ann's mind raced. She raised her shoulders so that she appeared even taller beside the dumpy figure of her neighbour.

'Shall I have Jessie fetch your cloak?'

'Thank you,' said Margaret as she headed for the door. She shook her head then stretched out to grasp Ann's hand. 'Let us hope that you have news soon. The waiting must still be horrid.'

Ann shrugged. 'I am resigned to it now.'

★ ★ ★

Ann dabbed a few drops of her favourite perfume on her neck, recalling how Robert used to love telling fellow jute barons at the dinners they attended that the 'Sweet Smell of Jute' was the city's very own perfume. He loved this poetic phrase, but it was basically the smell of his money he loved, money from the sweat and labour of hundreds of poor mill workers.

She rubbed it in then reached for the bottle once more. She could be generous with it tonight; it made her feel feminine, free, unleashed. She dabbed some more on her bosom and unfastened the top button of her cream silk blouse, taking pleasure in the feel of the silk between her fingers, then pulled her redingote over the top. With its high collar and formal style, she looked very much the respectable lady. She smiled as she pulled her hair into the loosest of buns and secured it with her favourite ivory clasps. She stood to admire herself in the mirror then nodded. Yes, she looked good, a real lady. But under this attire throbbed a heart ready to let go. She tossed her head back and a smile played on her lips. Now was her chance, she must not fail.

She stole to the door and opened it. Silence. She leant back inside to pick up the lamp then walked downstairs, through the darkness of the house towards the front door. She stood in front of the grandfather clock and peered at the face. It was ten minutes before ten in the evening, perfect timing. She opened the front door and tiptoed down the steps and onto the lawn. The grass was damp and she sighed as she realised how inappropriate her embroidered slippers were. She reached the summer house and unlocked the door. This was the ideal place, unseen from the house since all the bedrooms were at the back; and it could not be seen from the road. She pushed the door shut and placed the lamp on the little table. It was cold but not too chilly. She had filled two stone water bottles with boiling water and put them between the layers of blanket she had placed on the chairs once the children were in bed. She never felt the cold; the tiny Glenisla cottage had howling gales blow through it all year and in winter the snow even blew in under the door.

She looked around. It was dark but hopefully there was enough light from the lamp to reveal her face. He adored her face, she knew that. Every time he looked at her it was as if he was taking in every inch of its beauty.

There was a tap at the door. She took a deep breath and opened it. He stood there, a quizzical expression on his face.

'Come in, Archibald. I do apologise for the disarray in here. It is usually used to store things for the lawn in summer but I found two chairs for us to sit on. And there are warm blankets, should we require.'

She shut the door softly behind him and pointed to a seat. He sat down and stared at her beautiful face. 'Why have you asked me here, Ann?'

He frowned, looking apprehensive. She must take things slowly. He was attractive and sensitive, but in an unhappy marriage – well, who would be happily married to dumpy, dull Margaret?

'Archibald, do not look quite so scared.' She laughed then turned to the table where she had placed a decanter of Madeira and two glasses earlier. She poured and handed him a glass, the crystal sparkling in the candlelight. She never took her eyes off his face as she raised her glass to her lips.

He was buttoned up tightly in his overcoat.

'Might I take your coat?' She smiled and reached to help him shrug it from his shoulders. Underneath he had a tweed jacket and the mustard waistcoat she loved.

'Is there a problem, Ann?'

'Nothing at all. I simply wanted to see you, to have a conversation. How is the work at the morgue?' She took a large sip from her glass.

'Unpleasant. We received two more bodies today; we now have twenty-four.' He was staring at the floor. 'Still no sign of Robert.' He looked up at Ann who was taking off her redingote. She leant down to flick something off her slipper and as she slowly raised her head, she knew he was staring at her décolletage but when she smiled at him he averted his gaze.

'Archibald, you and I have been friends for so long and I know there is more than a neighbourly connection between us.' She leant over to his chair and placed her hand over his, not taking her eyes from his face. He flushed red. 'Are you warm? The hot water bottles at our backs are delightful, do you not think? It reminds me of picnics by the stream at Kirkmichael House when the children were little. They ran about splashing in the water while we sat on chairs lined with blankets with hot water bottles tucked in.' She tilted her head to one side and smiled. 'Let me help you remove your jacket, you will be more comfortable, I think.' She leant towards him and slipped her hand inside his jacket and pushed it off his shoulders. She looked up at him and knew her intoxicating perfume was beginning to take effect.

'Ann, I...'

She tutted and shook her head. 'Archibald, do not trouble yourself with speech, you are tired from your long stressful day. Your work is so important and you are always so busy, you must relax. Here, let me massage your neck.' Gently, she began stroking the nape of his neck, pushing his head down a little as she did. She saw his eyelids flutter and close.

'Let me help you out of this waistcoat, Archibald, you still look a little hot.' She slipped her hand onto the silk material and pushed her fingers between the buttons. She could feel his heart pounding. She undid the buttons slowly then looked at him again.

'Ann, I must go. I am so sorry.' He stood up but she tugged his sleeve down firmly so he landed back on the seat with a thump. She leant over him so that she could feel his hot breath. Slowly, she leant in to kiss him and as he closed his eyes again, she knew she had him. She smiled in anticipation of the conquest.

Chapter 44
2015

When her phone rang, she ran to the table from the window where she sat, waiting.

'Martha?'

'Who? Not unless I've had a sex change, Fi.' An Aussie voice chuckled at the other end. 'It's Ross from The Pier.'

'Oh, hi, Ross, sorry, bit of an emergency going on here, not quite with it.' She explained about her dad being rushed to hospital.

'Christ, sorry, d'you want me to phone back later?'

'Please, I'm waiting for Martha to call.'

'No worries, had some news about Debs that might interest you but not a problem.'

'Hang on,' Fi said, glancing up at the clock. The match was due to finish in five minutes. 'Got a couple of minutes, fill me in please?'

'Okay, here's the thing. The police have just left. They were after Debs and...'

'Why were the police after her?'

'Turns out she's a conman, well, conwoman. Fiddled the books when she worked here that first time and they reckon it might even have been her who set fire to the place just as they were onto her.'

Fiona gasped. 'She tried to pin that on Pete!'

'Doesn't surprise me. Anyway, she was never found out. Then the boss has been saying for the past few weeks how nothing was adding up in the tills at the end of the night and so she talked about it to Debs and me last night. We get in this morning and Debs is gone, taken all her crazy music from the kitchen and those weird sandals she left there. And the police said she's done it before.'

'So how come they didn't find her?'

'Changes her name, her hair, sometimes she looks like a respectable librarian, always gets away with it. She's originally from Orkney, name's Morag Quigley.'

Fiona looked at the clock. Two more minutes. 'Unbelievable. I met her for lunch, Ross, couple of months ago.'

'Yeah, she told me drunkenly one night.'

'She said not to tell you!'

'That's how she was. Devious. She said she told you how much Pete loved you and he was sure to come back.'

'Bloody liar. She told me they'd slept together and he'd got angry when she had asked for a pound for the bus home the next morning.'

'Christ, Fi, you didn't believe her?'

'Why not?'

'I wouldn't believe a word out of her mouth. She was nothing more than a bloody crook. She probably stole all his money too.'

Fiona sighed. 'Ross, I've got to go now, but thanks for this. Makes me feel a bit better about Pete.'

'No worries, hope your dad's okay. Keep me posted.'

Fiona looked up at the ceiling and shook her head. So, Debs was a liar and a crook and maybe even an arsonist. So, had Pete been taken in by her too? Her eyes opened wide as the implication dawned. Bloody hell, was he in it with her? Is that why he kept disappearing? She shuddered as she thought of the two of them, criminals working together...

The phone rang.

'Fi, it's me, game's just over. Jamie loved it. What's up?'

'Dad's had a heart attack, I've got to get to Skye as soon as possible. Can you bring Jamie over fast and we'll get going. Could be there for about nine tonight.'

'Oh no, sorry, Fi. But listen, why don't we hang onto Jamie? You don't want him at the hospital. Anyway, he's in love with Allie. We can stay at yours or he can come to us?'

'That'd be great, M. But I thought you were out tonight?'

'Not important, Fi. Your mum needs you. Just let me know about the key if you want us to stay at yours. Then get going.'

'Oh, okay, I'll leave the key under the back doormat.'

'Right, off you go. Drive safely!'

'Thanks, M. You're a star. Give Jamie a big hug. Oh, and make up something about why I'm off, don't tell him Pa's ill.'

★ ★ ★

As she crossed the bridge over to Skye, she felt hollow inside. It wasn't hunger, she had taken packets of nuts and a slab of chocolate with her. No, it was unmitigated terror. She looked at her watch. Eight twenty. It was pitch black and she could barely see the road signs but she knew she had to head north at the end of the bridge. The deep fear inside her was irrational, she told herself. Her dad was going to be fine. He was strong as an ox. This was just a blip, something brought on by too much wine. He drank too much; and as for that pipe, well, that would all have to go, no doubt about it.

Forty minutes later, she drove up the hill towards Portree Hospital and parked the car. She got out and ran towards the entrance. The receptionist directed her to the visitors' room where she was told her mother would be. She sprinted along the corridor and flung open the door. Her mother sat crumpled in a corner, a nurse on either side of her, one holding a cup of tea on a saucer.

'Mum!' Fiona ran over to her and her mother looked up, her eyes filled with tears.

'He's gone, Fi, about an hour ago.'

'What d'you mean, gone?'

One of the nurses stood up and patted Fiona's arm. 'So sorry, Fiona, your father passed away at eight o'clock tonight. The doctors tried everything they could, but it was already too late.'

'But that's impossible, he's strong, robust, he's…'

'The doctors said if it hadn't happened on the ferry, they might have been able to save him. Took too long to get to the ambulance and get that stent put in. Would you like to see one of the doctors?'

The nurse pushed her gently onto the chair she had just vacated and as Fiona nodded, she grasped her mother's hand and looked up into tear-filled eyes.

Fiona felt her chest begin to heave and she started to cry, gulping as tears flowed. She rested her head on her mother's lap and shook with silent sobs. Her mother stroked her forehead and began mumbling something, she had no idea what, but the noise was soothing.

'We'll get the doctor along for you now,' said the nurse as she and her companion tiptoed out of the room and shut the door firmly behind them.

Chapter 45
Friday 9 January 1880

Ann got down from the carriage at her husband's jute mill and spoke to the driver. 'Wait here. I'll only be a half hour, no more.'

Heading through the wrought iron gates at the entrance, she passed the night watchman's dingy office where Alec Smith used to sit, in a room the size of a cupboard with nothing but a candle for company. That was before he managed to get a job as station porter then soon became promoted through the ranks to manager. He worked so hard; he didn't deserve the tragedy he was having to deal with right now.

She creaked open the heavy wooden door of the mill. The sound inside was deafening. As she walked towards the production area, she heard the whirring of the spindles and the clatter of the looms; it was little wonder many workers went deaf. Above the noise of the machinery, she could discern the clamour of shouting and yelling. The women in Dundee's jute mills had their own dialect, developed over the decades to counteract the roar and clunking of the spinning frames and carding machines. Ann smiled as she heard the flat vowels, the only ones to carry across the cacophony. The memories came flooding back to Ann as she noticed the rags and tatters of the women's dresses, their bare feet, while she stood incongruously in her black silk gown and tall black velvet hat. As she looked over to the receiving area where the jute was batched, the smell of whale oil carried over the air and she began to feel nauseous. What used to be an everyday smell now made her gag.

A young girl, about twelve, came up to her and bobbed. 'You lookin' for someone, missus?'

'Thank you, child. I came to see Mr Johnston the manager.'

The girl looked over towards the roving machines. 'Over there last time I saw him.' The child ran away and Ann watched her stop at a carding machine where a woman skelped her across the head. Ann sighed as she looked around at the many children the same age as her own, working as 'pickers', cleaning dust from the machines. She lifted up her skirts a little and headed towards the roving machines. A man, dressed in dark brown, was pointing to something in the machine. Perhaps there was a problem with the twisting of the fibre, Ann thought, watching him lift a thick strand and wind it around a bobbin.

'Mr Johnston,' she shouted above the clamour. 'Excuse me, Mr Johnston!'

One of the workmen beside him pointed in Ann's direction and he turned round.

'Wait a minute please,' he shouted.

She watched him give instructions to the men at the machine then headed towards her. He was smiling.

'Mrs Craig, what a pleasure to see you here. Have you news?'

'Nothing specific but I should like a word. Please.'

He gestured to her to follow and together they walked up rickety wooden steps to his office above the mill. They walked inside and he shut the door and at once the babble and clatter below ceased.

She sat down at the chair he indicated and watched him go behind his desk. He took his seat slowly, all the while gazing at her. She had taken some time to do her hair and knew that it was attractive in this new bun, tucked neatly under her hat. The nape of her neck was shown to best effect. She knew that Johnston, with his piggy features and ruddy complexion, was taking her in, so she did not rush to speak.

'Mr Johnston, or might I call you Alfred?'

He flushed a little and picked up a pencil, which he began to tap rhythmically on his desk.

'You always used to call me that, Mrs Craig. Or shall I call you Annie?'

Ann took a deep breath and suppressed the urge to put him in his place. 'Alfred, you and I go back a long way, meeting at the Alyth mill when we were twelve. And I have forever been grateful that you have been so loyal both to me and to my husband.' She smiled at him. 'My husband is, we now are sure, dead. Hence my mourning attire.' She swept her hand slowly down her legs to her dainty black boots. She knew he was watching every movement. 'And so I feel, even before we have had a funeral or spoken to the lawyers, that I must inform you of something. Something that is not entirely pleasant, but which I feel duty-bound to relay.'

Alfred Johnston held up his hand. 'I just realised I don't have any refreshments up here to offer you, Annie.'

Ann smiled graciously and shook her head. 'This will not take long, Alfred.'

He sat back in his chair and gazed once more at her.

'I believe you're happy being manager of the mill and

that your family is doing extremely well. I hear you have moved out of the tenement in Lochee and now live in a fine house in Mains Road. Your children will do well at the new school nearby.'

'Aye, the wee one's just five and he'll be going next year. The other bairns all started last year.'

'How many children do you have?'

'Five and Bettie's having another one next month.'

'What wonderful news.' Ann twiddled with a jet earring. 'I am sure you should want to continue in this prestigious job for some time in order to support this growing family.'

Alfred Johnston grinned then stopped tapping his pencil. He moved forward on his chair. 'Why? Why are you asking all this?'

Ann thrust her hand in her pocket. 'Alfred, I'm so sorry, I seem to have misplaced my handkerchief. Could I bother you please?'

'Of course,' he said, thrusting his hand into his pocket. He passed her a freshly pressed handkerchief, which she used to dab her nose. She pocketed it and continued. 'Before my husband took the ill-fated train journey that led to his untimely death, he had been explaining some affairs of work to me. He told me there was a document to be drawn up by his lawyer that, in the case of his death, the mill would be taken over by Mr Clegg at Clegg Mills.'

'What would he do that for?' Alfred snapped.

'My husband and Mr Clegg never saw eye to eye on many matters, as you know. There was that dreadful issue of the whale oil shipment. But they had become reconciled in friendship of late and that was the plan. My husband had been so distressed when his colleague Mr Grieg had died intestate aged only thirty-five, leaving his family destitute.'

'Well, I don't see how letting Clegg take us over would help any of us.'

'That is exactly why I am here today, Alfred. And I am sorry to say it is worse.' She bit her lip. 'He also stipulated that Clegg's manager, Bert Lawson, would take over as manager running both mills.'

He leapt to his feet . 'So where would that leave me? Without a job? And me with another bairn on the way? Why did you not tell him he could not do that, Annie?'

'Alfred, I tried, believe me I tried, but as you know my husband is – was – a stubborn man, and he simply would not listen.'

Alfred sat shaking his head in disbelief.

She waited then said, 'I hope to speak to lawyers soon and shall petition on your behalf. I feel sure I can resolve this matter. If you could perhaps visit me at home one day?'

'Any time, Annie, any time you say I will be there. Whatever you think you can do. I can't lose my job with the new house, the bairns. And Bettie would kill me, she's got all these airs and graces now and...'

Ann pulled on her kid gloves and stood up.

'Meet me at the gate of my house on Monday, at nine in the morning. I should prefer if this was kept between ourselves, my servants need not know.'

'All right, Annie. I'll be there.'

She swept off down the stairs and back into the clamour of Dundee's jute.

★ ★ ★

'Sure you want to go this way?'

'Yes, just drop me over there and wait, driver. Again, I shall only be some half an hour.'

Ann climbed the steps towards the house, inhaling the pipe smoke as she went. She rapped on the door.

It opened slowly and the same girl, Elspet, stood there, peering up at her with wide eyes.

'Is Mattie in?'

'Aye, come in, she's been expecting you.'

'Expecting me?' She had made no arrangement.

Ann walked towards the fireplace where Blind Mattie sat, pipe in hand.

'Come away in.' She turned towards the girl. 'Is it the same lady?'

'Aye, just like you said, Auntie Mattie. But today she's wearing all black. Like a raven.'

Mattie patted the seat beside her. 'Draw near. You have things to tell me.'

Ann swept off some grime from the only other chair in the room and sat. She looked at Mattie, this woman she had known all her life, and felt a pang of emotion. Ann had no family, no connection with anything; only this woman knew everything about her origins, her childhood. She stretched forward to take Mattie's hand.

'How are you today, Mattie?'

'Doing away, same as last time. Why have you come here again?'

Ann paused as she thought about what she had planned to say. But there was something about speaking to Mattie that made all words futile.

'I've got a problem,' she said, staring into Mattie's dead eyes.

'Aye, I ken that. That's why you've come back.' She put down her pipe and turned to face Ann. She patted her hands around Ann's lap till she located her other hand. 'What do you want from me, Annie Robertson?'

Ann's shoulders slumped. No one had called her that for years. Alfred Johnston calling her Annie had unsettled her, but now this.

'Mattie, you and I have known each other forever. My mother said that when I was born, you were there to help the midwife and then assist my mother after.'

Mattie chuckled. 'Midwife. Assist. You never talked like that then, Annie. We called the midwife the howdie wifie, you ken that.'

Ann nodded.

'And yes, I gave your Ma a hand, but she did the most of it herself. Well, she had to do most things herself, with that drunken father of yours.'

Ann sighed.

'So are you happy in your new life, all that money and the big house and the new clothes? Never worrying about putting food on the table?'

Ann removed the handkerchief from her pocket and sniffed. 'Yes, I am. I have a wonderful family and I...'

'But if your husband's dead, how do you plan to keep the bairns in the only way they know?'

Ann sat up straight. 'Well, yes, but what if he wasn't dead but had come back to steal my bairns? My precious children. What would I do then, Mattie?' Ann's voice was urgent.

Mattie picked up her pipe and took a long, slow suck.

Elspet scampered towards the meagre fire and thrust in the poker. A brief flicker of red lit the embers.

'Annie, it's good you've come to me if you are in trouble, but I cannot tell you what to do. You must be guided by your own judgement. But if your bairns, your own flesh and blood, are in danger, then you must act quick, so he cannot do anything.' She put down the pipe again and lifted both of Ann's hands in hers. 'Here, let me see what you are feeling.' She repeated what she had done before with Ann, rubbing her hands up and down, as if by stroking them rhythmically she could enter her soul.

Ann eventually withdrew her hands and sat back with a thump. 'It's no good, I can do nothing. How can I, a feeble woman, challenge a strong man?'

Mattie lifted her pipe and took another long draw. 'Elspet, fetch the tin box from the mantelpiece.'

The girl brushed past Ann and lifted down a tattered old box from above the fire, handing it to Mattie. She put in her hand and patted around till she felt what she was looking for.

'Here, take this, Annie Robertson. It's been with me for some forty years now but I don't need it any more. You can use it to protect yourself from any harm. Here.' She stretched out her hand and placed something in Ann's.

Ann looked down.

'I cannot take this from you, Mattie. It's yours. You've had it for ever.'

'Take it, it will serve you well.' She gestured to the girl. 'Now, shall I play for you?'

'Thank you, Mattie, just one song,' said Ann, watching as Elspet handed her aunt the melodeon.

Ann gazed into the dying fire as Blind Mattie played

another song from her childhood. Yet again her face was awash with tears. She sat sobbing silently as she remembered the past. Yes, her childhood had been hard, tough, but there must have been good times too. People looked out for each other, there was a real sense of community, though no affection. That was why she hugged and kissed her children always. What would her children remember of their childhood? The luxury, the fine clothes, good food, yes... but hopefully also the love of their mother. The unconditional love that she had given her children all their lives. She was determined. She would never let them go.

Chapter 46
2015

The minister was talking about Struan's life; his school days, the pranks he got up to. There was a murmur of approval and even some laughter when he relayed what a naughty schoolboy he had been, but Fiona was barely listening. She had read the eulogy several times, in fact she had composed most of it with her mum, there was no need to hear it again. She knew what came next: art college, architecture, marrying Dorothy, her birth...

She stared at the coffin, laden with flowers. She had not wanted any flowers but Dorothy had insisted – anything except lilies, she had told the florist. Fiona glared at the polished casket that contained – she tried not to think of it – her father, her wonderful, funny, irreverent dad. How would she cope without him? Looking at the coffin only made her feel worse; she bowed her head. She was holding it together. She had to be strong, today of all days, for Jamie more than anyone.

She glanced to her right where Jamie sat, dressed in his sweatshirt and school trousers. He had refused to put on a smarter top, had insisted that Pa loved that sweatshirt with Dennis the Menace on it. He would wear it for Pa. He was looking up at the minister and seemed to be listening intently; he seemed, surprisingly, fine. And to her left was Dorothy. She also seemed to be coping, she had even heard her snigger when the minister was telling the story of Stru and Mark as students dismantling someone's Mini and getting it in the lift up to the top floor in their halls, where they reassembled it. But her mum had been on sleeping pills since he died twelve days before. She seemed strange, not herself.

Fiona stared at the long drapes hung from the ceiling at either side of the coffin, the purple velvet cascading onto the floor. There was a dark brown curtain hovering over the bier. This one would soon shudder into place above the empty space when the coffin was lowered down below to be cremated. She took a deep breath, she could not bear to think of it. She focused instead on the two arrangements of flowers laid out on the steps in front of the coffin. They were beautiful, white roses and those other waxy flowers with the unpronounceable name. Who would they be from? They had stipulated no flowers in the announcement.

Fiona and Dorothy had disagreed about what to write in the newspaper. Dorothy had wanted, as well as "loving husband, father and grandfather," to say that he had been adored by his friends and wider family. Fiona thought that was unnecessary, you were just meant to mention close family. Dorothy also tried to remove his date of birth, saying he had always been funny about his age. Fiona overruled that one, showing her dozens of other announcements, each with dates of both birth and death.

'You're making him out as someone who cared what others thought about him, Mum.'

'Well, he was actually quite a vain man, you know.'

'Don't be ridiculous.'

And so it went on. The week since they had returned from Skye had been strained, not loving and caring, as it ought to have been, not full of affection. Whenever Jamie was around, Fiona and her mum were civil and Jamie himself was the recipient of both women's hugs, but the strain was too much. When Jamie was in bed, and mother and daughter were having a glass of wine in the kitchen, Dorothy admitted that she was convinced Fiona blamed her for insisting on the Hebridean holiday, and if they hadn't been on that ferry for two hours, he'd have been fine, they could have treated him easily. Fiona tried to persuade her mum that there was no blame, nothing could have been done. Though, having spoken to the doctors in private, she knew he could have been saved if he'd reached the hospital within an hour. That's the islands for you, one of the doctors had said, a sympathetic look on his face.

She looked up as the minister mentioned her name.

'Struan's daughter Fiona and his grandson Jamie brought so much joy to his life, especially during his last few months when they lived back with them in the family house. He told a friend that he could now enjoy retirement properly, now he had a purpose, as a hands-on grandpa.'

She knew he was near the end. She must concentrate. If only she didn't feel so tired. God, she had all those people to speak to on the way out. Again, Dorothy and she had disagreed on this. Why did they have to do the 'meet-and-greet' at the exit to the crematorium? Could they not just see everyone at the tea afterwards? No, tradition insisted and so did her mother.

The final hymn was announced and everyone stood. She glanced round to look at the rest of the mourners. There seemed to be hundreds of people, how did he know so many? The organist began to play 'The Day Thou Gavest, Lord, Is Ended' and she put on her glasses and attempted to sing.

★ ★ ★

The line-up at the side door of the crematorium as mourners filed out was as awful as she had anticipated. Fiona and Dorothy stood side-by-side and were kissed or hugged by what seemed like hundreds of people, only half of whom Fiona recognised. Martha and Allie had taken Jamie out first, saying they'd keep him busy till the reception. Thank God for Martha, Fiona thought. What would she do without her?

'What a friend he was.' Mark had tears in his eyes. 'I will miss him so much. Even though we only saw each other once or twice a year when I was home on leave, we had such good times, Fiona. Well, you were there the last time we had lunch and…'

'Mark, you're holding up the queue,' Dorothy said, pointing to the long line behind him. 'We can chat longer at the reception.'

Fiona gave Mark a peck on the cheek and looked down the line of everyone she had yet to greet. She had no idea who they all were. As Mark was giving her mother yet another embrace, she looked towards the back of the crematorium at the end of the queue. There was someone standing alone, not in the orderly line like everyone else. In the dim light, he looked shifty, as if he were lurking for some reason.

'Fiona, darling, we've never met but your father designed our new house in Brechin. The atrium was the talk of the county, it was splendid – well, it still is.' The large elderly woman reeking of Chanel No. 5 gave her a slobbering kiss then a short man with a red knobbly nose, introducing himself as her husband, moved in behind her with a limp handshake. As Fiona smiled wanly at him she glanced again at the back of the crematorium. The lone figure was heading for the back exit. God, he looked like Pete. His hair, the way he walked...

'Fiona, this is Molly Melrose, her husband Bill played golf sometimes with Dad and we all attended a few charity events together.'

Fiona shook the woman's hand while looking at the back of the crematorium, which was now empty.

'Mum, sorry, I've got to dash out for a moment, not feeling well,' said Fiona as she darted for the back door.

She ran outside into the damp drizzle. The funeral directors were placing the flowers from the front of the coffin under the canopy. People were standing around looking at the inscriptions and she pushed past them, heading towards the car park. She looked right and left, her whole body tense. There was no one there; her shoulders slumped. How ridiculous, it couldn't possibly be Pete. He was in bloody Tasmania. She started to walk back towards the flowers at the exit, sweeping her windblown hair back off her face, when she caught sight of a figure walking away between the trees. It was the same person she'd just seen; could it be him?

'Pete! Pete! Is that you?' she shouted into the wind.

Chapter 47
Sunday 11 January 1880

'Ann, I do believe the last forty-eight hours have been the most wonderful in my entire life.' Archibald shifted his body onto one elbow and pulled the blanket round his shoulder. He gazed down at the woman who had just made love to him for the third night in a row. She lay there, languid, eyes shut and a hint of a smile on her lips. He leant down to kiss her eyelids and she looked up at him, her hair loose around her beautiful white neck.

'Oh, I am sure you have had other happy times, Archibald,' said Ann, fondling the nape of his neck and smiling up at him. She lifted her other arm and drew her hair onto the top of her head then let it tumble loose once more.

'Never, Ann, not like this,' he said, gazing at the curls cascading round her shoulders. 'I feel guilt at what I have done and yet I cannot possibly regret any of it, indeed I feel no shame, for ours was love waiting to happen. Do you not feel that, Ann?'

She threw back the blanket and stood, naked, in front of him. He had never seen a woman without clothes on. Certainly not Margaret, who undressed and dressed in her own room. He could hardly bear to imagine what her body looked like. His female patients never undressed fully in front of him. He was in a state of delirium. Ann was Venus, Aphrodite.

She began to reach for her clothes. 'It has been wonderful, I agree, Archibald.' She pulled on her stockings, then her skirt and sat, her blouse in her hand. 'I wonder if I might ask you something.'

'Anything,' he said, reaching out to her breast. She turned away and slipped her silk blouse over her shoulders and began to button it up, slowly.

'When you are working with Dr Anderson and a body comes in to the mortuary, how do you decide which one of you will do the examination?'

Archibald frowned. 'What do you mean, my darling?'

'Say, for example, that Robert's body was brought in, would you be able to be the one to examine him?'

'Well...' He coughed. 'Professionally, I should perhaps leave that to Dr Anderson since Robert is – was – a friend.'

She reached out and began to massage the back of his neck. 'But could you do a favour just for me, Archibald?'

'Anything, anything at all.'

'If you can attend to his body yourself, please, should it arrive at the morgue. For what if, for example, it was obvious that he had not been in the water for two weeks but was, in fact, more recently deceased. Would you be able to...' She paused and drew her face nearer, 'arrange things?'

'But I don't understand, Ann. Robert's body must be in the water and we are simply awaiting the time when it surfaces, if it ever does at all.'

'But, I am hypothesising, my darling,' she said, running the tips of her fingers across his lips. 'What if a body were to be found that had only been in the water a day or two? And it was Robert? You could perhaps write down on those very important documents you must write for each person, that he had indeed been in the depths for two weeks, that his fate was that of the other passengers on that most awful of nights.' She gazed into his puzzled eyes. 'You would do this for me.' She was so near him now, her heady perfume lingered round him like a mantle.

He gazed at her as she kissed his forehead lightly. 'I am not sure, I...'

She began to stroke his cheek.

'Of course I would do this for you, my darling. If you ask me, I will do it.'

She kissed him on the lips then turned and fastened her buttons up to her neck and slipped on her redingote.

'I must return to the house now.' She drew her hair up with her hands and clamped it in at either side with two clasps. Loose locks tumbled down.

'Even with your hair undone, you look more beautiful than ever.'

She smiled at him and kept him in her gaze as she slid on her slippers. 'I must go now, please shut the door when you leave.'

'Shall we meet tomorrow again, my darling?'

Ann kissed the top of his head. 'I shall send a note if Margaret continues to be away.'

'Oh, she will, my darling, we have another few days,' he said, as Ann swept out of the door into the dark night air.

* * *

Half an hour later, Ann peered inside her children's bedroom. All she could hear was the gentle rise and fall of contented breathing. She drew the door to and tiptoed down the stairs towards the front door. She pushed it open very slowly, so the hinges did not creak. Mrs Baxter had said to her at breakfast that morning that she thought she heard a noise in the night and had nearly sent her husband to scour the house.

How was that possible, Ann thought, from their cottage at the back – but she knew her housekeeper was a notoriously bad sleeper. Ann had reassured her by saying that their presence nearby made her feel calm at all times during the night and that she mustn't worry about a thing. Any noise must have been one of the children tossing around in bed. Mrs Baxter was becoming a busybody, Ann thought, she must be watched.

The chill night air enveloped her as she pulled the door gently closed. She tiptoed onto the grass, avoiding the noisy gravel, then headed for Riverside Drive.

Patting the large pockets of her voluminous cloak, she disappeared into the dark night. It was ten minutes before midnight – the timing was perfect.

She sat on a bench on the promenade by the riverbank and thought of all the times she had been there before, with her husband, her children, her neighbours. It was the ideal place to see the river, the sun sparkling on the water during summer. The children would run the length of the promenade with their hoops and watch the boats bob on the water. Now, though, the water was black and still and there were no other people to be seen. Ann looked to her left and saw a figure approaching in the light from the lamppost. He wore a top hat and walked briskly, his tall walking cane tapping in rhythm. It was Robert and he was shivering; he always felt the cold, having been brought up in large houses with roaring fires and swaddled in warm clothes. She continued to sit on the dark bench as he drew nearer.

He tipped his hat and sat down. 'As ever, you do not even shiver, sitting here in the freezing cold.'

'I am not cold, Robert.' She turned to look at him and smiled.

'How are the children?'

'They are well, as ever. How blessed we are.'

She delved into her pocket and brought out a little flask with a small tumbler on top. 'I have brought you a little drink, Robert. I had anticipated you might be cold and brought you a warming dram.' She poured some dark liquid from the flask into the tumbler and handed it to him. He tipped it all down in one then shook his head. 'My, that was strong. Where in God's name did Baxter buy that whisky from?'

'I believe it was a New Year's gift, Robert.' She took the tumbler from him and put it on the bench, then peeled off her gloves and took her husband's cold hands in her own warm ones.

'Tell me your plans, my dear. How was your journey?' She attempted affection, though all she felt was rage.

'First of all I must tell you the truth, unpalatable though it is. I do feel I owe that to you before what I am soon to do.'

She bit her lip.

'There was someone I was to take to Australia with me. A woman I planned to spend the rest of my life with.' He swallowed. 'It was Janet Clark, that poor girl Aunt Euphemia had to identify.'

Ann gasped out loud; she must feign shock. 'How

could you do this to me?'

He cleared his throat and continued, speaking quietly. 'We were perfect together, Ann. Not like us, a marriage of convenience for you, and for me a foolish youthful error, out of which the only good things to come were our two children.'

Ann began fumbling in her pocket, but said nothing.

'On Friday, I did not go to Glasgow. I travelled instead to Tayport, where Janet lived. I arrived at the cottage on the shore and was greeted at the door by a girl. I realised she was Janet's sister, poor soul, she is rather simple. Though I'd met her once before, she did not want to speak to me at first, for it was obvious she had something to hide. Eventually I got it out of her that her father, a mussel fisherman, had been at home on that fated Sunday when Janet had returned to pack. He is a violent man and so she had tried to avoid an encounter with him. She thought he would be at church, but he was at home, nursing a hangover. That Sunday was the day we were to meet at Leuchars station to take the train for Edinburgh and thence to Liverpool for the ship to Tasmania.'

Robert stopped speaking and turned abruptly to his wife. 'There is something else, Ann, something important. She was with child.'

'Oh, dear God.'

'Yes, she was expecting our child. It was all to be so good, a new life down in Australia, but then...' His shoulders slumped and he yawned widely.

Good, thought Ann, the tincture is taking effect.

'According to the sister, who was hiding, unseen, her father noticed her condition; how could he not, though she was some four months from delivery, she was slender as a willow. So she told him the father of her child was a great man, of reputable family, wealthy, a man who would make a lady of her and...'

'What, like he made of his wife? His wife, Robert, not some maid with loose morals!' Her voice rose to a crescendo. 'Who beds you without a thought for his family at home.'

They both looked around, but there was no one to hear.

Robert shook his head. 'You see, my dear, you have still never quite lost the cadence of the mill worker you are deep inside.'

'And you, Robert, have lost none of the priggish arrogance of your privileged background.' She wanted to slap him but clenched her hands together; she must wait.

'Mr Clark was so angry with Janet, he swung his fist at her and she fell and hit her head on the stone floor. She...' He stopped and snivelled. 'She died at once.' Robert was wringing his hands.

'So why did no one know anything of this? Surely it should have been reported?'

'No, nothing was done, according to the sister.'

'But, forgive me, Robert, I fail to understand how the body ended up in the Tay Bridge Station mortuary?'

'He threw the body from the back of the house into the Tay in a panic, that afternoon of the fated train crossing. The sister watched, terrified, from the window. And so what were identified as injuries inflicted by the rocks on the riverbank were in fact the head injuries poor Janet sustained on her own scullery floor. The sister is the only one who saw what happened and she was in a terrible state upon telling me. I had to promise her on my children's lives I would not say anything to the authorities.'

'Robert, that is horrible.' She looked at his face, trying to see his expression in the darkness. 'But why are you telling me all this?'

Robert gave a wide yawn and slumped down a little on the bench. 'I speak the truth to you now because I shall explain what is going to happen. I shall go to Tasmania in three days' time. The ship is booked, I have a berth for myself and my two children.'

'How in God's name do you think you can do that?'

'By law they are my children, not yours.'

'You expect me to say nothing at all? Allow you to take my children off to the other side of the world and simply say farewell?'

'Ann, if you do not, the consequences would not be terribly pleasant for you, I fear. The little cottage in Glenisla might no longer suit your ladylike constitution – perhaps one of the tenement flats in Lochee might be more appropriate. Indeed, you could ply your wares on the streets at night.'

She slapped him hard. 'How dare you, how dare you.'

He put his hand to his cheek then grasped her hands and drew closer. 'I do not imagine your wealthy friends would like to know that you are no more a lady than the whores down at the docks. I am drawing up contracts tomorrow regarding the mill and also your finances. I had thought to change ownership of the mill but I decided last night to keep things as they are, with Johnston in charge, he's a good man. I will be providing you with a generous allowance and leaving you the house and servants. Provided you say nothing malicious, you can invent some tale about being sent for at a future date, as you wish.'

He put his hand up to his mouth to stifle another yawn

and she pulled her hands away and reached into her pocket.

She put her other hand onto his coat and started to unbutton it. 'Robert, you are my husband, have you no heart?' She slipped her hand onto his thin silk waistcoat and rubbed his chest where his heart was. 'I cannot believe you would deprive me of my children. I love you and...'

'Love me, ha! You have never loved me, you used me,' he slurred, slumping further down the bench. His eyes were closing.

'You are so right, Robert Craig, I never have.'

She pulled out Mattie's gift. Now was the time. She removed the long, heavy, sharpened darning needle from its cloth and thrust it once, twice, three times into his heart.

Chapter 48
2015

The figure darted off over the road then disappeared. Had she imagined him? Fiona felt tears prick her eyes. She snivelled and headed back to the line of mourners, where her mother whispered, 'You okay?'

Fiona nodded and took up hand-shaking position again.

An hour later, she was doing the rounds of the tables set up for the funeral tea at West Park Hall where Jamie had chosen to sit between Martha and Allie. Fiona paused to speak to Doug and Mrs C. As the older woman chomped her way through the sausage rolls, egg sandwiches, ham sandwiches and scones, she said the only thing she'd had different at a funeral – mind you, it was Edinburgh and they're a bit uppity there – was soup. A wee cup of thick pea soup would be perfect on a day like this, what a cold wind. As she stretched across the table to the cakes, she proffered one to Doug. 'See, you always get a fruit cake and a sponge with jam. But now they're going in for those fancier ones, a chocolate brownie or a slice of carrot cake. Me, I think you can't get past a fruitcake. And this one's grand. How about you, Fiona, can you manage a bit? Bet you've hardly eaten a thing.'

'I'm off to do the rounds, Mum said we had to try to speak to everyone.'

She went to Martha's table first. She put her arms round Jamie and he smiled. 'Doing okay, sweetheart?'

He nodded and sipped his coke. 'Mum, will we still stay at Granny and Pa's house?'

Fiona and Martha exchanged glances. 'I think so, there are no plans to change anything yet. That suit you all right?'

He nodded. 'It's just, well, Allie says she can take me to the football any time it's a home game and I'd hate to miss it if we were back up at Glenisla.'

'No worries.' Fiona smiled and gave him a kiss on the top of his head.

'Want us to take him home after?' Martha whispered.

'No, thanks, you've been so good to him. We're going to get fish and chips tonight, just the three of us, then try to get him back into some normality tomorrow.'

'Good idea. But you know, any time we're not working, we love having him around.'

Fiona took Martha's hand. 'You're a star. Thanks.'

'And don't send us any more flowers. We don't need thanking!'

'Will do, boss. Oh, and I'll be back at work next week if that's okay?'

'Course. I've come to a bit of a standstill in my exhibition work, so got a bit of free time. I thought I'd start looking up that Craig family story in the archives for you. If you want?'

'That'd be brilliant, thanks, M. I'm even more keen to find out what it was all about, now Dad's gone.' Fiona smiled and walked on.

She headed for Mark's table next. He was sitting beside a small elegant woman with cropped white hair and they were face to face, engrossed in each other's conversation. She tapped his back. 'Hi, Mark, how're you doing?'

'Oh, Fiona, dear girl.' He gave her a kiss on both cheeks. 'This is Bunty Mackenzie, your Dad and I went to school with her. Not seen each other for, what did we say, forty-five years?'

'Something like that, but if you hadn't gone off to work in Bermuda, then, what might have been, Mark!' The woman smirked then reached out to pat Fiona's arm. 'How are you doing? We met outside the church, but not properly. Mark's been filling me in on what you're up to and that gorgeous son of yours. And I'm so sorry about your husband. What an untimely death.'

If another person mentioned Iain, thought Fiona, she would scream. Today was about her dad, not her husband who had died several years before.

'Thanks, Bunty.'

Another woman arrived at the table and shrieked loudly, 'Bunty Mackenzie, you've not changed a bit!'

'Yes, well apart from the colour of the hair,' said Bunty, getting up from her seat to speak to the other woman.

Fiona sat down next to Mark and watched him finish off a dram. Not his first, Fiona presumed, judging by the alcoholic fumes around.

He turned round at the sight of a waitress passing. 'Another whisky, please. And, Fiona, a sherry? Wine?'

'Just a Diet Coke please.' She had been persuaded at Iain's funeral to have a stiff drink and found herself unable to control the tears. So today she decided to stick to Coke.

'I always loved visiting Struan's house, when we were growing up. His family were all such fun, especially for me, being brought up by such strict parents. My mother was from Lewis and was a Wee Free and she ran a tight ship. Going to Magdalen Yard Road was an escape for me.'

'Dad always said it was a happy house.'

'Oh, it was. Stru's grandpa, a wonderfully eccentric old man, lived with them. He'd inherited the house from his older brother and sister when they died or emigrated or something. He had been brought up by an aunt, I think. His bedroom was downstairs, where Stru's study is now. Stru and I used to love going in there, listening to his stories and tales.' Mark chuckled then drew back as the waitress brought the tray of drinks.

'I remember one day Stru and I had been digging in the garden and come across some foundations so we went to ask Grandpa Archie what it was. He said that it was already gone when he was growing up but he'd been told about the summer house by his older siblings. It hadn't been that big but it had been a thing of beauty, post-Palladian style. God knows what possessed them to demolish it. Why get rid of a fine summer house? But then I think beautiful buildings, whatever their size should...'

'Fiona, sweetheart, the Morrisons are going, come and say bye!'

She turned to see her mother beckoning her over to the door.

'Sorry, Mark, got to go. Let me know if you remember anything else?'

He nodded, wrapped both hands round his tumbler, gazing into the whisky as if for clues.

★ ★ ★

Fiona slammed the car door shut and watched Jamie run ahead to the house, the key swinging from his hand.

'How did you think it went, Fi?'

'Okay, I suppose. But I don't know why you keep asking that, Mum. And why d'you need to know how many folk were there?'

'Well, it seemed to me like hundreds, so I asked the funeral director and he said about three hundred. Not bad going for an only child of only parents.'

'God, Mum, it's not a competition,' Fiona muttered, walking into the kitchen.

Jamie was sitting at the table with a piece of paper in his hands. He was very still.

'What've you got there?' Fiona asked as her mother brushed past her, mumbling about having been desperate for the toilet for hours.

Jamie looked up at her and held it out. 'It's a letter for me. It's from Pete.'

Chapter 49
Monday 12 January 1880

Robert's body slumped to the ground. Ann stared at it, eyes wide. Dead. He was dead and she had done it. Ann looked around; there was no one to be seen. She had to follow her plan through. Taking out her handkerchief, she wiped Mattie's needle clean then pierced it through the cloth again. She shoved it into her pocket then looked up as a cloud shifted, revealing a sliver of moon in the black sky. Something glistened in the silvery light. Blood, a pool of it. She pressed her handkerchief over his heart, to try to stem the flow.

The sooner she got his body into the fast-flowing river the better. The stab wound would not be noticed after the body was swept onto the rocks out there. Ann wrapped her handkerchief in the larger one in her pocket, Alfred Johnston's.

She knelt down and lifted her husband's legs and began to pull. Good God, how on earth could such a thin man weigh so much? But she had carried heavier weights, like the bundles of jute she used to lug from the delivery area into the mill. That was where she and Alfred, both aged twelve, had become friendly. It had been obvious that he liked her from their first meeting and soon he had fallen under her spell. She gave her first kiss to Alfred Johnston, and the rest sometime later.

Ann dragged the body towards the riverbank and

looked up. Dark storm clouds were scudding across the sky. She sniffed the air. Rain. It was driving east along the river. Thank God, she thought, as she thrust the body down the slithery slope. It caught on something on the bank, so she ran back to the bench and picked up Robert's walking cane. She jabbed at his shoulders and back until he suddenly came loose and shot down the slope, hitting the water with a splash. She looked around again. Nothing. A flash of moonlight glinted on the silver top of the walking cane in her hand. She saw the body jerk a little as the strong current picked it up and Robert drifted away into the dark.

Ann walked back towards the bench and pulled out the handkerchiefs. She began to wipe away blood from the ground then looked up as great drops of rain began to splatter all around. No need, the rain would do it for her. She rammed the handkerchiefs back in her pocket then stared at the walking cane in her fist. If she took it home with her, the servants would find it and questions would be asked. She ran over to the river and hurled the stick as far as she could. With a final splash, the last vestige of Robert Craig was gone. She patted the pocket with Mattie's needle and as she strode up the Green towards Magdalen Yard Road, she began to work out what to do with that. The rain, which had begun softly, was now pelting down. Heavy rain clouds swept over the sky and as she turned round to look one last time at the river, the moon shone with startling brilliancy.

Chapter 50
2015

Fiona sat at the kitchen table reading the note for the third time. She didn't get it, why would he write to Jamie and not to her?

Jamie snatched the letter from her again.

'So can we go and see him tomorrow or Saturday, like he says? He's back, Mum, back from Australia!' Jamie beamed.

'I've got to get my head round this, Jamie. But I very much doubt you'll be coming with me.' She heard a noise upstairs. 'And don't say a word to Granny, it will just upset her. Okay?'

'Okay, but I don't see why I can't go too. He invited me first!'

'Let's chat about it tomorrow, Jamie. Now go and get your PJs on and I'll order the fish and chips in a minute.'

She stared at the note again.

> *Hi Jamie, how you going, mate? I'm back in town, would be good to catch up for a bit of footie or something. I'll be down on Magdalen Green the next two afternoons if you fancy catching up.*
> *Cheers,*
> *Pete x*
> *P.S. Bring your mum too.*

She still didn't understand why she was a mere P.S. That must have been him at the funeral, after all. What the hell was going on?

'Fiona, I'm not sure I can be bothered to stay up for anything to eat, I might go off to bed early.' Her mum stood in her bare feet at the kitchen door. Fiona covered the note with her hand. 'You and Jamie get the fish and chips though. I've got a busy day tomorrow, need to try to get a proper night's sleep.'

'You're not going to carry on with the sleeping tablets, Mum, are you?'

'No, don't worry, I'm not becoming an addict. I intend to stop from tonight.'

'What have you got on tomorrow anyway?'

'Got to see the lawyer again.'

'I can come with you?'

'I'm fine on my own,' she snapped. She slumped down onto the chair beside Fiona. 'Sorry darling, of course you can come, if you want.' Dorothy reached out for Fiona's hand. 'I'm so sorry I've been such a grumpy old cow, I think these tablets have been doing something to me. I feel so down and then suddenly I'll be on a bit of a high, like I was at the service.'

'It's what happens with those pills. So you're going to give up now?'

Dorothy nodded. She had tears in her eyes. 'Fi, sweetheart, it's just the two of us now Dad's gone, we've got to stop bickering. Come here.'

Fiona reached over and the two women hugged. They were both crying.

'I should have been less crotchety and more grateful for everything you've done for the past fortnight, darling.

You've run the house and I have done nothing. Thank you, my love.'

'Mum, it's all fine. And if you'd prefer to go to the lawyer's alone, that's also fine. I'm here if you need me.' Fiona gave her mum a kiss.

'Granny, d'you want me to make you some hot chocolate with that special whizzing stick Allie gave me?'

Jamie stood in his Desperate Dan pyjamas at the door, taking in the scene of his mother and grandmother in tearful embrace.

'That would be just lovely, darling. Thank you.'

Jamie ran to the fridge for the milk, then to the cupboard for the chocolate. 'I'll put marshmallows on top too!' he shouted, excited.

Dorothy stroked Fiona's cheek and smiled. 'We'll speak tomorrow, sweetheart. I'm off to bed once our little chef has done my hot chocolate.'

★ ★ ★

Fiona took the fish-and-chip wrappers out to the bins in the garden and looked back up at the house. Lights were on downstairs and in Jamie's top floor bedroom. Shabby neo-classical, that's how Stru used to describe the grand Victorian exterior as it slowly became more run-down.

What was it he used to tell her mum when she berated him for ignoring her pleas to repair the masonry? Fiona chuckled as she remembered his ditty: 'Your house will still be here once you're gone.' And now he was gone and here was this solid house. Okay, it was a bit tatty round the edges but still, it was her dad's family house, the Craigs had lived here forever. It didn't seem possible that he was no longer with them. How could they get over his loss?

Well, at least things seemed better between her mum and her, so hopefully that was a start. She turned towards the Green and thought about what her dad would have made of Pete's note. It was so strange that he had addressed it to Jamie, not to her. A recurring thought came back to her. What if he had been that guy at the school gates, some kind of paedophile and he wanted to take Jamie away with him. Maybe he and Debs were going to abduct him.

It just didn't seem plausible, any of it. The Pete she knew was a kind, gentle guy – not some sort of crazy psycho. But then, she never thought he would run out on her like he did either.

She wandered back into the house and locked the back door. She would go and meet him, but by herself. No way was she taking Jamie along. She would go tomorrow, when Jamie was at school. When she thought of seeing him again, she felt a shudder of excitement, then shook herself out of it.

For God's sake, she told herself, he left me, stole all my money and disappeared without a trace. He's got some explaining to do. His excuses better be good.

Chapter 51
Monday 12 January 1880

Once she was sure that the Baxters and Jessie were all busy round the back of the house, Ann pulled on her shoulder cape and stepped onto the lawn so her steps would not be heard on the gravel as she headed for the gate.

There he was, waiting. He whipped off his cap.

'Good morning, Alfred.'

'Morning, Annie. Do you have news?'

'I do. It is good news. The lawyers have had no instructions from my husband before he died to hand the mill over to Clegg. Your job is safe.'

Alfred Johnston clasped his hands together and beamed. 'Thank you, Annie, thank you. That you have done this for me, in your time of grief and mourning, is too kind.'

'I have a small favour to ask of you, in return.'

'Anything, Annie.'

'Can you can find Blind Mattie for me and give this back to her? Today if possible.' She handed the cloth to him and he peered down at it.

'That's one of the mill worker's darning needles.'

'It's Mattie's. I want her to have it back. You are nearer Lochee than I am.'

'Aye, I can do that,' he said, taking the cloth. 'But why do you have it?'

'She gave it to me, I had forgotten it was still in my possession.'

'Oh, sorry to ask, Annie, but d'you have my handkerchief? I had to tell Bettie I left mine at the mill. It was one she embroidered for me, special.'

'It is inside, being laundered. I shall have it sent to the mill.' She turned upon hearing a noise. 'I must go. Goodbye, Alfred.' She swept back over the lawn and reached the front door just as Baxter crunched slowly over the gravel towards the back gate.

★ ★ ★

'Mamma, may I get down from the table please? I am doing a special drawing in the nursery. It's of our house and I am trying to get the pillars at the front door just right.'

'Of course, dear boy. What did Pappa call them?'

'Ionic.'

'That's it.' Ann beckoned to her son with a smile. 'Come and give your Mamma a kiss.'

James slunk towards his mother. 'The twins say it's not right to do kisses now I am ten.'

Ann shook her head. 'What the Donaldsons do is their business. In this house we show each other how very much we love each other.' She ruffled her son's hair then planted a kiss on his head.

'Pappa never kissed me.'

'Nor me,' said Lizzie, putting down her spoon with a clunk.

'Your Pappa is – was – never a man to show his emotions. But I am sure he loved you, in his own way.'

She must say nothing against him; she must forever be the grieving widow and loving wife.

'That black hat pudding was very good,' said Lizzie as she clambered onto her mother's lap.

Ann pulled Lizzie's dainty satin slippers off. 'Black cap pudding, darling girl,' she said, tickling her feet.

'The rain's stopped, Mamma. Can we go out later? Please?'

'No, I would prefer if you stay at home this afternoon.'

'But Mamma, we had to stay in the nursery all morning, you always say fresh air's good and...'

'Sorry, my dear, not today. Though the rain has stopped, it will be too wet underfoot. Perhaps tomorrow.'

Even though he was gone, she felt his threatening presence, she wanted to keep her children close.

The door swung open. Mrs Baxter hobbled in and frowned as she looked at them. 'Lizzie, you are too big to sit like a baby on your mother's lap.'

'I think that is something for us to decide, thank you.' Ann started to pull Lizzie's slippers back on. 'Off you go up to the nursery. I shall pop up later.'

Mrs Baxter stood back to allow Lizzie and James to run past her then she approached the table. 'Mrs Craig, I noticed your heavy cloak was damp. I hung it in the drying room earlier.'

'Oh, thank you. What a good idea.'

'I didn't hear you go out last night. Did you go far?'

'No, not far,' said Ann, flustered.

'I'll clear up the lunch things then fetch your coffee in the drawing room.'

Ann nodded, thinking about the coat and what was in the pocket. She had completely forgotten about it. Last night, she had just flung it on the coat stand and gone straight to bed, too exhausted to think straight. And now she could not get to the drying room without passing through the kitchen where Mrs Baxter resided all day.

There was a loud knock at the front door.

'Shall I see who that is, Mrs Craig? I can bring them to you in the drawing room.'

Ann stood up and went out, head bowed, thinking about what to do.

She could hear her voice before she reached her favourite window seat. Good God, Margaret was back.

'Mrs Donaldson to see you, Mrs Craig,' said Mrs Baxter as Margaret swept past her, carrying a large carpetbag. Her face was pale, her expression austere; she did not greet Ann as she took a seat.

Mrs Baxter pulled the door to, but did not shut it completely.

'Margaret, how nice to have you back. You have been missed. How was your sister?'

'My sister was fine.'

Margaret's expression was thunderous. Ann had never seen her be anything other than charming.

'You are back earlier than you had thought. Was all well, my dear?'

'In fact no, all was not well. Yesterday morning we received a message from Aggie to say the dog had disappeared during the evening and she was worried. She had tried to waken Dr Donaldson in the night to look for her but he was not there. It was not an evening he was on duty, he had told her he had no work until Monday morning.'

Margaret glared at Ann who stood and went to the

door. Take your time, Ann told herself. Be careful. 'Shall you join me for coffee, Margaret, dear?' She opened the door wide and, as she thought, her housekeeper was hovering in the hall.

'Thank you for awaiting orders, Mrs Baxter. You may fetch in the coffee tray now.'

Ann went to sit beside Margaret on the sofa. 'I do hope Bridie is safely home now?'

'Yes, she is. It was as if she was emulating the cat, prowling around at night, trying to find a male to mate with.'

Ann's eyes opened wide. She had never heard Margaret be so base.

'Well, that is good she is home, the children do love the dog.'

The door swung open and Mrs Baxter shuffled in with the tray.

'Leave it there, Mrs Baxter. And shut the door tight.'

Ann reached to pour the coffee. 'You like just one spoon of sugar, do you not, Margaret?'

Margaret nodded; Ann noticed that she was strumming her fingers on the side of the brocaded armrest. She took the coffee and turned to Ann so they were face to face. 'Ann, first I hear my husband is not at home in the middle of the night. Then I find this!'

She delved into the carpetbag at her feet and pulled out a mustard-yellow waistcoat.

'What is it, Margaret?' Ann tried to speak normally but found her voice was croaky.

'It is my husband's silk waistcoat. His favourite.'

Ann looked at her, expectant.

'Smell it,' Margaret said, a disdainful look on her face.

She thrust it into Ann's hands. She took it and sniffed. Dear God, it was too obvious.

'The aroma – no, I must call it an odour – is one of jasmine with a hint of bergamot, the stench of someone who wears more perfume than a common whore.'

Ann gulped.

'It has a strong and lingering smell and my husband's waistcoat is reeking of it. Do you have any suggestion as to how this might have happened? While I was away?'

'I have no idea, Margaret. Perhaps when I saw him last week I had too much perfume on and it lingered on the fine silk.' She stroked the material.

'Take your hands off it, woman!' Margaret yanked it from her.

Ann blinked and looked deep into Margaret's eyes. 'What are you suggesting, Margaret?'

'I am not suggesting anything. I am confirming what I know happened during my absence.'

'I do not seem to be following you, Margaret.'

'Let me spell it out so you are in no doubt. You and my husband were cavorting together during the nights I was away.'

Ann gasped. 'Oh, such accusations, Margaret!'

'Your girl Jessie told my Aggie that there were blankets and hot water bottles in the summer house at the weekend. Why would you, in January, wish to heat the summer house? My contention is that you and Archibald were in there.' She looked away, eyes narrowed. 'Together!'

Ann's heart hammered against her ribs but she sat quite still. 'I am sure there is some misunderstanding, Margaret.' She thought fast. 'What does Dr Donaldson say about this nonsense?'

'He is out at work. I have not yet seen him but he will return at teatime, overjoyed no doubt to see us back. But he will not be overjoyed when I confront him.' She stood up.

'Margaret, please do not go, let us talk further. There has been some misunderstanding. You know how servants talk. I am sure...'

Margaret was already at the door and flung it open to find Mrs Baxter there, stooped down at the keyhole. The housekeeper straightened up and hurried to open the front door for Margaret.

Ann watched Margaret sweep down the path then stop and cross the lawn to the summer house, where she tried the door. Thankfully it was locked. But then she saw Margaret look enquiringly towards the back of the house, as if she had heard something. Ann peered round and saw her walk round towards the kitchen where Mrs Baxter stood, beckoning. The two women spoke and the housekeeper handed something to Margaret. She held it, whatever it was, in her hand for a moment as if examining it, then stuffed it into her carpetbag before stomping down the path. Ann slumped down onto the window seat as the realisation sunk. It was the bloodied handkerchiefs from last night.

Chapter 52
2015

'What on earth are you doing, Mum?' Fiona had just returned from the school run and heard harrumphing from the study.

A huge pile of papers and documents surrounded Dorothy as she sat in the middle of the floor.

'Sorting Dad's things. I know he has a will, we both did that about twenty years ago, so it's just a matter of locating it. But do you know, I have no idea where his birth certificate is.'

'Why d'you need that?'

'He was always funny about his real age and I reckon he might have been older than he was.'

'Don't be ridiculous, Mum, we've been through this. He's the same age as Mark and that Bunty woman at the funeral. Born in 1944.'

'But there was no one who knew him from his infancy. They all knew him from age six. I need to know the date.'

'Why? Why the bloody hell does it matter? He's gone.' Fiona was exasperated.

'Watch your language, Fiona. Just because your father's gone doesn't mean you have to take up his swearing mantle.' She sighed. 'I have to write the birth date on the plaque thing at the crematorium and I don't want to just invent the year he was born.'

Fiona shook her head and sat down on the floor beside

her mum. 'What are you going to do with his clothes and his things. What about his pipes?'

'Well, the pipes can be flung, the constant inhaling of noxious fumes can't have helped his health one bit.'

'I may hold onto that one pipe, you know the one he always had in his pocket, I'll chuck the others. And clothes?'

'Let's wait a bit,' Dorothy looked at her daughter, eyes full of tears. 'No rush on those.'

Fiona nodded. 'How did you sleep?'

'Terrible, tossing and turning all night, but I'm determined to come off those pills for good. Like I said, they made me cranky and not quite with it. I felt as if I was hovering, not quite landing in real life. Think I was becoming a bit addicted actually.'

Fiona peeked up at her mother whose face had softened. She was back to old Mum, Fiona thought.

'Mum, if I tell you something, will you promise not to get angry?'

Dorothy put down the paper she was studying and peered over her glasses. 'What?'

'Well, I'm off this afternoon to meet Pete. Now, don't get mad and…'

'Pete? Pete Gibson? Fancy that.'

Fiona stared at her mother. 'That all you're saying? Aren't you going to make more of a fuss?'

Dorothy shrugged. 'Is he back in town, then?' She continued to study the sheet of paper in her hand.

Fiona's mouth opened wide. 'You knew, didn't you? You knew he was back and you knew he was at the funeral and…'

Dorothy took off her glasses and eased herself up from the floor to the chair at the desk. 'He got in touch a couple of days before we left for the Hebrides, said he wanted to see you to explain everything. He knew you'd be so livid and proud and would probably refuse to see him, so he asked me what I thought was the best way.'

'You knew, Mum, you knew he was back and didn't tell me?' She shook her head. 'I can't believe it!'

'He loves you, Fi. He really does and I have no idea, truly, what he did and why he did it but all I know is that he's terribly sorry and wants to woo you back. I think that's why he sent Jamie the note. He thought you'd never want to see him so he hoped to get Jamie involved to lure you to a meeting.'

'But Mum, I ran after him at the funeral, could he not have spoken to me then?'

Dorothy shrugged. 'I didn't know anything about that. It was maybe just not appropriate. But all I said to him was to wait and I would get back to him once I had thought it through, then it was the holiday, then poor Stru...'

Fiona stood up from the heap on the floor and sat on the little sofa opposite the desk. 'It's unbelievable that you kept this from me. And, hang on, how come you know about Jamie's note?'

'Grannies can be useful confidantes sometimes, darling.' Dorothy swivelled round on the chair. 'So are you going to meet him today?'

Fiona nodded and looked at her watch.

'Yeah, I'll go over to the Green after lunch. Might need a large glass of wine first.' She smiled. 'Did he really say he loved me?'

★ ★ ★

Fiona left the house and headed for the Green. She had on her boots and raincoat, as Dorothy insisted rain was forecast. Also, she didn't want to look as if she'd made too much effort. She could hardly eat at lunch, her stomach was churning. But she did manage to glug down a large glass of wine, as did Dorothy, who had cancelled her appointment and was going to continue trawling through Struan's affairs.

As she crossed the grass, Fiona spotted a figure sitting on the old bench overlooking the river. She got nearer and saw it was him. Even from behind, he looked as if he'd not changed much. His hair was a bit shorter and he looked a lot thinner, but apart from that, it was the same old Pete. He turned round and beamed. Oh, he was handsome. She smiled and resisted the urge to run. No way would she just fall into his arms, he had six months of explaining to do.

He got up from the bench and stood, leaning on something. What on earth was it? When she saw it was a cricket bat, she smiled. It must be a present for Jamie. Pete had always said he'd buy him a bat in Australia. He put the bat down on the bench and came towards her. She continued walking towards him, taking in his dimple and the way his eyes crinkled as he smiled, trying to tell herself not to get carried away, not to forget how he'd hurt her and Jamie. But he looked like the same gentle, loving Pete she remembered. She stood in front of him and he gazed at her.

'Christ, Fi, you look nervous!'

'I've not seen you for so long, I was terrified I'd forget what you looked like.'

He smiled and leant in towards her. 'I've never forgotten anything about you, Fi.'

Chapter 53
Tuesday 13 January 1880

'There's a note for you, Mrs Craig.' Jessie bobbed and held out a silver tray.

'Thank you. Where is Mrs Baxter this morning?'

'Says she doesn't feel good, she's staying in the kitchen.'

'I see. And are the children still upstairs with Miss Graham in the nursery?'

'Aye.'

Ann took the note into the drawing room and turned it over. It was his writing. She must calm herself before reading it. She poured herself a glass of Madeira which she quaffed in one, then headed over to the window seat. Ripping the letter open with the paper knife, she began to read.

> *My darling Ann,*
>
> *I have two pieces of news. Firstly, Robert's body came into the morgue late last night. It was instantly recognisable and so I took over the work. Dr Anderson had gone home for the night and my colleague, Dr Macdonald, does not know the connection. Even though it was obvious the body had only recently been in the water, I drew up all the necessary paperwork and the body is still there with his date of death certified as 28 December 1879.*
>
> *There were lesions to the heart but these were not*

noted on the official records. Fortunately the thickness of his chest hair makes it less obvious to the eye. You will receive the official letter notifying you that the body lies at the morgue and the undertakers await instructions.

The second piece of news is not good. Margaret thinks she has evidence about us, my darling, and our love trysts. There is nothing she can prove and so I intend to stay away from home for now. Indeed, the morgue is busy, we now have thirty-seven bodies, many came ashore overnight.

But I cannot wait to lie in your arms once more. With fondest love,
A

Ann looked out at the Tay, sparkling in the early morning sunlight. So, Archibald, dear sweet Archibald, had served his purpose well. What would happen with Margaret? Somehow she doubted it would blow over.

Now all Ann had to do was await the official letter telling of her poor husband's death on that ill-fated train, then deal with the funeral arrangements.

What would she wear? She would need to have a new gown made, perhaps taffeta? Or would silk be best?

There was a noise on the gravel. It must be the courier with the letter from the morgue. She turned and saw two policemen crunching up the drive towards the front door.

Ann froze.

She had planted the needle on Alfred so that she would never be implicated. And Alfred would say nothing that might incriminate her, of that she was positive, even if he were to be arrested. Surely they couldn't find anything from the handkerchiefs if Margaret had handed those in?

'Mrs Craig, two gentlemen to see you.' Jessie's eyes were wide, as if she had never encountered a policeman at close quarters – and there were now two in her mistress's house.

Ann took a deep breath to compose herself, then nodded as Jessie showed them in.

'Sorry to disturb you, Mrs Craig,' the older one said, as he nudged the younger one and whispered to him to remove his hat. 'We have some questions to ask if you don't mind.'

'Of course, please be seated.' Ann glanced up at the door. 'Bring us some refreshments, Jessie, and ask Mrs Baxter for some yellow cake.'

The policemen smiled then the older one coughed. 'Mrs Craig, we are here regarding a murder. Nasty business, sorry to bother you about it.'

'Madeira? Can I offer you a glass?' Ann rose and rushed, with too much haste, to the table and began to pour. Her hand was shaking so she steadied it on the table before handing each man a glass. She sat down and took a sip from hers.

'Murder, did you say? How awful. How might I be of any assistance, gentlemen?' Be your most charming, Ann Craig, without being coquettish.

'I don't know if you recall but the first body to be found after the tragedy on the the twenty-eighth of December was a serving maid. One Janet Clark of Tayport.'

Ann's breathing slowed down a little. 'Yes, I believe I do recall.'

'Her father has just made a dreadful allegation, Mrs

Craig, and one that will come as a shock to you.'

Just then, Mrs Baxter shuffled in with a tray of tea and cake. 'Ah, Mrs Baxter, you must be feeling better?'

'Aye, that I am,' she muttered as she placed the tray on the table. She looked round at the policemen and nodded then did a double take. 'Is that you, wee Jimmy Hutchison?'

The younger policeman flushed bright red and stuttered, 'Aye, it's me, Auntie Jeannie. Did you not ken I'm now a policeman?'

'Your mother and I have not spoken for five years so no, I did not. Look at you!'

'Mrs Baxter, it is wonderful you have rediscovered your nephew after all these years, but these men are busy people and must go about their business.' Ann nodded towards the door.

'Aye, right. Bye then, Jimmy, grand to see you. Remember me to your big sisters.'

'You were saying something about a servant girl?' Ann was cursing the big village that was Dundee, where everyone either knew or was related to everyone else. How on earth could Mrs Baxter turn out to be the policeman's aunt? How unfortunate.

'Aye, well William Clark's allegation is...' The older man looked towards Ann. 'I'll read his statement aloud, if that's all right, Mrs Craig, for I fear it will be more shocking in my own words.' Ann stretched to pick up her fan.

'Here is the statement of William Donald Clark of 5, The Cottages, Tayport, dated Monday the twelfth of January, 1880. "My daughter Janet Clark, a twenty-five-year-old servant at Kirkmichael House, Fife, began a relationship with the nephew of her mistress, Lady Cruickshank. After several weeks, Janet became with child to her Ladyship's nephew, one Robert Craig of Dundee. On hearing the news of the child to be, Robert Craig, in a rage, hit my daughter, her head cracked open on the kitchen floor, then he threw her in the sea on Sunday the twenty-eighth of December, 1879. It was all seen by Janet's sister Edith."'

Ann sat, her breathing shallow. Good Lord, was that why they were here? She took her time to speak.

'Gentlemen, I do not know what to say. All this leaves me simply speechless. My husband having intimate relationships with a servant is already too much for one to bear but the fact that he supposedly then killed her on hearing she was with child is simply unbelievable.'

Ann said nothing more; reticence was required here.

'Mrs Craig, did you at any time suspect that your husband was in a relationship with Janet Clark?'

'No, I did not.'

Jimmy scribbled in his book.

'And do you have any reason to believe your husband might have murdered Janet Clark?'

She hesitated. 'No, I do not.'

'Mrs Craig, where has your husband been since the night of the twenty-eighth of December?'

Ann frowned. 'Do you not know? Are you not aware that he was one of the train passengers that went down into the river that night?'

The two men looked at each other.

'No.'

'That is why I am in mourning, gentlemen, and even now await a letter from the morgue telling me his body has been washed ashore. I believe it will arrive soon. I miss him terribly but I am resigned now to the fact he will never return.'

'We will check at the morgue after this.'

'I can send Jessie to you with the letter when it comes,' she said quickly. 'Which police station?'

'Union Street. Aye, if you don't mind doing that for us, Mrs Craig.'

Thank God, she did not want policemen snooping round the morgue until Robert was buried.

'And now, Mrs Craig, we will take our leave of you and apologise for this. Mr Clark is obviously either mistaken or lying. And both would have serious consequences.'

They stood up and Ann inclined her head as they went to the door. Instead of going to her window seat to watch them leave, she stood in the hallway, as she knew Mrs Baxter would be there, hovering. But they were taking forever to put on their cloaks so she reluctantly went back inside; it was not seemly for a lady to see guests out. She ran to the window and saw the older man walking down the drive alone. That meant that the young one was speaking to his aunt. Soon she saw young Jimmy run down after his colleague, waving at the door where the housekeeper must have been, gossiping.

Ann stamped her foot. Damn the woman, she was becoming trouble. She sighed and looked out at the river. The wind was getting up and the waters were beginning to swell and heave.

Chapter 54
2015

Fiona and Pete broke apart from their kiss and sat down on the bench. She lifted the cricket bat up. 'What's with the bat, Pete?'

'Present for Jamie, remember I always said I'd bring him one from Aus.'

Fiona was silent.

He looked into her eyes. 'I know, I know, what the hell was I doing running off there anyway. Okay, here goes.'

She looked down at his hands. They were shaking.

'So you told me that night the review was coming out in the paper. Good for me professionally and for the hotel of course, but terrible on a personal front.'

'Why?'

'I suddenly realised they'd see it online back in Tassie. They've been Googling me for ages, trying to find me.'

'Who?'

Pete's shoulders relaxed and he stroked Fiona's cheek and pulled the scarf round her neck as the breeze got up.

'My mum died eleven years ago, I never told you.'

'Why?'

Pete clenched his trembling hands together. 'My dad killed her. Suddenly went crazy, smashed her head with a hammer. It affected me pretty badly. Well, obviously.' He glanced at Fiona, who was glowering at him.

'I left home soon after Mum's funeral, had to get away.

My sister thought I'd died, killed myself, with the grief and...'

'What? Why would she think that?'

'She tried for quite a while to find out what happened to me but I never got in touch. She presumed I was dead. She even put my name on Mum's gravestone, no dates or anything, but just so folk would think, like her, that I was dead.'

Fiona swallowed.

'So, once I knew that she would see my name online, I had to go to Tassie and see her, explain – which I did, courtesy of, sorry to say, our savings. I don't suppose you'll ever forgive me for that and why should you. Anyway, I slowly got everything sorted between us. But I had to come back here, I had to see you and Jamie again.'

Pete raised his hand and caressed Fiona's cheek. She flicked his hand away and sat back, scowling.

'I don't understand any of this, Pete. Why would you pretend you were dead?'

'I'm not proud of any of this, but, being back there, I had a bit of a breakdown. I needed some meds to set me right, and my sister helped me out, took care of me. By the time I was better, so much time had passed... I thought it would be better to apologise in person.'

'Pete, what's your sister's name?'

'Her name? Sam, my wee sister Sam.'

Fiona snorted. 'Of course, your sister.' She shook her head. 'Why the hell could you not have told me about her – and about your mum being dead?'

'I know, I know. To be honest, I was kind of ashamed. Christ, Fi, my dad's a murderer.'

'What happened to him then?'

'Prison, in for life.'

Fiona sighed and looked straight at Pete. He looked so vulnerable.

'Okay, so you used our savings to fly there, you saw your sister Sam. But how does Debs fit into this?'

'Debs?'

'Yeah, Debs from the Old Chain Pier in Edinburgh. I met her and she told me you slept with her, then she took a photo from your passport when you got really angry with her and...'

'Why on earth would you think we slept together?'

'Well, why did you spend time with her?'

'I didn't. We were colleagues, that's all.' He tucked her hair behind her ear, brushing her cheek.

'But she had a picture of yours. It looks like he's your son.'

'What, you think I've got another family or something? Don't be daft, Fi. You and Jamie are my family.' He tipped his head back then nodded. 'I had a photo in my wallet of me as a wee boy. She stole all the money in my wallet one night when she was drunk and she must've taken the photo too.'

Fiona leant her head onto his shoulder and inhaled. It was so good to smell his wonderful smell again.

'Please, Fi, please believe me, I'm not a lying, thieving bastard.' He turned to look at her and smiled. 'Fi, the only bad thing I did was take the money from our account for the fare, but I was desperate. It was terrible and I should never have done it. I can't imagine you'll ever forgive me.'

'Did you fly first class? I mean, all that money?'

'No, I didn't fly first! I spent nearly a thousand on the fare then saved the rest. And I got some temping chef jobs while I was away so I've brought it all back – and a bit extra.'

Fiona frowned. 'But if you were just doing something as, well, worthy as you say you were, at last letting Sam know you were alive, why the hell could you not have got in touch? Emailed me to say, "Sorry, Fi, I stole all our savings and here I am back in Australia reconciling with my sister, but I'll be back soon."'

'I know, I handled it all badly, I'm rubbish. Sorry.' He stroked her hand. 'I should have got in touch. Thing is, Fi, the breakdown meant I had to see a shrink a few times, but I've got myself totally sorted out now. I felt ashamed of that too, like I wasn't coping well, so, kind of, unmanly.' He took a deep breath. 'But when I was fit again and ready to come back, I got in touch with Dot and then your dad died.'

He turned to her. 'I'm sorry about the funeral, it was me there at the back, but I just wasn't ready for the talk with you and I didn't think it was a good time for you. But I wanted to be there, he was a great guy your dad, a legend.'

'So how come Dad said you got really angry and shouted at Jamie one night when you were online?' Fiona scowled at him.

'Oh, Christ, did he bring that up? What an idiot I was. I'd been trying to find my sister online and I just got so stressed out about everything. I think I made up something about Facebook to Stru, I was so ashamed I'd bawled at Jamie. Sorry.'

Fiona frowned. 'How come all those football exercises you taught Jamie were from Sam? I thought Sam was a boy.'

'Sam was always a bit of a tomboy. She's coach of a women's footie side out there. She's ace.' He smiled but Fiona was still scowling. 'I'm sorry, Fi. I let you down. A lot.'

'Who d'you reckon the woman was who phoned Doug and said to him you were always leaving people in the lurch like that? Was that Sam?'

'Yeah, that was Sam.'

They sat looking out at the water, side by side, until Fiona said, 'D'you want to come back to the house for a cup of tea? I think Mum'd like to see you.' She looked at her watch. 'And Jamie'll be home from school soon. He'll be so excited.'

'Of course. But, Fi, can you ever forgive me? I'm so sorry I did this, to hurt you so much – and Jamie. I've been a shit, really useless. But I'm going to make it up to you.'

'What are you going to do, Prince Charming?' Fiona smirked.

'Wait and see!'

They walked together over the Green towards Magdalen Yard Road. Though inside she felt a flicker of hope, Fiona warned herself to stay calm. Even though Pete was back, she couldn't just forget the months of hurt he'd caused her and Jamie. It would take time, probably a very long time, to get over what he'd done. But... She loved him. Wasn't that enough? They reached the top of the Green and Pete stopped and stamped his foot.

'Christ, I bring it all the way from bloody Aus then I leave it on a park bench,' he said, laughing. He ran towards the bench where the cricket bat lay.

Fiona watched him go, remembering that long slow

stride, when she heard her phone ping. It was a text from Martha.

Found all your family history stuff in the archives, made copies to give you later. You up for a Friday drink? M x

Fiona hit reply and tapped out a quick message.

Yeah, come round to the house, big surprise here. F x

Chapter 55

Wednesday 14 January 1880

'Jessie, go and call Mr and Mrs Baxter and Miss Graham into the drawing room.'

Jessie bobbed and headed upstairs. Ann heard her taking the stairs two at a time. She strode into the drawing room, the letter in her hand, thinking of what she might say. This would not be easy. She reached for the decanter on the table and then paused. No, she must keep a clear head.

It was a cold winter's day; frost lay thick along the branches of the magnolia tree and on the ground. She gazed at the summer house and sighed. Damn those interfering servants and their chatter. She stood up straight and looked out beyond, to the river. It was calm, there was a stillness upon the water that was unusual. On most days, the Tay flowed gently from the hills in the west, through Perth, then at Dundee it began churning up as it approached the sea. Downstream of the bridge the waves were beginning to roll down towards the North Sea.

As she watched the little fishing boats bob about, she thought of Janet Clark's father who fished for mussels at the other side of the river. What would become of him now? What did he think he would gain by blaming Robert for his daughter's death? The simple sister must have told him about Robert's visit and this was his attempt to deflect any blame. But now it would backfire as he would no doubt be arrested and his family would bear the shame of both the affair and the murder. Should she feel sorry for him? Perhaps. He had tried in vain to shift the blame for a crime he had done onto someone else. She felt her heart race as she thought of how she had done the same with Alfred Johnston. She hoped he'd already given Mattie back the needle so that, even if the police visited the morgue and insisted on a re-examination, there would be no evidence with which he – or she – could be implicated. No one would suspect an old blind melodeon player.

There was a tap on the door and in walked the Baxters and Jessie. Ann nodded at them. 'Please, take a seat. Is Miss Graham coming, Jessie?'

'Aye, said she was on her way, just settling the bairns.'

The three servants shuffled and looked at their feet while Ann sat down in the wing chair before them. There was a flurry of movement at the door and in rushed Miss Graham, her skirts flapping.

Ann cleared her throat. 'I have news that you must all hear. Just before breakfast, I received this letter from the morgue. It tells me that my husband's body was washed ashore with the other poor passengers from that fated train that went over the bridge last month. He was found on Broughty Ferry beach late on Monday night. He was identified by the doctors and his body will lie there until the funeral.'

She glanced up at the faces. The Baxters were glowering at her. Jessie snivelled and wiped her nose on her sleeve. Miss Graham was shaking her head.

'So, once the funeral is over, you are all free to continue

working for me in your present roles. Or, should you wish to leave, I shall arrange a small sum of money and excellent references. It will be your choice.' She smiled graciously, every bit the munificent employer.

'After we have finished in here, I need you, Jessie, to take this letter to the police station in Union Street and hand it to the police. Wait for them to copy down the details and bring it back here. Do you understand?'

'Aye, I'm to take it to the police then wait and bring it back.'

'Precisely. It is an important document.'

'Whatever decision you reach on your futures here, I should be grateful to know soon please. I intend to begin to make funeral arrangements today.' She looked at each of them in turn.

'Condolences, Mrs Craig,' mumbled Mr Baxter. 'Our condolences.'

'Thank you, Baxter. You have been particularly helpful to me, especially in those early hours after the disaster. I shall not forget that.'

She heard a low growling noise from Mrs Baxter and looked towards her, expectant, but the older woman remained silent.

'Mrs Craig, may I also pass on my sincerest condolences for your loss.' Miss Graham was blinking, as if stemming back tears.

'Thank you. There is just one more thing: I want the house to remain as it is, calm and peaceful for the sake of the children. Is that understood?'

They all nodded. 'Jessie, take this letter. Go and do as I've bid.'

She handed Jessie the envelope and turned away as

they filed out. Mrs Baxter's hand locked onto Jessie's arm as she guided her out the door with a tight grip.

★ ★ ★

Ann stepped out of the carriage and paid the driver. What a long and arduous afternoon. The minister had taken forever as he pondered the most suitable choices of hymns and paraphrases and she had not expected the undertaker to have so many questions. But she only wanted the finest casket for her husband. This would be a funeral many would attend, everything must be well taken care of. As she walked up the drive, she worried about what to do with the children during the funeral. Ordinarily she would have asked Margaret to keep them but she did not want to ask that woman anything. She would have to ask Miss Graham to stay at home with them.

She opened the door and noticed there were two black capes on the coat stand. Who could possibly be here when she was not at home?

Upon entering the drawing room she saw that there were two policemen on the sofa, the older one from the day before and another, this one with more braid on his shoulders. They both stood up but did not smile. Her heart began to race.

'Gentlemen, what an unexpected pleasure. I do hope you have been offered refreshments?'

Her legs were trembling; she sat down with a thump in front of them.

'Mrs Craig,' said the unknown man. 'I am Detective Inspector MacCallister. You know my colleague Sergeant Donnelly.'

'Yes, yes I do.' Ann clasped her hands on her lap.

'There have been some allegations made, relating to yourself, that are extremely serious. I shall itemise these and then you may speak. Do you understand?'

She clenched her hands tight and nodded.

He cleared his throat then looked directly at her. His face was grey as granite.

'It is alleged that Robert Craig was never on the train over the Tay on the twenty-eighth of December, 1879. That he returned here at some time over the past few days. That, on realising he was alive, you conspired to murder him. During this undertaking, you involved two otherwise innocent men, both of whom are now also party to a crime. First, you had intimate relations with Dr Archibald Donaldson and he falsified the death certificate to state that your husband had been on the train and his body in the water for two weeks, when in fact he had three lesions in his heart, suggesting that he had been stabbed, and was in the water for less than two days. Secondly, you involved the manager at your husband's mill, one Alfred Johnston. He had the murder weapon about his person. He insisted he did nothing apart from relieve you of this.'

Fool, the man was a fool.

'In case, Mrs Craig, you are about to fabricate excuses, I shall relay the facts. Your neighbour Margaret Donaldson found out about you and her husband and says the relations took place in the summer house in the garden. She has evidence upon her husband's clothing.' He stared directly at her, his steely eyes unwavering. 'Your housekeeper Mrs Baxter found two bloodied handkerchiefs in your coat pocket, one yours, one belonging to Alfred Johnston; his initials were on them and the housekeeper recognised them. She brought those to Mrs Donaldson who then accompanied Mrs Baxter to the police station this morning along with the letter from the morgue. The letter which was certified by one Dr Archibald Donaldson.'

Traitors, the lot of them.

'I expect Mrs Baxter spoke to your assistant, her nephew Jimmy, Sergeant Donnelly?'

'Aye, she did that,' mumbled the Sergeant, looking at his feet.

'Is there anything you would like to say, Mrs Craig?'

Donnelly got out his notebook and had his pencil poised.

Ann's heart was pounding, yet she felt defiant. 'Yes, what if my husband was trying to abduct my two dear children? What if he was attempting to kill me and so I had to kill him in self defence?'

Why? Why did she mention the very possibility that she had killed him? Now she was the fool.

'These, Mrs Craig are all matters for the court to decide. But for now, we must ask you to accompany us to the police station for further questions.'

She felt stifled. 'Can I see my children first?' She could hardly breathe.

'They are at the Donaldsons' house. The doctor is elsewhere but Mrs Donaldson has kindly agreed to take care of them until further notice. It is best that you do not see them.'

Ann got to her feet and stumbled into the hall. Where usually a servant would rush to open the front door, there was no one. All was silent. She pulled her black velvet hat firmly down to meet her high collar as the men put on their capes. Outside, she looked back up at the house and saw a curtain twitch upstairs in the nursery. So, her entire staff was in on this.

Chapter 56
2015

Fiona and Pete walked into the kitchen and sniffed the air.

'Your mum been baking, Fi?'

'No idea. If so, it's the first time for ages. She's been kind of weird on the sedatives from the doctor, but she's coming out of it.'

Fiona went to the foot of the stairs and hollered, 'Anyone home?'

'Just changing out of my school uniform. Granny's made scones.'

Pete's eyes crinkled on hearing his voice.

They both sat down at the table and waited. The thud on the stairs was followed by a sudden halt. They both looked up at Jamie standing at the door, immobile, his mouth open.

'Pete, you're back!' He ran into the room and flung himself at him.

'Hi, mate, how're you doing?' Pete bent down to give him a big hug then pulled his ear the way he used to.

Dorothy joined them at the door and Pete stood up and went to give her a kiss on the cheek.

'Do they not eat in Australia? Look how thin you've got.'

'I know, lovesick.' He smiled at Fiona. 'Dot, I'm so sorry about Stru, what a loss. How are you doing?'

'I'm fine just so long as no one is too nice to me,' she said, as she went to put the scones from the wire rack on a plate. 'Put the kettle on, Fi.'

'So why did you leave, Pete?'

'Jamie, it's a long story, but it was really bad of me. I hurt you and your mum and Granny and Pa too. You remember I used to tell you that some boys were just idiots? Well, turns out I was an idiot too.'

Jamie giggled.

'No, I was, really. I'm not proud of what I've done but I'm back here now and I hope we can be a family again.'

Jamie grinned from ear to ear.

After tea, Dorothy said she was going to continue sorting through the papers in the study – she was making good progress.

'Is it okay if I take Jamie out to play with his new bat? There's enough light from the lampposts over on the Green. Stru had a cricket ball in the shed I think, didn't he?'

'Key's there, go and see,' Fiona said, pointing to the fruit bowl. 'I'll wait here for a bit then join you. Martha's on her way.'

'Someone else to make me eat humble pie,' said Pete.

'Yes, you'll need to butter her up big time, she's been my crying shoulder since you left.'

Pete bent down and kissed Fiona then rootled around under the apples in the bowl and picked up the shed key. 'Come on, Jamie, let's practise a few strokes.'

'Put your jacket on, Jamie,' said Fiona. 'It's getting cold!'

'Leave him be, Fi, he never feels the cold.' Pete looked down at Jamie, grinning. 'Unless you've changed while I've been away?'

Jamie shook his head, grabbed Pete's hand and pulled him towards the door.

★ ★ ★

Martha rang the bell then walked in the back door.

'Why d'you ring the bell when you just breeze on in anyway, M?'

She shrugged. 'Done it since I was little, why change now! So what's the big surprise?'

'Wait and see. Glass of wine?'

'Please.'

Fiona poured two glasses and Martha got some photocopies out of her bag. 'Here's the newspaper piece from The Courier, found it at last. From the seventh of May, 1880, the day after the court case. Look at this bit here. There's a lot of preamble about the nitty gritty of what exactly each witness said – you can read that later– but the last paragraph's the one to check out first. Look!'

'What are you talking about, Martha? What court case?'

'Just read it!'

Mrs Ann Craig of 73 Magdalen Yard Road, Dundee was tried and found guilty of murdering her husband, Robert Craig, of the same address. The murder took place on the promenade south of Magdalen Green on the 11th of January, 1880.

Two accomplices, Doctor Archibald Donaldson of 75 Magdalen Yard Road, Dundee and Alfred Johnston of 40 Mains Road, Dundee were found guilty of collusion. Doctor Donaldson was sentenced to two years in prison for falsifying a death certificate. He is also barred from practising as a medical practitioner for three years. Alfred Johnston was sentenced to two years in prison for aiding the accused in disposing of the murder weapon.

Ann Craig was sentenced to hanging by the neck until dead. Given her condition, the timing of her hanging is deferred until her child is born and weaned. In summing up, Judge Kennedy said he had never known such a vicious and wicked crime, and certainly not one conducted by a woman.

'Bloody hell, M! So she killed her own husband. And just over there on the Green.'

'Some genes you've got, Fiona Craig!'

'Wonder if Mum knows all this. Mum! Come and see this.'

'Be there in a minute,' called Dorothy. 'I've just found something.'

'So this Craig woman was what relation to your dad and you?'

'Well, this took place in 1880 so let's assume that baby was born that year. God, it must've been born in prison. So, if Dad was born in 1944, then his dad was born some twenty-five to thirty years before that... So, looks like that baby could have been Dad's grandpa maybe? Or his great-aunt or uncle?'

'Wait till you see what I've found, Fi!' Dorothy stood at the door in an old pair of dungarees. 'Hello, Martha, love. How're you doing?'

'Grand thanks. More importantly, how are you?'

'Okay, keeping busy, it's the best way. Now, look at these, girls.' She spread three certificates on the table. 'I found them fastened together with an old wooden clothes peg, hidden away. Here's Struan's birth certificate. So he was born in 1944, Fi, I don't know why I was worrying about that. Then here's his dad's certificate. William Craig, he was born in 1910. And here's Stru's wonderful grandpa, the one Mark was going on about.'

'Grandpa Archie?'

'Yes, look, here he is, Archibald Craig, born on the ninth of September, 1880.' She pointed at the place of birth column on the certificate and her eyes gleamed. 'Look where he was born, girls. Dundee Prison!'

'Of course, this is the baby from The Courier article.' Fiona peered closely at the birth certificate. 'It says his mother was Ann Craig, née Robertson, formerly of 73 Magdalen Yard Road, Dundee and his father was Archibald Edward Donaldson, formerly of 75 Magdalen Yard Road, Dundee.'

'A fling with the next-door neighbour!' Dorothy sat down.

'So Grandpa Archie was born in prison but presumably brought up here in the house. Mark said he'd lived here all his life, brought up by some aunt. How strange is that.'

'Look, Mum, read this article,' Fiona said, pouring her mum a glass of wine and pushing the photocopy in front of her.

Dorothy peered through her glasses at the piece, her mouth opening wider with each paragraph.

'Goodness gracious me, I never knew all that. So she was the woman who brought the Craig family to shame. It's all so incredible.' Dorothy sipped her wine. 'I wonder if Stru knew. Maybe that's why the certificates were hidden at the bottom of his desk drawers. But why would he be ashamed of it, all these years later?'

'So that's my big surprise, Fi,' said Martha, leaning back on her chair. 'What's yours?'

'Don't say a thing, Mum, she doesn't know yet.' Fiona beamed. 'Let's all head down to the Green and see Jamie. I'll take the red kite down. In fact, Mum, why don't we take a bottle of that bubbly in the fridge and we can toast Dad on the Green overlooking the river?'

Dorothy smiled. 'Why not, I'll get four glasses.'

Martha looked around. 'Wow, a glass for Jamie? You guys are pretty liberal with that boy. Allie and I think giving him Irn Bru's a bit risqué!'

The three of them began to walk over the Green towards the shore, the water shimmering in the fading light. Fiona's phone rang.

'You guys carry on. Look, there's Jamie trying to bowl, down by that bench.' She tucked the bottle under her arm as she put her phone to her ear. She could hardly hear the voice at the other end.

'Sorry, can you speak up? Who is this? Sam who?'

She turned round and bent down against the wind, trying to hear better. 'Sorry, what? What on earth are you talking about?'

Fiona jerked her head round to look over the Green. In the dying light she could make out Dorothy, standing with her hands raised. Martha was bolting over the grass towards the two figures down by the river. There was Pete, slowly swinging the cricket bat high above his head as if he was about to hit something hard. Fuck, there was Jamie, standing beside him, turned the other way, pointing out a train on the bridge. Sam was right, Pete was...

She flung the champagne to the ground and broke into a sprint.

'Jamie!' she howled into the wind.

Chapter 57
Thursday 9 June 1881

'Get up, Annie, she's here, the Countess is on her way.'
The jailer stood at her cell door and rattled his large ring
of keys.

An elegant figure stopped at the door and waited as he
pushed the key in.

'Lady Camperdown, can I get you anything?'

'No, thank you, Wallace. I shall call when I am ready.'

Ann Craig rose from her bed, slowly, ensuring that the
bundle nestling in her arm was not disturbed. The dank
room was lit by only one tiny window but today there
was a beam of bright summer sun. She looked over to her
benefactor and, as usual, admired her choice of clothes.

'Good morning, Isabella.'

'Good morning, Ann, how are you today?'

The Countess of Camperdown sat down on the
rickety wooden chair. Every time she visited, as wife of
the Prison Visiting Committee's chairman, she looked
incongruous. Dressed in her finery – always a silk or
taffeta gown, velvet hat trimmed with feathers or fur,
and dainty slippers or soft calf skin boots – she was a
contrast to Ann Craig in her tattered, grubby dress and
bare feet.

'Oh Ann, I gave you shoes at the last visit, did they not
fit?'

'They were perfect, thank you. But I gave them this

morning to Maggie in the next cell. She's got another month or so before her time.'

Isabella sighed and looked into Ann's eyes. 'Are you ready for this?'

'How will I ever be ready? Isabella, you are a mother, how can you possibly give up your child? Your baby?'

The Countess shook her head. 'I have no concept, Ann, truly. I cannot begin to imagine.'

Ann clutched the sleeping child close to her. 'Did they not permit a visit from James and Lizzie?'

The Countess shook her head. 'The Earl tried to intercede on your behalf, but his fellow members on the committee, Sherriff Cheyne and those do-gooders, were adamant. They said it would be detrimental to the children. I am so sorry.'

'You tried. Thank you, Isabella.'

'Ann, I checked with Wallace and he says your time is this evening, at six. Is there anything else I can do for you before then? Apart from pray.'

'You are already doing the best thing with Archibald here.' Ann looked around as if searching for something. 'I have given you letters for James and Lizzie already?'

The Countess nodded. 'They will now have the joy of their little brother being brought up with them in their own house. Lady Cruickshank is overseeing their care with the governess. They will want for nothing.'

Ann reached into her pocket and drew out a handkerchief. 'I have also something for the woman who plays the melodeon in the streets of Lochee. If one of your servants could find a way to give this to her, please? Her name is Blind Mattie, everyone knows her.' She passed the handkerchief to the Countess.

'It is beautiful. There are some initials embroidered upon it. But it says A.R., not A.C.?'

'That was my maiden name. She will remember.'

'Very well, Ann. And now, it is time for me to take little Archibald.'

The Countess stood and stretched out her hands. Ann kissed the baby's soft forehead and placed him in her arms. 'Thank you, Isabella, for arranging this. My little Archie will be fine growing up with his brother and sister in the house in which I had many happy memories.'

The Countess headed for the door and called out, 'Wallace, it is time.'

At the sound of the jailer approaching with his keys, Ann's face crumpled and she rushed to give her baby one last kiss. She shut her eyes and inhaled his sweet innocent smell before turning back to her cold, bare bed.

'Thank you, Isabella. You have been a friend for the past year.'

'God bless you, Ann,' said the Countess, as she took the sleeping baby out of the squalid prison cell. Once they reached the street she paused to take a long, deep breath, happy to be in the fresh air once more.

'Magdalen Yard Road, number seventy-three,' she told her driver, stepping into the cool air of the carriage. She peered into the baby's face and, as the carriage began rattling over the cobbled streets of Dundee, he opened his eyes and gazed directly up at her. She tickled his chin and smiled. 'It's all right, little one, you're going home now.'

Chapter 58
2016

'I just keep thanking God that Mrs C gave you my mobile number. She's never done that before.'

'I had to tell her what I was about to tell you, Fiona,' Sam said. 'It was the only way.'

Dot shook her head and poured the three of them more tea. 'So are you ready to tell us about Pete's past?'

'Yeah, the truth.' Fiona finished her cake. 'I mean, how could I have lived with someone all that time and not had a clue who he really was?'

'Well, I mean, more will come out at the trial, if they let him out of the secure hospital.'

'Hang on.' Dot raised a finger. 'He was sectioned under the Mental Health Act after that hellish afternoon. Why did that never happen in Australia? There must be a similar law there?'

'He didn't have to be, his psychosis was always under control. He'd been on Risperidone since he was nineteen, when he had the first symptoms – aggression, agitation, hearing voices tell him to do stuff.' Sam sank back into the sofa. 'The week after Mum died, he drowned my pet rabbit and told me she'd told him to do it. That's when the docs got involved.'

'So did the meds stabilise him?'

'Yeah, he was on them every day. I can't believe you lived with him for three years and didn't know.'

'I knew he took pills every day but he said they were for his high blood pressure. Why would I question that?'

'And you never thought anything was, you know, not right, or a bit weird?'

'Nothing physically, I mean he got fatter but he was a bloody chef, it was hardly surprising.' Fiona sipped her tea. 'And emotionally, well, sometimes I used to think he was a bit heartless, when we talked about Iain, but I just presumed it was his way of preventing me getting all weepy – or him being jealous. Now, having read all about the side effects of the meds, it says blunted emotions are part of it. Everyone just used to think he was Aussie cool.'

'Yeah, Risperidone has horrible side effects,' said Sam. 'Weight gain, limbs shaking – but his body must've got used to them after so long. God knows why he stopped taking them – or when.'

Fiona shivered. 'And when Martha rugby-tackled him to the ground, the first words he said were, "They told me to do it!" Was that his voices?'

'Suppose so.' Sam shrugged. 'It's a horrible, horrible illness.'

Fiona sipped her tea. 'I've been Googling all about psychosis; it can be genetic too. Was that what your dad had?'

Sam wrapped her hands round the mug. 'Yeah. They say you can be predisposed, but a traumatic event can trigger it.' She looked at Fiona over the rim of the mug. 'You know he saw Dad kill Mum?'

Fiona shook her head.

'They reckon that brought it on, so they got him onto the meds. The funeral was a month after Mum died because the post-mortem took forever. And the day after the funeral I woke up to a note under my door. It was from Pete saying he'd had enough and he was sorry to leave me too but his life was no longer worth living.'

'A suicide note?'

'Everyone thought so. We tried to track him down but nothing. We'd no idea he'd gone to London, where he trained as a chef. And then eventually he ended up in Edinburgh where he met you. We presumed he was dead, I even put his name on Mum's gravestone. Then about four years ago, everything changed. I started getting regular payments into my bank account. A lot of money, about five hundred dollars each time. There was no name but I realised pretty soon it must be him. His way of kind of saying sorry, I guessed. So when I knew he was alive, I started searching for his name online. Then I saw the restaurant review, which he reckoned I'd see, so he decided to come home. The guilt must have been too much.'

Fiona sighed.

'The thing is, Fiona, he wasn't rational. When the meds were going fine, he could appear so, but he said to me when he was home last summer he still often heard voices telling him to do things.'

'I'm just so relieved Jamie was unaware of the whole horrible thing. He thought Martha was playing around, launching herself at Pete like that.'

'That bloody cricket bat's going in the Tay, once the trial's over. Allie, Martha and I are going down to the shore and we'll throw it in,' Fiona said.

The door was flung open and Jamie burst into the room.

'Sam, you promised we'd go and play football after your tea.'

'I know, Jamie, just give me two ticks to finish it.'

Jamie went to sit beside Dot who enveloped him in her arms and gave him a large noisy kiss. He pulled himself away, wiped his face with the back of his hand, and rushed towards the window.

'Look, Mum, there's a train on the bridge.' He glanced up at the wall clock. 'It's the four fifteen from Edinburgh.'

Acknowledgements

Thanks to MaryAn Charnley, Anne Dow, Elisabeth Hadden and Isabelle Plews for reading and advising.

Thank you to Jennifer Hadden, Sophie Hadden and Iain Lamont for their professional expertise.

And thank you to the helpful staff at the University of Edinburgh Library and the National Library of Scotland for allowing me to peruse their archives.

Finally, thanks as ever to my agent Jenny Brown for her encouragement and support, and thank you to Julie Fergusson for her insightful editing.